The time: the present. The setting: an imaginary New England seaside town, seedy and slightly sinister. To the town comes Robert Cameron, an AWOL soldier who is tricked into taking a job as a stunt man with a movie company on location there. The movie, improvised from day to day, becomes a mirror of Cameron's own plight. He is pursued by the Army and local police, pushed by the director and a malevolent cameraman into more and more dangerous stunts that lead him further away from the real world and deeper into the unreality of the film, where life itself becomes the most intricate stunt of all . . .

"An absolutely first-rate novel . . ."
—*Library Journal*

MELVIN SIMON PRODUCTIONS PRESENTS
A RICHARD RUSH FILM

PETER O'TOOLE
STEVE RAILSBACK
BARBARA HERSHEY

THE STUNT MAN
Starring ALLEN GOORWITZ
ALEX ROCCO
ADAM ROARKE
SHARON FARRELL
PHILIP BRUNS
And CHUCK BAIL

Music by
DOMINIC FRONTIERE

Lyrics by
NORMAN GIMBEL

Associate Producer
PAUL LEWIS

Director of Photography
MARIO TOSI, A.S.C.

Executive Producer
MELVIN SIMON

Screenplay by
LAWRENCE B. MARCUS

Adaptation by
RICHARD RUSH

Based upon The Stunt Man by PAUL BRODEUR

Produced and Directed by
RICHARD RUSH

The
STUNT MAN

Paul Brodeur

BALLANTINE BOOKS • NEW YORK

Copyright © 1970 by Paul Brodeur

Front cover artwork copyright © 1980 Melvin Simon
Productions, Inc.

All rights reserved. Published in the United States by Ballantine Books, a division of Random House, Inc., New York, and simultaneously in Canada by Random House of Canada, Limited, Toronto, Canada.

Library of Congress Catalog Card Number: 80-66170

ISBN 0-345-29601-X

This edition published by arrangement with
Atheneum Publishers

Manufactured in the United States of America

First Ballantine Books Edition: March 1973
Second Printing: November 1980

*To Leonard Wallace Robinson
and Frederick L. Keefe*

1

There was no doubt that his fellow passengers welcomed the interruption of the journey, but Cameron was anxious to be under way again. Already impatient with the forced hilarity that echoed around him, he was restless above all with the terrible heat. Ever since the bus had broken down, it had been filling with hot air that rebounded in waves off the macadam of the highway, which, too far inland to be bathed by the salt smell of the sea, yet too close to shore to benefit from the shade of real trees, was lined on either side by one of those tenacious forests of scrub oak and pitch pine that grow in sandy coastal regions where the sun stunts everything. Now, twenty minutes later, Cameron withdrew a letter from the breast pocket of his shirt, inserted it into a mystery story he had started at the beginning of the trip, and placed the book on the empty seat beside him. The letter was written on pale blue stationery, and the margin that protruded from the pages of the book revealed a column of words inscribed in the tiny, rounded hand with which she sought to assure him that she would wait for his return. For a moment, he was tempted to read the letter again, but he had already gone over it often enough to know its contents by heart. Instead, he read the column of words, and, reordering them slightly, formed a tender, awkward sentence that stood for all the rest. Then he leaned back in his seat, closed his eyes, and tried to shut out the phony merriment that, together with the stifling heat, seemed to be inflating the interior of the bus to the point of bursting. Remember they're just a bunch of kids, he told himself, but the fact that he was older than his companions, which allowed him to keep his reserve and to maintain a certain distance, also filled him with despair. By refusing to participate in the false hopes raised by the failure of the bus engine, was he not admitting that they were all in the same boat and bound for the same destination? Yes, this interim period in which, still wearing civilian clothes, he found himself in transit from one life to another constituted an unbearable limbo for Cameron, who wanted desperately to resume the journey if only to get it over with. Now he opened his eyes and stared morosely at the barren landscape beyond the window. Fitting scenery for contemplating a future in which he would pass interminable days by waiting for her other letters. In this mood, he looked forward to his arrival at the training camp, where, having been issued gear and assigned to a barracks, he would fall exhausted into a bunk and know even as he lay awake in the darkness that the past—his books, his studies, and the small apartment near the graduate school in which they had lived together—was finally and irrevocably over.

At this point, the sergeant in charge—a massive Negro who had gone outside to inspect the engine with the driver —climbed aboard and looked down the aisle with eyes that, because they appeared to be permanently bloodshot, held a perpetual glare. Authority, Cameron thought with a sinking heart as the laughing and the singing ceased, and the bus fell still.

The sergeant, whose suntans were soaked with perspiration, picked up a travel roster that was attached to a clipboard, and started calling roll.

"Abrams?"

"Here."

"Anderson?"

"Here."

"Barrientos?" said the sergeant, looking up as he called each name and accenting the last syllables with a melodic voice that rose in pitch to the point of shrillness.

Cameron listened to the roll call with expectation and amusement. Can the sergeant be worried that somebody's run away? he wondered as he heard his name pronounced in the manner of a phonetically similar African republic.

"Here," he said.

When the sergeant came to the end of the roll, he studied the list for several minutes as if he were double-checking for omission. Then he looked up. "Cameron?" he called.

"Still here," replied Cameron, drawing a ripple of laughter from his fellow passengers.

"I want to talk to you, Cameron," the sergeant said softly.

When Cameron advanced to the front of the bus, the sergeant led him outside and around to the rear of the vehicle, where the driver, a civilian, was peering into the housing of an engine that gave off smoke and the stench of burning oil.

"We've thrown a rod," the sergeant said. "Means somebody's got to find a telephone. Driver and me got to keep an eye on things here, so you got the detail."

"How far will I have to go?" Cameron asked.

"How would I know?" the sergeant replied. "Neither me or him has ever been up here before." At this point, the sergeant produced a road map, which he opened and held against the side of the bus with the palm of his hand. "I got an idea we're right about there," he continued, pointing vaguely with his index finger. "But we could be nearer to the camp. Anyway, your job is to find a telephone and call us some assistance."

"Who'll I call?" said Cameron, who noticed that the highway, which ran roughly parallel to the coast, was nearer to the sea than he had imagined.

"Nearest military installation," the sergeant answered. "That'll probably be the camp. Ask for the O.D. at the transport center."

"O.D.?"

"Officer of the Day," the sergeant said patiently. "Now listen, Cameron, make sure you transmit the proper information to him. First off, tell him we've broken down. Then tell him where we're at, which, since we don't exactly know, means you got to find out, doesn't it?"

"Yes, it does," replied Cameron, who was somewhat irritated at the sergeant's patronizing manner.

"To find out where we're at means you got to keep an eye

out for signs and exit roads. That way you can give the O.D.
the right fix on our position, right?"

"Right," Cameron said, and, glancing at the bright cam-
paign ribbon on the sergeant's chest, suppressed a smile. The
sergeant ought to be back in the jungle calling in air strikes,
he thought.

"Okay, now what's the last thing you do?" the sergeant
asked, turning his bloodshot eyes on Cameron with a quick,
sideways glance.

"Come back to the fold," said Cameron with a shrug of
resignation.

The sergeant gave his head a weary shake and folded the
road map. "Hot day like this," he muttered. "Older fella like
you should have more sense. Last thing, Cameron, is tell the
O.D. your own position. That way, when they send down
another bus, we'll know where to stop by and pick you up,
right?"

"Right," Cameron said with sudden appreciation for the
sergeant's methodical approach to military problems. "What
shall I do about my gear?"

"Take it or leave it," the sergeant replied.

"I guess I better take it," said Cameron, who climbed
quickly into the bus, retrieved a small duffel bag containing
his personal effects from the rack above his seat, and hurried back along the aisle. Having deduced the nature of his
mission, several of his fellow passengers exhorted him not
to hurry on their account. Cameron responded with a smile
and a wave of his hand as he went down the steps to the exit
door.

The sergeant was waiting for him outside, his baleful stare
fixed on the ribbon of highway that stretched ahead through
the scrub. "Try hitchhiking if you want, but wait'll you get
down the road and out of sight," he said. "I don't want any
of these chickens getting ideas. And another thing, Cameron.
This is a hot mother for all of us, so don't exercise yourself
but don't dawdle either."

"Okay," Cameron said. "Anything else?"

The sergeant grimaced up at the sun and wiped a sleeve
across his brow. "Take off," he replied.

Only when he looked back did he remember that he had

left her letter behind. For a moment, he was tempted to return, but the thought of the sergeant's displeasure deterred him, and in any event it was too hot to indulge oneself in sentimental gestures. The bus was still in sight—an ark stranded upon a horizon that was already obscured by heat and haze. Maybe it's a mirage, he thought. Suddenly he felt the relief of a sailor who has swum ashore from a shipwreck. He was no longer in the same boat with the others. He had been deflected from his course by chance. Might this not allow him to alter his destination as well? The idea appealed to Cameron, whose literary tastes tended toward the works of ironists, and, quickening his step, he hurried along the highway. When he looked back again, the bus was out of sight, and all at once he realized that the sergeant's last words could be construed to have a double meaning, and that there was nothing to stop him from interpreting them in their most vernacular sense. Take off . . . Yes, there was absolutely nothing to prevent him from simultaneously obeying the order and satisfying his deepest wish. Why, then, did he choose this moment to think again of her letter? It nagged at him, that letter. It was holding him back. He resented its hidden implications. Why should he feel tied to a letter and, by extension, to a future in which a succession of letters would inevitably become the most important events in an endless string of dreary days? No, it was best to leave her letter where it was—a bookmark in a mystery he had no desire to finish—and, having closed that story, look to another future. Yet the detachment with which he contemplated this act of abandonment gave him pause for thought. Had he ever loved her? Could he in the future? Was he capable of it? Too early to tell. There was too much in the way. There were too many obstacles in the present, and not the least of them was this initial tendency to be maudlin about a letter. For some moments longer, Cameron remained at the edge of the highway, wondering if he should try to flag down one of the automobiles that came hurtling over it. In lulls between the whining noise of their passage, he could hear insects humming in the forest at his back. Turning, he approached a curtain of gnarled trees. Then, quickly he stepped behind it.

He was amazed at how easily he disappeared. The world and its ugly sounds subsided as if some hidden fault in the crust had opened up in back of him, yawned, and taken a swallow of geological proportions. Now, with determined strides, he plunged ahead through a crackling undergrowth of laurel and huckleberry bushes that soon gave way to thick stunted stands of pine and oak. Except for an occasional trunk that, still black from some old fire, lifted itself like a charred spar above the rest, the trees were less than twice his own height. Everything seemed to spread sideways in this parched wilderness, as if the heat of the sun were a lid that stifled the possibility of vertical growth. Cameron plowed on, using his duffel bag to fend a passage through scrub whose dead lower branches broke off at the slightest touch, but gradually the screen grew thicker until, unable to penerate it by continuing straight ahead, he began to detour, crouching low and following tiny avenues that appeared in the maze of trunks. Finally, he was reduced to scrambling on all fours over a thick carpet of needles and fallen cones that covered the forest floor. When he stopped to rest and consulted his watch, he was surprised to discover that he had been traveling for nearly half an hour. Above him, he could scarcely see the sky; behind him, he made out a long, gouged trail through the needles which marked his serpentine progress. Stupid, he thought. Stupid . . .

He went on, carefully lifting and planting his feet in order to leave no tracks. But his new caution was tiring. His breathing grew labored. Sweat poured into his eyes. Blinking, he pulled an undershirt out of his duffel bag, tore it in two, and tied one half around his forehead. Then he went on again until he reached a small clearing in which he thought he discerned the shallow ruts of an old road. Following the traces until they petered out, he came to a mound of needles, which, when he uncovered it, revealed a heap of rusted cans. Cameron touched one of the cans with the toe of his shoe, and watched it disintegrate. The forest beyond grew thicker than ever. He returned to the clearing, which seemed smaller than before. Stop and think, he told himself, and, looking up at the sky, tried to get his bearings. But the sun, nearly overhead, told him nothing. Were there no perspectives in this desolate maze? He remembered reading somewhere that branches grew longest on the southern sides of trees, and for several moments he examined the gnarled and mutilated scrub that surrounded him. It was useless. How futile to seek ecological truth in this godforsaken wilderness.

Only the idea that the sea could not be far away gave him hope. He plunged off into the woods. Twenty minutes later, utterly spent, he sat down to rest again.

The squirrel, which appeared out of nowhere, brought his heart to his throat. It was a red squirrel that, having spent the morning scratching over acres of slippery needles in search of acorns, had simply stopped to look at him. "Get lost," Cameron said wearily. "Better still, get yourself a new home." The squirrel disappeared with a jump. A moment later, Cameron heard it chattering in a thick stand of pine. Suddenly, he imagined the sergeant freezing in his tracks and opening his bloodshot eyes wide as he listened to the squirrel's scolding and searched the woods for movement. Don't be ridiculous, Cameron told himself. The sergeant is still at the bus keeping an eye on his brood. But he sat perfectly still, scarcely daring to breathe as he peered into the forest around him.

How on earth he had overlooked the sheen of light directly ahead of him he would never know. Perhaps the squirrel, triggering off his fear of pursuit, had distracted him. Or perhaps it was not a clearing he saw at eye level through the trees, but the illusion of it. No, there was a clearing, all right, and, judging from the amount of light, a large one. Getting to his hands and knees, Cameron crawled through the scrub until, emerging from the tree line, he found himself at the rim of a large, shallow bowl that had been carved out of the forest. The bowl contained sand and no vegetation. Not even a blade of grass. A black tar road bisected it, and in the middle of this road, beneath a flag that hung motionless from its pole in the appalling heat, stood a cubicle of glass and concrete. Cameron could scarcely believe his eyes. It's a sentry post, he thought. I've stumbled upon the camp. . . .

2

Ten minutes later, it was all he could do to keep from laughing out loud. A sentry for the middle of nowhere, he thought, gazing with delight and astonishment at the toll collector, whose booth was swollen with hot air like a jar at the end of a blowpipe, and whose prattle revealed an intense desire for companionship. Judging from the hospitality the toll collector insisted upon tendering in his absurd and stifling cubicle, there was little doubt that he welcomed company. Ever since Cameron had arrived there—faint from the heat and disheartened by the assumption that his long flight through the woods had merely led him to the camp—he had been resting on a stool vacated by his host. Now, realizing that he must have gone in circles and that the toll booth sat at the end of an exit road from the highway, he stirred as if to leave. The toll collector, a man of indolent bulk, was quick to interpret the move correctly.

"Be patient," he said. "Maybe somebody'll be along."

Cameron nodded and sipped at a glass of lemonade the toll collector had poured from a gallon jug. The jug sat upon a small counter beside a defective radio that gave off a steady crackle of static which was occasionally surmounted by a piercing squawk. The lemonade, too saccharine to be refreshing, had the consistency of sugar syrup, but outside nothing moved except waves of heat that shimmered above the macadam.

The toll collector poked his head through the door of the booth and peered along the roadway as if to assure Cameron of continued vigilance on his behalf. "Somebody may come along," he repeated, but without conviction.

"How far is it to the nearest town?" asked Cameron, setting his glass on the counter beside the radio.

"Sit tight," the toll collector advised, "or the heat'll get to you again."

8

"I ought to be moving on," Cameron said. "Anyway, there doesn't seem to be much traffic on this road."

"It's not open is why."

"If it's not open," said Cameron, "how can you be expecting anybody to come along?"

"Not open to the public," the toll collector explained. "Didn't you see the barricade down at the highway?"

"No," Cameron replied "I took a short cut."

"Well, the road's been closed while they make repairs on the causeway over the river. Only people in authorized vehicles are allowed to come through."

"I'm on foot," said Cameron with a smile.

The toll collector shrugged, indicating peril on Cameron's part and *laissez-faire* on his own. Then, dropping his voice to a conspiratorial whisper, he said, "Look, young fellow, you can get arrested in this state for hitchhiking. I'm just trying to do you a favor."

Cameron gazed at the man with distaste and made up his mind to leave. The large pair of sunglasses which, at first glance, seemed to lend his face an impassive look of authority now merely accentuated a weak mouth that, even while delivering words of caution, trembled upon the brink of recrimination. This is a very bored and lonely toll collector, he thought. "I'm in sort of a hurry," he said politely. "How far did you say it was to town?"

"Stay awhile and help yourself to some more lemonade. If a car comes through, you'll have a lift and I'll be able to find out what's happened on the radio."

If it has a radio, thought Cameron, who glanced at his watch and got to his feet. He had been gone nearly two hours. Was it possible that an alarm had already been put out for him and that the toll collector was attempting to delay his departure? "What makes you think something's happened?" he asked. He did not really care to know, but, reminded now that he had accepted the toll collector's beverage to begin with, he felt it was only sensible to cloak his leave-taking with conversation.

"Because when my set went on the blink, they were breaking in with a special announcement," replied the toll collector, who stepped outside again and, like a captain on his bridge, scanned the horizon in all directions.

Cameron took this opportunity to shake the radio, which

protested with a screech. Come on, he thought with a smile, it's time you replaced me in your master's affections. "The radio must help you pass the hours," he said.

The toll collector turned in the doorway and, pulling the soaked shirt of his uniform from his chest with thumbs and forefingers, made it flutter up and down. "This job's not so boring as you might expect," he replied. "I mean, there are compensations. One thing is I collect coins."

Cameron barely suppressed a laugh. "Yes, yours is a redundant profession," he observed.

"Don't knock it," said the toll collector solemnly. "There's good money in coins. The 1916-D dime is worth a hundred dollars these days."

Cameron was in a hurry to be gone, but fearful of arousing suspicion if he left abruptly. Now, reaching into his pocket, he withdrew some change, and turned the coins over in the palm of his hand. "Here's a 1958 Roosevelt," he announced.

"Worthless," the toll collector replied.

"How about the 1924-S buffalo nickel?"

"If it's in good condition, it'll bring you three or four dollars."

"In that case, I'll hang on to it," said Cameron, who picked up his duffel bag and started toward the doorway.

The toll collector was still fluttering his stained shirt front with feminine indolence, but now he moved with surprising speed and, shifting his bulk, blocked the exit. "Listen," he said hoarsely, "coins aren't the only thing you come across on a post like this. When the road's open, it's a regular parade of open blouses, unbuttoned halters, and miniskirts hiked all the way up past—" The toll collector gasped in the stifling heat, broke into an ocean of perspiration, and, leaning toward Cameron, told of having taken money from hands whose blandly hidden counterparts supported crouched and squirming girls. Staring into the convex lenses of the man's sunglasses, Cameron saw a grotesquely distorted and bloated reflection of his own face, which seemed to be a caricature of the toll collector's vicarious lust. A moment later, he shouldered his way brusquely through the door and found himself standing in the road.

"Thanks for the lemonade," he said.

"And don't think I haven't learned to take my own good time making change!" shouted the toll collector as he finished a series of lurid reminiscences. Now, breathing heavily, he leaned against the wall of the booth and fixed Cameron with a look of avarice. "How about selling me that nickel? I'll give you a dollar for it."

Here's a chance to placate this nut, thought Cameron, who reached into his pocket, pulled out the nickel, and handed it over. "It's yours," he said. "With many thanks for your hospitality."

The toll collector accepted the coin as matter-of-factly as if Cameron had used it to pay for passage. "You're crazy to go running off in this heat," he said.

"I'm supposed to be looking for a telephone," Cameron replied, and swung the duffel bag up on his shoulder.

"Suit yourself, but next time you go out in weather like this, young fellow, better wear something on your head."

"Good luck with your collection," said Cameron, and started away. As he did, the radio came briefly to life, giving off a peal of electronic guitar music that was followed by a barrage of static. Cameron turned around, expecting to see the toll collector dash inside; instead, he found himself looking at the deprived and reproachful face of a minor functionary.

"I wish I was going with you," the toll collector muttered. "All that stuff strutting around in bathing suits. Why, the beach'll be a regular paradise on a day like this."

"What's the best way to get there?" asked Cameron.

"There's only one way. Around the bend and straight ahead across the marsh. But keep your eyes open. Like I told you, the causeway's under construction and no one's supposed to use it."

"Thanks for the advice," Cameron replied. "Thanks for everything."

"Hey, you didn't give me your name!"

Cameron looked back. He had only taken a few steps, but already the heat rebounding from the roadway was obscuring the booth and its proprietor. "My name?" he said. "Why d'you want to know my name?"

"That way if a cop comes through I can tell him who you are and not to bother you."

Cameron tried to make out the nature of the smile that was playing across the toll collector's face, but the heat and the sweat that was trickling over his brow had contrived to make everything vague and indistinct. Was it a smile to match the toll collector's helpful tone, or a smirk to mask betrayal?

"You've got a name, haven't you?"

"My name is Jackson," Cameron replied evenly. "Richard Jackson."

"Well, Jackson, good luck to you!"

So long, Cameron thought. So long, gateman to paradise. But the alias, flung heartily back, stayed with him as he continued along the road, weighing upon him even as his memory of the toll collector's senseless lechery made him profoundly aware of his own youth. In this mood, his journey took on a picaresque quality. The adventures of Richard Jackson, he reflected lightly, but he was filled with a sense of relief, as if he had run a gantlet. Now he quickened his pace, hurrying toward the first salt breath of the sea, and felt the full infernal force of the sun upon his head. The toll collector doesn't need a radio in that caldron, he thought. What he needs is a Doberman pinscher named Cerberus. . . .

When he looked back from the last turn in the road, the booth had diminished in the glare, but even so he could make out the figure of the toll collector, who was popping in and out of the doorway as if in the throes of some terrible agitation. "A bird in a cuckoo clock," Cameron said aloud, and shuddered as he thought of the man and his fate—a heat-struck numismatist doomed to coining sexual fantasies in the confines of his scorching cubicle. Because of this, the toll collector's first shouts seemed strangely muffled, but when they continued—hoarse and insistent—Cameron strained to penetrate the blazing light, and saw that the man had run out of the booth and was standing in the middle of the road, dancing and waving his arms. *"Whoa!"* came the shout, more distinct and louder now—*"Whoa!"*—as if it were the command of some ancient porter trying to halt an errant chariot. Cameron turned away, shaking his head. The poor devil must want to flag down everybody, he thought. Now he continued out of sight with quicker, more determined steps until he came to the causeway leading across the marsh, which he took with scarcely a moment's hesitation and without any thought whatever of the toll collector's warning or the signs on some carelessly arranged sawhorse barricades that pronounced it closed to use.

3

Only later would he wonder why he had taken this forbidden road over which, as the smell of hidden roses is wafted over a garden wall, came the intoxicating odor of the sea, whose salty exhalation was mingled with the sweet-and-sour stench of marsh grass and mud flats. At the moment, it seemed perfect—a route prohibited by workmen who could scarcely have expected their flimsy barrier to be honored, and by a guardian whose cry to halt lacked the ring of authority. In any case, it's the only road to paradise, thought Cameron, who, certain that he was under no other surveillance than that of the dazzling sun, struck out across it with confident strides. Far away, a sandbar shone in brilliant light that also sparkled upon a stretch of open water where the river that drained the marsh emptied into the sea. Inland, in the opposite direction, the marsh narrowed between headlands covered with lush trees whose tops were wreathed in haze. Ahead of him, also indistinct in haze, lay a low ridge that no doubt concealed the town. As he trudged over the causeway, Cameron kept his eyes upon this last horizon, with which the heat was playing tricks, but long before he reached the half-way point, where the cut of the river exposed layers of muck beneath the marsh grass, he felt the sun again and lowered his gaze to the roadway at his feet in the manner of a long-distance runner who, with perspectives forcibly shrunken by the agony of his effort, bends his head to concentrate upon what is gained by each weary jog.

It was a new road, freshly glazed with an asphalt coating that had not yet been rolled into the gravel bed beneath, and as a result it was filled with tiny perforations that formed patterns of minutiae, which, like the designs in sickroom wallpaper, proved idly intriguing. It was a straight black road that, because of the tricks the heat was playing with the horizon, seemed to be getting no place. Someday it would be a road with speed limits, directional signs, and median markings, and would be buttressed by acres of dirt fill supporting gas stations with strings of flapping pennants and bedroom cabins with elfin porches, gaudy trim, and tiny windows into which the sweep of headlights would steal at night and whisk across the gleaming backs of lovers. But now, like all newly tarred roads, it was unspoiled by debris, skid marks, and other traces that bear witness to the speed of passage. As yet, there were no carcasses upon this road, no corpses of small animals that have been mesmerized by glare in one instant, struck dead in the next, and then pulverized between the mortar and pestle of wheels and macadam into pulpy mats of fur and hide, which, after a few rainstorms, are reduced to stains that soon become indistinguishable from crank-case drippings. As yet, there had not even been the hopeless passage of a turtle upon this road, nor had seagulls begun to drop mussels torn from their marsh beds upon its surface. A totally uninitiated road, without even an Aesopian history, Cameron thought as, spent from the sun, he arrived at the bridge that spanned the river.

The bridge was unfinished, but lacked only curbs and railings. A small air compressor sat baking in the sun beside a few pieces of lumber, and several peach stones were strewn about as if in reminder that a few lazy workmen would repossess the bridge and, moving slowly to conserve energy and prolong tasks that were no longer demanding, contrive to stretch out their labors for still another week. It was a simple bridge supported by girders and flanked by a pair of concrete abutments that flared back along either side of the causeway to protect it from being eroded by the current. The abutments were stained by the flow of brackish water, and tiny strands of mermaid's-hair clung to a wainscoting of green scum that showed the high-tide mark. Cameron sat down with his back to the air compressor, looked into the water that was moving toward the sea, and decided that it must be very deep. A good place to fish, he thought, for surely there were eels down there, as well as sea robins, cunners, and rock cod. Now, dangling his feet above the current, he found himself wishing that he had a line to unwind from its wooden brace, a line smelling of tar and weighted with a lead sinker, a line to be held between thumb and forefinger and bounced along the bottom, the kind of line with which small boys plumb the mysteries of murky waters that surround dock pilings, railroad trestles, and rock jetties. It was a fleeting wish, however, for Cameron soon found himself preoccupied with the idea that his period of grace was nearly over, and that he was fast approaching a point of no return after which his options would be decided for him. For some moments, he tried to imagine himself working his way up the coast and slipping across the border into Canada; then he saw himself entering a telephone booth, dialing the operator, and asking to be connected with the camp. But even as he attempted to decide upon a course of action, he knew that he would never be able to choose either of these alternatives. In this mood, trapped in the present and uncertain of the future, he felt suspended. I've got to do something, he told himself, but with the sun beating down upon his head, he found it hard to concentrate. For a while longer, he tried to overcome his lethargy; then, all at once, he saw the helicopter.

Capricious as a dragonfly, the helicopter skimmed across the marsh from the direction of the sea, swooped out over the river, and, tilting on end, came straight upstream toward the bridge. Cameron listened to the chatter of the rotor blades with a sinking heart. They're looking for me, he thought. He was tempted to make a run for it, but when he glanced along the open causeway, he realized he would have no chance. Now, shrinking back, he flattened himself against the air compressor and drew his duffel bag in beside him. The helicopter passed overhead, perhaps forty feet above him, with a terrible racket and a downdraft that sent a cloud of dust swirling over the roadway. Cameron rubbed his eyes and watched it continue toward the headlands on the other side of the marsh, where it pivoted on the horizon and started to return. Here's your chance to run, he told himself, but even as he started to get to his feet, he saw a car approaching from the other end of the causeway.

Cameron sank to his knees and watched the car come toward him. Then, with a shrug of resignation, he decided that he might as well step out into the middle of the road, flag down the vehicle, and ask to be taken to the nearest telephone. Why not pretend to welcome the inevitable? he thought. You're still in the clear. There's no way in the world they can prove you were on the run. . . . But as the car drew closer, he suddenly realized it was moving much too fast to stop. It's not going to stop! he thought with astonishment as, still on his hands and knees, he watched the vehicle flash past him and, accompanied by the helicopter that appeared to be towed in its wake by an invisible string, continue at terrific speed to the far end of the causeway. At that point, the car came to a screeching halt, made an abrupt U-turn in the roadway—a maneuver that was matched effortlessly by the helicopter—and started back.

The helicopter was now flying just above the marsh at eye level with the car, and, realizing that no matter what he did, he would be exposed to the view of one or the other, Cameron simply crouched beside the air compressor and watched their swift approach. When the car drew abreast of him this time, however, it suddenly veered toward the edge of the bridge, passed within a few feet of his hiding place, and with a squeal of tires that could be heard over the racket of the helicopter, swerved crazily back into the middle of the roadway and came to a stop. Cameron immediately jumped to his feet and started toward it at a hesitant hitchhiker's trot that became a dash of gratitude. The car was an ancient model whose once-black paint, pitted by long exposure to salt air, had turned an oily iridescent blue, like the skin of a fish. It was a hulking car with a high, hump-backed trunk beneath an oval window through which Cameron, running, saw a head slip sideways as the driver reached across the empty seat beside him and opened the door. Assuming that this was an act of accommodation, Cameron shouted a breathless "Thank you" as he swung his duffel bag in beneath the dashboard, planted his left foot beside it, and, sliding onto the seat, grasped the handle of the door to shut it. And it was in this moment of complete entanglement (for he had wrapped the cord of the duffel bag around his wrist) and of hasty motion based upon the assumption that his benefactor was in a hurry that he opened his mouth and, even while framing words to announce his destination, saw that the driver—a young man of about his own age—was trembling with fright.

"What's the matter?" Cameron asked.

"Lost my nerve," the driver muttered.

Cameron was not sure that he had heard correctly because the helicopter hovering just ahead and above them was filling the car with an angry buzz. "Look," he said, "I've got to get to the nearest telephone as quickly as—"

"Don't worry," the driver exclaimed. "I lost my nerve is all."

Cameron gave his head a puzzled shake. "D'you want me to take the wheel?" he inqured politely.

"I want you to get the hell out of here," the driver replied.

"But I have to find a telephone."

"Listen, I'll go through with it!" the driver said angrily, and placed a hand on Cameron's shoulder. "Now get out of here before the—"

"But I—"

"—whirleybird gets set—"

"—think you must be making—"

"—to start—"

"—some kind of—"

"—shooting."

"—mistake."

For a second, Cameron and the driver stared at each other with identical expressions of disbelief. Then, just as Cameron was about to ask the clarifying question that had formed in his mind, he received a violent shove that sent him flying.

Now the preceding order of things was reversed in ludicrous fashion as he was catapulted out of the car, with left foot following right and the duffel bag, whose cord was still wrapped around his wrist, coming last. And it was somersaulting through the air, or just after he had landed and lay flopping on the concrete apron of the bridge like a fish swung out of water, that he had his first reaction, thinking (or, afterward, thinking that he remembered thinking) the phrase "ass-over-teakettle" to describe what was actually the rather graceful parabolic arc of his ejection from the vehicle. So it was chagrin that he felt first of all at this absurd turnabout, which, in the fashion of a Keystone Kop film, seemed all the more comical for having been speeded up, and then pain, for he had landed upon his side and then skidded along the rough, freshly poured concrete until the friction of his body had brought him to a halt. As a result, one whole side of him was bruised, and he was bleeding from a scrape on his cheekbone, which the sun and salt air did nothing to assuage. So pain followed close upon the heels of chagrin, but gave way in the next instant to terror when, looking up at the black car on one side and sensing the depth of the water on the other, he began to tug frantically at the cord of the duffel bag which had become knotted around his wrist. His terror subsided as the car drew slowly away from him, but was suddenly replaced by outrage as he saw a hand reach out, grasp the handle of the door, and pull it shut. The lackadaisical gesture of this hand—the same hand that had so rudely unseated him to begin with—unnerved Cameron completely. Untying the last knot that bound him to the duffel bag, he delivered a curse at scream pitch; then, having freed his wrist, he tried to sit up, gave a cry of pain, and rolled over on his back. In this position, gasping for air and blinded by tears of anguish and rage, he saw nothing but the sky, which was filled with harsh light and the roar of the helicopter. It was as if he were tanning himself upon the roof of the world—a hot roof, however, that was already burning his bruised shoulderblades. When he tried to sit up a second time, he was successful. Then, as he struggled to his feet, he saw the black car circling in the road, a hundred yards away.

Now, like a lazy shark, the car swam back toward him through the haze that shimmered above the asphalt, with something so predatory in its slow approach that Cameron's nerves contracted within his flesh as if flinching in preparation to flee his body. He was vaguely aware from the sound of the rotor blades that the helicopter was still somewhere above him, but his whole attention was focused upon the vehicle. The sun glinting off its windshield pierced his eyes, and he stood upon the bridge, filled with the immobility of disbelief. They're out to kill me, he thought, backing to the edge, where he began to perform a macabre little dance as, teetering above the water, he tried to keep one eye on the approaching car and the other on the current flowing beneath him. At this point, everything in Cameron urged him to jump. Then, unaccountably, he stumbled over a loose rock —a jagged piece of roadbed that had escaped submergence when the concrete was poured—and, stooping to pick it up, lurched away from the edge of the bridge and into the path of the car. Clutching the rock in his fist, Cameron now ran the angling run of a bullfighter toward his adversary but away from the direction to its thrust. He was thinking as he ran that he should try to take shelter behind the air compressor. Too late. The car was upon him. For an instant, he could see the face of the driver behind the windshield as, with an immense effort, he jackknifed himself to one side and, leaning off-balance like a pitcher throwing side-arm, hurled the rock with all the detestation with which he might have driven home a knife. Afterward, he went sprawling flat on his face upon the roadway.

There was a thud. Yes, unmistakably, there had been a thud—one of those soft-pulpy thuds that are produced on radio serials by the sound man's hammer striking a grapefruit—but whether it was the rock hitting something, or himself landing on the bridge, or simply an auditory trick played upon him by fear, Cameron would never know. Lying dazed upon the concrete apron, he sensed the car roll past him, and the thud—that mushy sound as if his rock had struck a mudbank—had no other immediate reverberation. What he came to remembering was the smell of old upholstery—a musty smell of dust and decay which had stayed with him from the brief time he had been inside the car, and which, similar to the odor that emanated from his father's ancient, dome-shaped Philco radio, recalled now the times as a child that he had been allowed to come down into the living room late at night to hear broadcasts of championship boxing matches. Later, he would decide that if, while lying in the roadway, he could remember the excitement and fear generated in him by the brutal tattoo of Marciano's fists upon the heads and bodies of Charles and Walcott, there must also have been sufficient time for the car to have driven off and disappeared. At the moment of raising his head, however, and of seeing the bridge and the roadway utterly deserted, he felt only a profound sense of relief and triumph.

The notion that, like David, he had overcome his adversary with a rock was brief, for when Cameron rolled over and looked at the duffel bag beside him, he saw that it had been neatly creased and imprinted with the tread mark of a tire. Following the direction of this mark, his gaze traveled to the edge of the bridge, where, only minutes before, he had sat dangling his feet above the current. But he rejected the implication almost as quickly as it intruded upon him, for if he had truly heard the thud—no matter *what* its implications—would he not also have heard a splash? Yes, it seemed impossible that he would not have heard such a splash. So it was just another trick being played upon him by the excessive heat and his throbbing head. Yet the duffel bag was creased by the unmistakable imprint of a car tire, and the edge of the bridge lay only a few feet beyond it, and now, crawling forward, Cameron looked down into the water and saw that the surface of the current that swirled toward the sea was frothing with bubbles. It must be gas, he thought. It had to be gas—a pocket of decayed vegetation and sea life that had been released by the sudden shifting of a mud-bank. But the bubbles—an effervescence as agitated as that of soda water—continued to burst the surface, and even as he watched, this exhalation was carried out upon the current until, gradually diminishing, it popped up only in sporadic gasps, as if a huge pair of lungs were discharging their final precious cargo.

So the car had gone off the bridge and the implications of the thud would continue to reverberate long after the bubbles ceased to find the sky. Cameron waited for the bubbles to be followed by a head and flailing arms to which he would throw one of the workmen's pieces of lumber. (Yes, why not be generous with the workmen's lumber, especially since the current was too swift to swim against?) But nothing appeared, and he was soon overwhelmed by the terror and comfort of those diminishing bubbles, which, filling him with the horror of drowning, also provided the incontrovertible evidence of his complete and final triumph, thus contriving to carry him beneath the surface to a bed of silt and mud, where he imagined up-ended wheels turning slowly in the depths. Then, emerging from the river, he heard the clatter of the helicopter overhead, and suddenly became aware of his fantastic visibility on this deserted causeway that nothing cloaked from view.

The helicopter was wheeling in the sky above him—a predator, he decided, waiting for its victim to make a move —but after a single, furtive glance, he forced himself not to look up at it. Try to think, he told himself. Try to figure things out. . . . To begin with, there was no question of flight, and even as he realized this, he sat down beside the air compressor and allowed his legs to dangle, as before, above the current. Yes, he would have to stay, simply on the supposition that whoever was in the helicopter had witnessed what had taken place. The question now was what to tell the police. Already his story seemed ludicrous. It was a story no one would believe. The kind of story that required improvement. Perhaps he could say that the car had struck him a glancing blow as he tried to flag it down, thus explaining his injuries and implying that the driver—no doubt blinded by the sun—had lost control. Now that was a better story, one that would not only explain his injuries but also the tire print on his duffel bag—that telltale mark of passage that only the most thorough job of laundering would remove. A better story in every way. Except that it did not take into account the possibility of being contradicted by the pilot of the helicopter. Was it not entirely possible, however, that the pilot had been too busy at his controls to have seen everything that happened? Certainly it was possible that the pilot had not seen him throw the rock. For that matter, it was even possible that the pilot had missed seeing the car go into the river, and that he was now circling overhead and shaking his head in puzzlement. In any case, the car had disappeared entirely, if not forever, for now Cameron saw that the current had slackened and that even at ebb tide the river was too deep and murky to reveal its secrets. Sit tight, he told himself. Keep your head. . . .

As he sat upon the bridge, conjuring up the image of the policeman to whom he would tell his story, Cameron suddenly remembered the toll collector, whose false identification of him would surely plant doubt in the mind of even the most stupid cop. But who would think to question the toll collector, who must still be sweating in his cubicle, poring over his dimes and scanning the roadway—a voyeur ever hopeful of obtaining a rare coin or a forbidden glimpse of thigh? No, only the pilot of the helicopter that was still circling persistently overhead could place him in jeopardy—a pilot who, even now, might be calling over his radio to report with dismay and disbelief that, incredibly, a black sedan had rolled off a bridge at a point southeast of . . . If it has a radio, Cameron thought as lazily as he had entertained a similar notion in the toll collector's booth. Now, gazing up at the helicopter, he gave a wave of his hand—the kind of wave designed to assure any pilot that what he thought he had seen from the corner of his eye on this overwhelmingly brilliant day was merely an errant shadow, or a trickle of sweat, or one of those unaccountable spots that play tricks on the periphery of vision. It was a gesture that carried all the magic of his deepest wish, for no sooner had he lowered his hand than the helicopter flew off straight as an arrow to the north. The pilot is either bored with the mystery of the disappearing auto, or he has gone for help, Cameron thought, and, deciding that he would have to wait at least half an hour to find out, resumed his patient vigil above the river that, with the tide at ebb, had become smooth as glass.

When, to his vast relief, the time he had allotted himself was up and no one had appeared, he got to his feet and retrieved his duffel bag, which was still lying where the car had creased it. Except for the current that had begun to flow gently in the opposite direction, everything was as it had been when he arrived. Cameron found himself filled with a strange and profound calm. With luck he would gain the end of the causeway, melt into the merciful obscurity of the trees, and make his way to town, where Richard Jackson would vanish and he, Robert Cameron, would be free to select another alias. Now, as he prepared to start away, he thought of her letter again, and was glad that he had left it behind. After all, the alias would cut him off from everything in the past, including the possibility of receiving mail, and since the story he was now embarking upon was not the kind that could be conveniently laid aside, it seemed unlikely that he would find himself in need of a bookmark. Yet he could not help wondering if his vanquished antagonist—how easily those words came to mind!—might also have had a correspondent who was anxious about his future. Cameron shuddered as he thought of how cold and dark the river must be. For some moments longer, he stood at the edge of the bridge; then he saw a newspaper tucked into the interior of the air compressor—a newspaper whose week-old banner headline already seemed absurd. Perhaps it was a newspaper that had been put there by some workman who had not had time to finish the sports page. Cameron glanced at the headline that hinted of new bombings as retaliation for fresh provocations that, if continued, could only lead to a breakdown of negotiations and to further escalation. Afterward, folding the newspaper in three parts, and tucking the last edge inside in the style of newsboys, he tossed it in a gentle arc out over the water.

Once he had crossed the bridge, he did not look back.

Five minutes later, he reached the end of the causeway, and ten minutes after that, he climbed out of a laundry truck (from whose driver he was careful to keep his face averted) at the outskirts of the town that nestled against the sea.

4

Cameron found himself at the head of an avenue that descended in a gentle slide to a waterfront amusement center, where an ocean pier continued out to sea to which was tethered, like a giant crab, a dance casino supported on a maze of spindly stilts. Broad and treeless, the avenue was lined on either side with shops, bars, and restaurants whose dilapidated façades contrived to give it (perhaps because of the automobiles that, parked nose to curb, appeared to be hitched to the meters on the sidewalks) the look of a main drag in a western movie set. Nearby stood a church surmounted by a fake lighthouse instead of a steeple, and an ornate gingerbread police station with scalloped shingles and a blue globe above an entrance from which now emerged a patrolman who wore the short-sleeved white shirt and matching hat of an ice cream vendor. Cameron turned away from the policeman's line of vision and walked down the avenue to the amusement center, where a Ferris wheel, a fun house, a merry-go-round, and a whip ride were spinning, rocking, and whirling full tilt for a crowd of tourists. Here, the atmosphere was saturated with an homogenized odor of frying clams, grilling frankfurters, and baking pizzas, which, emanating from a few short-order stands, was carried in visible suspension on a greasy smog that formed an essential oil for the saccharine smell of spun-sugar candy, and that was pulsated over the entire area by shock waves of electronically produced rock and roll coming from competing public-address bellows in the various arcades. Cameron headed toward the ocean pier through a gantlet of pinball machines and nearly ran headlong into another of the town's harmless-looking policemen, whom he managed to avoid at the last instant by veering off to the entranceway of a shop that sold comic postcards, straw beach hats, bottles of suntan lotion, and the kind of inflatable and improbably shaped plastic sea animals that expire quickly and lead gaudy afterlives among

24

flotsam at the high-tide mark. Pretending to examine the postcards, he found himself looking at the caricature of a bleary-eyed and obviously hung-over blonde who, clad in panties and bra, and having just got out of bed, was studying herself in a mirror and saying to the accompaniment of a stream of effervescent bubbles that were supposed to represent the matinal effect of some heavy drinking, "Gee, I hope I had a good time last night." At this point, the policeman turned away, but Cameron scarcely noticed, for he was staring at the idiotic card whose bubbles signified an alcoholic evening and, according to the caption, who knew what else? Who knows what those or any bubbles signify? he reflected grimly, and started out across the pier.

Halfway to the casino, he stopped to rest on one of the wooden benches that lined the railing. The pier was swaying gently from the waves that washed against its pilings, and he had a sudden desire to curl up and fall asleep. Instead, he kept his eyes open by scanning the coastline—a sandy, crescent-shaped beach that stretched away for miles on either side to a horizon that was soft with haze. To the south, the beach was lined with cottages, and to the north with a row of large wooden hotels that looked like excursion boats stranded upon the sand. Stifling a yawn, Cameron examined a sign opposite him that admonished passers-by to THROW ALL CIGARETTES OVERBOARD, and another sign that urged them to look at moray eels and piranha fish in an aquarium on the top floor of the dance casino. LE PLUS GRAND AQUARIUM MARIN DE LA NOUVELLE-ANGLETERRE—PASSIONNANT ET INSTRUCTIF, read a third sign for the benefit of French-Canadian visitors. 250 VARIÉTÉS DE POISSONS, VIVANT QUI NAGENT SOUS VOS YEUX. VOYEZ AUJOURD'HUI LA VIE MYSTÉRIEUSE DES PROFONDEURS DE L'OCÉAN. An aquarium on a dead-end pier, Cameron thought. What an unlikely place to hide! But he was beginning not to feel any longer like a fugitive in this make-believe town with its carnival stenches, its gyrating appendages, and its good-humorously uniformed cops. No one's going to come looking for me here," he told himself.

". . . *la vie mystérieuse des porfondeurs de l'océan*"—the phrase kept returning to his mind. How comforting to be reminded of one's darkest secret in a language other than one's own! And to be assured of the proximity of a border on the other side of which he would find safe haven. Cameron closed his eyes and listened to the water lapping against the pier. Then he dozed.

He was awakened by the sound of a helicopter flying low above the beach, and, bolting to his feet, looked wildly along the pier. But there was nothing accompanying the helicopter except a quick shadow that swept across the roof of the casino, skimmed the water's edge, and scuttled in beneath the rotor blades as the machine settled upon the sand, half a mile away. It can't be the same one, Cameron thought, trying to dispel the disorientation of having awakened to a bad dream. His head was aching, and the shoulder that had cushioned his fall had begun to throb. Now he inserted the dime pronounced worthless by the toll collector into the slot of a pair of sightseeing binoculars mounted on the opposite railing, and, adjusting the lenses to his eyes, focused upon the helicopter and saw a man alight from it and walk across the sand toward one of the hotels. The helicopter took off at once and flew out across the water. Cameron watched the man disappear into the hotel. Then there was a faint clicking sound in the binoculars, and everything went black.

For a long time, he stood at the railing, torn between caution and curiosity. It's probably a helicopter that shuttles between the local airport and the beach, he told himself. There had to be some such explanation. Some rational explanation. But he was in no mood to take anything for granted. He had had enough mystery for one day. Still, he would have to be careful. Simple enough. He would pretend to be looking for a job.

The hotel had the silhouette of a lopsided layer cake. The ground floor was encompassed by a wide veranda; the second story had once been similarly girdled, as was indicated by several door-sized windows and a joint mark that showed through the painted façade like a water line; and the third floor was topped by the peaks and valleys of a bastard mansard roof from which sprouted dozens of dormer windows. Cameron crossed the veranda, pushed through a screen door, and entered a shuttered, stucco-walled lobby that was air-conditioned. For a moment, he stood just inside the doorway, shivering in the cool and squinting into the darkness; then, heels clicking on tile and echoing into the hushed chill as if he were traversing the nave of some dank church, he walked to a semi-circular counter that enclosed the gloomiest portion of the room, and picked up a small silver bell beside a neatly lettered sign that read, "RING FOR SERVICE." Cameron gave the bell a shake, and was rewarded with the kind of tinkle that announces Mass, but even as the delicate sound dampened and died away, he sensed that he was not alone. A second later, he made out the dim outline of a man sitting at a desk behind the counter, a man whose head seemed to materialize from nowhere, disembodied, in illusory suspension, like the head of some religious masterpiece that is both the vanishing point of perspective and the focus of concentration. Now, having become more accustomed to the darkness, he found himself peering at the spare, gaunt face of a man of about sixty whose eyes, which failed in disconcerting fashion to focus properly, gave him the look of Vermeer's astronomer confronting the prospect of infinity.

"Sorry," said Cameron, replacing the bell on the counter. "I didn't see you."

"What d'you want?" the man asked softly.

"I'm looking for work."

At this point, the man pulled on a pair of dark glasses and proceeded to flick a series of switches on the desk which turned on a spotlight affixed to the ceiling above Cameron's head, another mounted upon a wall to one side, and a third that shone directly into his face from somewhere in front of him. "Very well," he said. "Speak."

Squinting uneasily into the glare, Cameron saw that he was being studied through lenses of extraordinary thickness, which created a sense of oversized scrutiny. There's something wrong with his eyes, he thought. "My name's Arthur Coleman," he said stiffly. "I've just arrived in town and I'm looking for work."

"Keep talking. What are your credits?"

"Credits?"

"Television, summer stock, repertory . . ."

"There must be some mistake," Cameron replied. "I'm just looking for a job."

"Actors usually are."

"But I'm not an actor," said Cameron, shaking his head.

"I need work—desk clerk, waiter, dishwasher—even if it's only temporary."

A soft laugh came from beyond the glare. "I think we've made simultaneously incorrect assumptions about one another. You're not an actor and I'm not a hotel manager. I'm a director."

"A director?"

"Of films. My name is Gottschalk. You've heard of it?"

"No, I'm sorry I haven't. Is the—"

"Well, that proves you're not an actor, yet I could have sworn—"

"—manager around?"

"—simply because, like so many prospective young actors who appear before me favoring what they consider to be their photogenic side, you've kept your face partially averted."

"I had an accident," Cameron explained, running a finger tentatively over his swollen cheekbone. "Could I speak to the manager?"

"But there is no manager! This is a film company on location. Now, about your accident . . ."

"It's a long story," said Cameron, lifting his duffel bag. "I won't take any more of your time."

"Stories," Gottschalk observed, "are my profession. You're looking for work? Well, there's a chance I can use you. So please continue. The accident, for example. Where did it take place?"

"On a causeway," Cameron said.

"On a causeway," echoed the director, turning off the lights. "Speak slowly and clearly. Tell me what happened."

For a second, Cameron stood mute, trying to resist the command of a voice that was full of quiet authority, like the voice of a priest exacting confession. He had forgotten completely about the helicopter. "The damnedest thing," he murmured. "You won't believe it."

5

When Cameron finished telling his story, the director remained silent, facing a window whose bamboo shade, drown against the flat trajectory blaze of the late afternoon sun, admitted just enough light around the edges now to dispel the gloom that had earlier pervaded the lobby. Leaning his elbows on the counter, Cameron also faced the window shade, and found himself wondering if the sun falling behind the headlands at the western end of the marsh were not surrounding the dark outline of the bridge with similar light. Yes, it was comforting to believe that the pocket of water on its seaward side—a pocket too deep to reveal its bottommost secrets even at low tide—was being overlaid with shadow, and now, with his entire spirit, Cameron faced west and imagined himself bathed by the cool passage of a whole series of shadows cast by the gnomons of the day. It was as if some part of each of them—the toll booth, the bridge, the pier, and this ark-like hotel on the sand—were fleeing toward the sea whose immense presence and infinite capacity for silence he felt at his back. Time is passing, Cameron thought, welcoming his shadowy incremental sense of it and wondering how a man with faulty eyesight could possibly conjure up in all their brilliance the sun-struck settings of his noonday narrative. But if the director could not be expected to imagine the terrifying glare of such illumination, what point was there in dragging in the iridescent explosions of those incriminating bubbles which had not been preceded by a splash that even a blind man could hear? No point at all, Cameron decided. So he had left them out of his story, just as he had neglected to mention his flight from the bus, the rock he had thrown at the car, and the helicopter which, as he told his tale, he had remembered in time to delete. Now, glancing at Gottschalk, he wondered if it would be up to him to break the silence.

But the director, who had listened to his story without

interruption, suddenly remarked that it contained several aspects for further consideration. Then he added that they might as well be taken up in the order in which they had occurred, since things were usually easiest to sort out that way. "Yes, first things first," he said. "Let's start out by examining the belated attempt of the toll collector to bring you back."

"Okay," replied Cameron, who was puzzled but secretly relieved at this unlikely point of departure. "But I ought to make it clear that I included the toll collector only as a kind of introduction."

"My own work is free of such constrictions," Gottschalk observed. "I avoid stories with a beginning, middle, and end. For me the interesting thing is fragments and the order in which I choose to put them."

"Perhaps I should scramble the sequence and start again," said Cameron with a laugh.

The director smiled and shook his head. "No, the prologue as it stands presents an intriguing mystery, and since there are subsequent ambiguities in your story that need clarification, we can perhaps benefit from the practice of solving this one, which, though it seems insignificant, occurs at the outset."

Cameron answered with a shrug that the actions of the toll collector could probably best be chalked up to the heat.

"You've already blamed a great deal upon the heat," Gottschalk said. "Let's absolve the weather wherever possible, however, in order to strengthen the rest of your case."

Cameron nodded without reply, but he had taken note of the legal quality of the director's language. He suspects something, he told himself moodily. Somewhere along the line, you must have given yourself away. . . .

"Now if I understand you correctly, the toll collector tried to delay your departure by emerging from his booth and shouting 'Whoa!' "

"That's right," Cameron said. "And what else except for frying brains could have led him to confuse me with a horse?"

"If the heat was to blame at all, it was probably not its effect upon the lucidity of the toll collector, but upon your own ability to hear what he was saying."

"As far as I know, there's nothing wrong with my hearing."

"Nevertheless, I think I can safely assert that when the toll collector emerged from his booth, he did not shout 'Whoa!' but something that was phonetically similar."

"What makes you so sure?"

"Because all radios carry the same news."

Cameron took a deep breath, but found that he could not control the sudden trembling in his knees. He remembered having mentioned the toll collector's radio, but he was certain that he had said nothing of his fear that the pilot of the helicopter might have used his set to report an accident on the causeway. In fact, he was absolutely certain, for had he not deliberately exorcised all mention of the helicopter from his tale? "Did you say *all* radios?" he asked.

"Yes, but with special reference to the toll collector's and my own."

"The toll collector's radio was out of order."

"A matter of crossed wires or a loose tube connection. These old radios are all alike. When you left him, the toll collector must have gone into his booth, given his set an impatient slap, and been rewarded with the latest news."

"I don't follow you," Cameron said.

"The noonday broadcast reported that negotiations had broken down and that advance units of two divisions had driven through the demilitarized zone and launched an invasion of the North. In short, that full-scale war had broken out."

Cameron was on the verge of saying that he still did not understand, when he was suddenly overtaken by his recollection of the toll collector calling to him through the heat, and repeating over and over the absurd and futile shout that was indeed phonetically similar to the one Gottschalk was suggesting he had heard. Yes, the director must be right; the shout was false—its meaning distorted by the same heat that muffled the splash that had to be the only logical sequel to the pulpy thud made by the rock—and this realization now trampled Cameron's train of thought and echoed in his head with the kind of sound effect that accompanies the most terrifying and implausible dreams.

The director had pulled on his thick spectacles, and was peering intently at him. "No need for alarm," he said. "The broadcast was refuted a short while later by official denials that described it as an elaborate hoax. So as it turns out, there's no war. At least, no full-scale war. Just a bad scare resulting from someone's odd notion of a joke. A bad scare from which you were spared by an error of your own making. Either way, you see, the toll collector's shouts were false."

"False," Cameron mumbled. His head was reeling as if his mind had been dissected into fragments and placed upon the viewing plate of a kaleidoscope for his own inspection.

"How d'you feel?" the director inquired.

"Tired," Cameron replied.

"Only natural after such an experience. Why don't you come in behind the counter and take a seat? Yes . . . And now, having unraveled one mystery, let's proceed to the next, which occurs after you pass the barricades and take the causeway, does it not?"

"Yes," Cameron answered, as readily as a witness being led through prepared testimony by his attorney.

"Or, more precisely, on the bridge."

"Yes."

"Now the driver of the car—the man whom you so promptly assumed was trying to kill you—he came from the opposite direction?"

"Yes."

"And were there barricades at that end of the causeway?"

"I forget."

"Try to remember."

"I think there probably were."

"So the driver had to stop his vehicle, climb out, and pull aside a sawhorse in order to cross the causeway."

"What does it matter?" said Cameron, who was thinking that the director had a fondness for indirection. "What are you after?"

"Motive," Gottschalk replied. "You've described a whole series of events culminating in an attempt upon your life, but what's the explanation?"

"I have none."

"You mean you have no interest."

"Perhaps there isn't any explanation."

"Skepticism is always a convenient mask."

"Why not arrange the fragments to suit yourself?"

"You young people have no curiosity," the director observed. "That's because you have no hope. You're simply spectators."

By way of reply, Cameron held up a hand in mock self-defense, to which Gottschalk responded with a laugh that they should get back on the track. "In this case, the causeway across the marsh," he went on. "But let's make an assumption about the driver. Let's assume for the sake of argument that he knew what he was about when he removed the sawhorse."

"You mean that he had some motive for trying to kill me?"

"No, just that he had some reason to cross the causeway."

"Anything is possible."

"Exactly."

"But who would act the way he did except . . . ?"

"A madman?" said Gottschalk, supplying the word as easily as he might have proffered a light.

"Well, isn't that the obvious conclusion?"

"Not so obvious in this case. If this so-called madman really intended to kill you, why on earth did he disappear when you were lying helpless in the road?"

"Who knows?"

"Unless, of course . . ."

"Unless what?" asked Cameron, who hoped that the most unearthly reason would appear to be the least possible, and was not prepared to hear the director begin a surmise for which every fiber of his being had already supplied corroboration.

"It was not a madman to begin with."

Cameron heaved an audible sigh of relief.

"But someone in perfect control of his faculties, who had a perfectly legitimate reason for being on the causeway."

"What are you suggesting?"

"Merely that you may have mistaken the driver's intent in the same way you mistook the toll collector's shout," Gottschalk replied. "Remember, it was you who said anything is possible."

"Yes," Cameron said wearily. "But where does that lead us?"

"To further conjecture," replied Gottschalk with a smile. "Endless conjecture."

"I'm tired already," said Cameron, who was thinking that the director had an extraordinary tendency toward complications. But he was grateful, too, for it seemed to him that Gottschalk had taken over his story, and that he had merely become an actor reading from an unfinished script which no longer bore the burden of a single conclusion but contained the promise of multiple endings. Yes, there were all manner of endings to his story, and he could now relinquish the task of their selection to the director and his penchant for putting fragments together. "There's just one thing," he said. "Something I forgot to mention. While all of it was going on, there was a helicopter. . . ."

"A helicopter?"

"Overhead."

"Interesting," Gottschalk murmured. "What d'you suppose it was doing there?"

"How would I know?" said Cameron with a shrug. "At first, it seemed to be racing the car. But I really couldn't tell. Because of the sun."

"Ah, yes, the sun! The sun is certainly an accomplice in this tale of yours."

"All right, let's not play cat and mouse," Cameron replied evenly. "It so happens I saw the helicopter land out front a while ago."

"So you want to know about the helicopter," said Gottschalk with a smile. "That's simple enough. The helicopter's mine, which is to say I rent it."

"You rent it!" Cameron exclaimed. "What for?"

"The answer to that is going to explain a good deal. But first, let's go on to what is for me the most puzzling aspect of all. In short, why, having miraculously escaped with your life, did you not notify the police when you got to town?"

"I was afraid they wouldn't believe me. Also, since I'd been hitchhiking, I was afraid of being arrested and charged with vagrancy."

"But surely, under the circumstances—"

"Take it or leave it," Cameron snapped.

"—it's your duty to notify them now," Gottschalk continued, and placed his hand on the receiver of the telephone that sat upon his desk.

"No," Cameron said. "I can't go to the police."

"Can't?"

"It's another story."

"Longer than the one I've been listening to?" asked the director, lifting the receiver off its cradle.

"Look, I can't go to the police because—"

"Yes?"

"—I've gone over the hill. I'm A.W.O.L. I'm going to desert."

"A deserter," Gottschalk murmured. "Perfect! I should have thought of it myself."

"Listen, in a few more weeks I would have turned twenty-six. I would have been too old. They couldn't have touched me. Instead, at the last moment, they withdrew my deferment."

"Well, now you've got it back."

"What?"

"Your deferment," said the director with a smile. "Haven't you been granted the best deferment of all?"

"What are you talking about?"

"The one you received on the causeway," said the director, hanging up the phone.

This man's got more than a fondness for indirection, Cameron thought. It's a positive vice with him. "Then you're not going to report me," he said.

"Certainly not. In fact, I'm going to hire you to work for me."

"Doing what?"

"Replacing a stunt man."

"I don't understand."

"Who suddenly disappeared."

"You mean . . . ?"

"Gone off the deep end, as it were."

"Oh, my God," said Cameron. "You mean the helicopter . . ."

"Yes," the director murmured. "The helicopter was filming a scene in which a car goes off a bridge and into a river."

"But how was I to know?"

"You couldn't have known," said Gottschalk sympathetically. "I'm convinced that you made perfectly honest and, under the circumstances, natural mistake."

"But I don't deserve—I mean you've no right, really to let it go at that."

"I'm not letting it go. The stunt man has disappeared, so I'm hiring you to replace him. Nature always fills a vacuum."

"But I know nothing about stunts!"

"On the contrary, it seems to me you've demonstrated a certain natural talent for them."

"You mean you're just going to give me his job? Like that?"

"Like that."

"But who was he?"

"A young man like yourself," said the director with a shrug. "Someone hired on the spur of the moment for a temporary job."

Cameron shook his head. "You're forgetting I'm a fugitive," he protested. "It's just a matter of time before they come looking for me."

"By then you'll have disappeared. You'll have become another person—a stunt man doubling for an actor who, in turn, is playing a role. In fact, the role of a fugitive."

Is this bird as crazy as he sounds? Cameron wondered. "I don't see how we can get away with it," he declared.

The director made no reply, but lifted the receiver of the phone, dialed a number, and, after a moment's pause, said, "Chief Broussard? About that accident. A ridiculous mistake, as it turns out. The cameraman was blinded by the sun." Here, Gottschalk smiled at Cameron. "Yes, indeed he did. Just now. Perfectly safe. Sound as a dollar. Nine lives, those fellows. Yes, yes . . . Very sorry for having troubled you. Very sorry indeed . . . Yes, certainly. Everything as scheduled. Tomorrow night on the pier . . . Good . . . Fine . . . Many thanks."

When Gottschalk hung up the phone, he turned to Cameron and gave a shrug. "Well," he said, "now you've been given still another deferment. A whole new chance at life."

Cameron shook his head in wonderment. "I hardly know what to say," he murmured. "You've no reason to be so kind."

"Take it or leave it," the director replied. "Not that you have much choice."

"I see."

"Do you?" Gottschalk exclaimed softly, and began to chuckle. At first, it was an almost soundless laugh; then, rising on a crescendo of suppressed mirth, it broke into a guffaw; and, finally, the director simply threw his head back and gave way to gales of infectious glee that filled the lobby.

"What's so funny?" Cameron said.

"Ha, ha . . . what a crazy mistake!"

"You mean thinking that the stunt was real?"

"No!" cried the director, nearly choking. "I mean the toll collector telling you there was war. And you convinced he was a lunatic shouting 'Whoa!' Ha, ha, ha . . . Aaaha, ha, ha!"

Cameron also had begun to laugh. Then, cued by the director—in fact, triggered as if by an exploding device—he was suddenly overtaken by a paroxysm of laughter. Leaning back in his chair, he thought of the toll collector popping in and out of his cubicle like a cuckoo on the hour of twelve, and laughed until he thought he would be sick. Finally, when Gottschalk had stifled his own hilarity long enough to hand him the key to a room on the top floor, he ran laughing from the lobby and up three flights of stairs. But even when he had entered his room and flung himself face down upon the bed, he had difficulty suppressing his immoderate joy. He was still trying not to laugh, fifteen minutes later, when he spied a chambermaid passing down the corridor with a load of dirty linen, and gave her his duffel bag to be laundered.

6

During the night, he awoke from a dream and, lying perfectly still upon his bed, tried to orient himself in the dark. Then, remembering where he was and what had happened, he sat up, swung his legs to the floor, and stumbled to the window. Beyond the peaks and valleys of the rooftops, the amusement center was bathed in light. The pier and its dance casino were illuminated by floodlamps, and the Ferris wheel, strung with incandescent bulbs, was spinning in fits and starts as if it were being fingered by a croupier. Cameron was reminded that he had been dreaming of a conflagration. It was not clear where the holocaust was taking place, but Gottschalk was there, wearing the crested, sloping helmet, rubber coat, and rolled-down boots of a fireman, and shouting into a megaphone. . . .

When he awoke again, it was morning. Sunlight was streaming through the window, and standing in a shaft of it at the foot of his bed was a girl in a white dress who carried a black satchel and some towels.

"Make-up," she said softly.

Cameron sat up, blinking, and found himself looking at an astonishingly well-built girl, with broad hips and heavy breasts that were revealed in nylon outline beneath the kind of semi-transparent dress worn by nurses and beauticians. "I'm awake," he replied. "Who're you?"

"*Make*-up," she said with a laugh, and put the bag and towels on the bed. "As in Max Factor. I'm going to give you a new face."

"A new day, a new face," said Cameron with a yawn. To go with my new role, he thought, reaching for his pants.

"First you have to take off those whiskers."

Cameron climbed out of bed and slipped into his pants with the same motion; then he went to a washstand and shaved. A few minutes later, he was sitting in a chair—eyes shut, chin on hands, and hand on sink—as the girl shampooed him vigorously with peroxide. "What am I going to look like?" he asked.

"A beach boy," she told him. "Malibu-style."

"You from California?"

"Uh-huh."

"What's your name?"

"Denise."

He hesitated, not wanting to appear inquisitive. "Been here long?"

"Couple of weeks."

"I just arrived," he said. "What d'you know about this film?"

"Strictly low-budget and B-grade."

He suppressed another question and, for several minutes, submitted to her ministrations in silence.

When she had given his hair a final rinse, the make-up girl told him to sit up. "Now comes the gunk," she said. "Eyeshadow, pancake, sideburns, the works. Hey, what happened to you? To your face, I mean."

"A funny thing," Cameron replied. "On my way to the movies."

"Well, that'll take some covering up. But I'll be laying it on thick, anyway. They're going to be shooting you in the water, so the stuff's got to stick."

Cameron started to ask another question, but once again thought better of it. Instead, he sat patiently as Denise—alternately patting and painting—applied several layers of cosmetics to his face.

When she had finished, she stepped back and studied him with cool professional appraisal. "You sure look different," she told him cheerfully. "Your own mother would have to sand-blast."

Cameron stood up, looked into the mirror above the sink, and found himself staring at the slightly corrupt face of an aging surfer. "My God, you're right?" he exclaimed.

"How does it feel?"

"Like plaster of Paris."

"You'll get used to it."

"I don't mind," said Cameron, smiling to himself. I'm transformed, he thought, glancing again at the face in the mirror. I'm another person. . . . "It's perfect," he told her. "By the way, *who* am I supposed to look like?"

Taking his arm, Denise led him to the window. "There you are—the tall one in swimming trunks. That's Lee Jordan."

Cameron looked down at the beach and saw a bronzed, blond man standing at the water's edge with a woman who was wearing a bikini and a large straw hat. "Never heard of him," he said.

"A television cowboy and God's gift to women. When I made *him* up, the other day, he had his hand up my skirt the whole time."

"What did you do?" Cameron inquired.

"Kept my legs together."

He laughed, amused by her frankness. "Who's the girl beside him?"

"That's Nina Mabry."

"Nina Mabry," Cameron said. "Wasn't she the mistress of—"

"—that's the way the—"

"—at the time he was—"

"—rumor—"

"—shot?"

"—goes."

"Huh," said Cameron.

"After the assassination, she disappeared for a long time. They say with a nervous breakdown. Mr. G is supposed to have rescued her. Now he's writing a movie for her to star in. His great opus, I hear."

"Funny, you know, but I've never heard of Gottschalk either."

"He was on top thirty years ago. Then he got washed up. Now he's trying to make a comeback along with Nina Mabry, speaking of whom I've got to locate her panties."

"Her what?"

"A dozen pair. The chambermaid put them into the regular wash by mistake, and Miss Mabry threw a fit. Gave me holy hell. See, I'm also wardrobe mistress. I'd probably be script girl, too, except there's no script to this flick. Mr. G's doing it out of his head. As he goes along."

Cameron looked out the window again, and saw that Jordan and the actress had been joined by a short, bandy-legged man with an immense torso, who wore a pair of chino pants cut off raggedly at the knees, and a white handkerchief knotted around his head.

"That's Bruno da Fé," Denise told him. "As in Santa Fe. He's been with Gottschalk for years. They're practically inseparable."

"What does he do?"

"Bruno's the cameraman. He's always wanted to be a director, but he hasn't got the imagination for it, so he makes porno films on the side. Supposed to have a flair for them. Five men and a girl with her ass in the air—that kind of thing."

Cameron studied Denise's face. There was a weariness and sense of fatality in it that he found exciting.

"It's a whole other world," she told him. "You haven't been a stunt man very long, have you?"

"No," he said. A whole other world, he was thinking happily.

"How'd you get to be one?"

He smiled at her and shook his head. "By accident," he said.

She gave a shrug and a knowing nod. "C'mon while I collect Miss Mabry's dainties. They're just next door."

Cameron followed her down the corridor to the chambermaid's room, which was awash with a mountainous pile of linen, and stood inside the doorway as she waded about, flinging bed sheets, towels, and pillowcases to the right and left of her. The she held up between thumbs and forefingers for his inspection a pair of blue lace panties whose brevity and diaphaneity came straight from the pages of some covert magazine for men.

"Nice, hmm?"

"Yes," he replied thickly.

"Tiny, though."

Tongue-tied, he gave a shrug.

Denise gazed into his eyes. Then, moving her lips, she asked a short and soundless question.

"Yes," he said.

"Well, do something," she told him with a smirk. "You're beginning to look like a hatrack." Now, enjoying his confusion, she peeled off her dress, undid her bra, and, leaning slightly toward him, stepped out of her panties with a quick bicycle motion that brought each knee toward her chin.

Stunned, he simply stood there, flabbergasted by the size of her breasts, which, though floating on hips of sufficient breadth and buoyancy, completely capsized his own sense of proportion. Then, just when he was beginning to recover himself, she astonished him again by diving into the pile of linen, where, thrashing her arms and wriggling her legs, she promptly disappeared from view. Cameron hesitated, as if worried that undressing might unmask him, and found himself thinking of those other breasts that, like her handwriting, were small, rounded, and delicately tipped. It was a fleeting, almost subliminal memory. His new face assured his annoymity and obviated any thought of restraint or regret. For a moment longer, he stood beside the pile of laundry beneath which Denise had disappeared. Then he took off his clothes, waded into it, and, like a man clamming in deep water, began to grope for her.

She eluded him by staying close to the bottom, until, with a mixture of amusement and exasperation, he made a deep dive, found a foot, and held it fast. Now, parting some linen with his free hand, he uncovered a leg. When he released her foot, however, he was rewarded with a kick that sent him reeling. At this point, circling in the wary fashion of a skin diver seeking to avoid the tentacles of an octopus, he reached below the surface and, with a quick, deft thrust, found the juncture of her thighs. For a brief interval, she struggled to get free, but the weight of the bedclothes upon her and the gentle yet insistent pressure of his fingertips soon produced the immobility he desired. Pushing aside the remaining linen, he parted her thighs and, crooking his elbows behind the backs of her knees, leaned forward until the calves of her legs were resting upon his shoulders. For a second longer, he hovered above her, groping to support his hands; then, with a swift descent that encountered no resistance, he plunged them into the depths of the pile, from whence came a series of cushioned shudders and smothered cries that were accompanied by delicate pressure from the deliciously cold soles of the feet she somehow contrived to place against the small of his back.

Afterward, they lay side by side, floating upon a sea of laundry that by now covered most of the room. Cameron shut his eyes and thought of the freshly laundered duffel bag that must be somewhere beneath him.

Gently, dexterously, Denise awoke him from a brief doze,

and, straddling him at the waist, leaned forward and lifted her eyebrows in another silent question.

Marveling at her breasts, framed in the cavity of her diaphragm, Cameron placed his hands upon her hips, and said, simply, "Yes."

Smiling dreamily, Denise bent over him and, with easy oscillation, offered first one and then the other of her nipples.

"Yes," he said.

Sitting back, she removed his hands from her hips, placed his arms at his side, and, anchoring them with her knees, began to travel over him.

Cameron watched her face disappear beyond his view, and lay perfectly still—a prisoner in contemplation. Then, raising his head slightly, he saw the door of the room between her thighs. When her knees reached his shoulders, Denise straightened, and, gazing up at her, he saw a strange expression—a mingling of contentment and contempt—upon her face.

"'Stunt man," she murmured, and, cupping his head with both hands, drew him to her.

7

Sunlight poured through the front windows of the hotel and advanced like tide across the lobby floor until stemmed, as if by a sea wall, at the edge of the counter where the director, his head nodding with the monotony of a metronome set for adagio, sat beside a man to whose conversation he was paying the respectful but weary attention one accords a piece of classical music that is too well known to hold surprises. Cameron had come halfway down the stairs; now, catching sight of the hat sitting upon the desk between Gottschalk and his visitor—a hat that under other circumstances would have evoked nothing more sinister than a Popsicle—he retreated slowly to the landing and stood beside a dumb-waiter shaft.

". . . so you've got to admit it sounds queer," said a gravelly voice from below. "Your cameraman—this Dufee fellow—his story's weird. Yesterday, he was sure something had gone wrong. Today—"

"He's equally sure that nothing did," Gottschalk interrupted with a laugh. "But don't forget that in the meantime the stunt man showed up safe and sound."

"I know. What I don't get, though, is why Dufee—"

"Da Fé," Gottschalk corrected.

"—da Fé not only failed to recognize the stunt man when he was sitting right below him on the bridge, but was convinced that it was someone else!"

"Consider the circumstances," said Gottschalk coolly. "First, the blinding sun; secondly, da Fé's preoccupation with his camera; then the suddenness with which the whole carefully arranged sequence went awry; and, last but not least, the appearance of the stunt man himself."

"What d'you mean—'the appearance of the stunt man'?"

"Simply that he was a frightened fellow—disheveled and badly shaken from his last-second leap from the car. He'd lost his nerve, you see. Happens every once in a while. Even to the best of them."

44

"You mean he was supposed to go into the water?"

"It would hardly look right otherwise, would it? On film, I mean."

"Jesus, what a way to make a living!"

"They take certain risks," the director admitted. "Which, of course, is what we pay them for."

"Well, I'd like to ask him a few questions. About this other business."

"Certainly," the director replied. "But what makes you think he'll be able to tell you anything about that?"

"A question of timing. The military police have come up with a witness who saw their suspect heading for the causeway just a short while before your man got there."

"You don't say," said Gottschalk.

"So it's possible the stunt man passed him on the road."

"Anything is possible," the director murmured. "I'll ring up his room. His name is Coleman, by the way."

"That's funny. I thought you told me yesterday it was—"

"Coleman," said the director, firmly, "Arthur Coleman."

The intercom on the wall beside his bed was buzzing insistently when Cameron, having raced up two flights of stairs, burst into the room and, panting for breath, removed the receiver from its hook.

"Coleman?"

"Yes, I know," Cameron gasped. "Arthur Coleman . . . I was standing on the steps. I—"

"Coleman, Chief Broussard of the police is here."

"Listen, I've got a new face," Cameron said. "But is it new enough?"

"He wants to talk to you."

"I'll be right down. Now look, about that witness . . ."

But the director had already hung up.

The chief of police was a heavy-set man in his early fifties, with piercing blue eyes, blunt features, and gray hair that, sparse to begin with, had been cropped close enough to his scalp to look like the stubble of a beard. There was a meld of cunning and crudity in his face, but these elements remained oddly unblended at the mouth—a full, feminine mouth from which sprouted, incongruously, a frayed cigar that the chief shifted orally from one side to the other as, leaning forward in his chair, he proffered a hand whose grip Cameron barely managed to endure without wincing. Now, sitting back, he regarded the younger man with a curious frown that Cameron fervently hoped was not the harbinger of recognition.

"About yesterday, Coleman. See anything out there? Anything out of the ordinary, I mean."

Cameron gave a shrug that was also a stall for time, for racing through his mind was the realization that he must pretend ignorance without playing dumb. "No," he replied. "Nothing."

"Funny," the chief muttered in his hoarse voice. "The M.P.'s found somebody who swears he was headed for the causeway. At noon, too."

"And who was that?" the director asked.

"Toll collector on the other side of the river. Told the military police and me the same story. And made a positive identification to boot."

"You see," said Gottschalk, turning to Cameron, "Chief Broussard and the military authorities are looking for a young man who has decided that army life is not exactly to his liking."

"An A.W.O.L.," explained the chief, who produced a passport-size photograph from a pocket behind the gold badge that was affixed to his shirt, and handed it to Cameron.

Why, it doesn't even look like me! Cameron thought. Now, pretending to examine the photo, he remembered the sullenness with which he had faced the cameras at the induction center, and gave his head a shake.

"Doesn't ring a bell, hanh?"

"Never laid eyes on him," said Cameron coolly, and handed back the picture.

"Think it's possible you could've missed him?"

Cameron considered his answer carefully. "It's possible," he said finally. "But not likely. I mean, where could he hide out there?"

"That's exactly what I've been wondering," the chief replied.

"Perhaps your fugitive decided not to cross the causeway to begin with," Gottschalk suggested.

"Perhaps," said the chief, who seemed lost in reflection. "Tell me something, Coleman. How come you lost your nerve?"

"Why, I—" Stunned by the sudden thrust of the question,

Cameron broke off and shook his head. "—don't know. I mean . . ."

"I guess you were pretty shook up, hanh?"

Cameron tried to speak, but only succeeded in giving out a croak.

Working his jaws, the chief shifted his cigar again. "So it's possible you weren't paying much attention, right? To the road."

"Well, no. I mean, *yes*."

The director had started to say something, but the chief held up his hand. "I'm getting an idea," he said. "This fellow da Fé—he was up in the helicopter with his camera, you say?"

"That's correct," Gottschalk replied.

"Taking pictures?"

"Yes."

"Then it could be on film."

"What could be on film?"

"What he and Coleman here may have overlooked."

"Well, anything is possible," the director said with a laugh. "Would you like to see the rushes?"

"Might as well, hanh?"

"Might as well, indeed! One admires your professional thoroughness, chief. The film is presently being developed, of course, but when it comes back—tomorrow or the next day— I'll be glad to arrange a special screening for you."

"Much obliged," the chief replied, and got to his feet.

"Of course, Coleman here is going to be embarrassed. He'd probably just as soon forget the whole affair, wouldn't you, Coleman?"

The chief gave Cameron a nod that was intended to convey sympathy. "Nothing personal, hanh?"

"Sure," Cameron managed to reply. "Business is always business."

"Exactly!" said Gottschalk with a chuckle. "I must say, chief, you seem to be pursuing the business at hand—this young fellow—with a vengeance."

"Nothing personal there, either," the chief replied. "It's just that if we don't nab him in a day or two, we'll have the feds in town. And the longer those birds nose around, the more they're liable to turn up."

"I hadn't thought of that," the director murmured. "Smart operators, I expect."

"Not so smart as they like to think," the chief said sourly. "Pair of them came around a few months ago looking for the Picard boy who took off when his draft number came up. They went to the old man and spent half a day tough-talking him. Finally scared him enough so he told them where the kid had gone. Bordeaux . . ."

"Bordeaux?" Gottschalk echoed.

"Bordeaux," the chief said softly. "Which sent the smart boys tearing off to Portland to look through sailing lists and shipping manifests for all the tramps and trawlers that had gone out of there in the last six months. Figured the kid had shipped out for France, see? Nice theory. Only one trouble with it."

"What was that?"

"Bordeaux," said the chief with a faint smile, "is also a town on the northwest side of Montreal."

The director threw his head back and gave a laugh. "So you made the feds, as you call them, look bad, eh?"

"Me?" said the chief in his grating voice, chewing on his cigar, and deadpanning the reply. "I didn't do anything. Picard is a great-uncle of mine. Besides, the war's a crock. It isn't worth a boy's toenail."

"Still, you're going to hunt down this young fellow you've been telling us about."

"That's different. I got reason to believe he's holed up in my bailiwick."

"To think," Gottschalk murmured, "that his greatest danger is your professional pride. It doesn't seem fair, does it? Let's at least hope that he's had sense enough to head north."

The chief pursed his lips around the cigar and shook his head. "State police are watching all the roads. He doesn't have the chance of a snowball in hell."

"But you say you have reason to believe he's here."

"I've got a hunch is all."

"Like looking for the proverbial needle, isn't it? I mean with all the tourists."

"Not so hard as you might think," said the chief. "No different from the rest of us, is he? Got to eat and sleep, hanh? Means he's got to show himself. Fact, if he's here, I bet we'll take him tonight."

"You don't say."

"Counting on you is one reason."

"Me?" exclaimed the director. "Ah, ha, now that's a good one."

The chief narrowed his shrewd blue eyes and stubbed out his cigar in an ash tray. "This scene you people are shooting out on the pier," he said. "Going to draw a big crowd. Liable to give our man a false sense of security."

"It would never have occurred to me," Gottschalk replied. "You're a clever fellow, Chief Broussard. I'd hate to have you looking for me."

The chief shrugged a modest disclaimer, picked up his white, peaked cap, and set it upon his bristling head. "Routine," he declared, and started for the door.

"Since you're counting on us," Gottschalk called after him, "we'll try to do our best."

The chief paused at the door, looked back, and grinned at Cameron. "Keep your chin up tonight, young fella, hanh?"

Gottschalk waited until the chief had gone. Then he said, "Well, we can be sure of at least one thing."

"What's that?" Cameron asked.

"Your face," the director replied with a smile. "It's new enough."

"Listen, why on earth did you tell him he could see the film?"

"My dear young man, what else was there to do? If I had refused, he would simply have confiscated it."

"But it's a giveaway. It'll show everything!"

"Everything? No, that would be much too literal. In the end, one never shows or tells everything, does one? Take, for example, the story you told me yesterday. But then, my point is simply that all our stories require deletion."

"Let's get down to cases," Cameron said. "What about the film?"

"The film is just another story," Gottschalk replied. "It will come back from the developing lab in the roughest of versions, so we'll undertake to make some improvements in it."

"You mean deletions," said Cameron with a grin.

"Yes, with a bit of cutting here and there, and by switching a few frames this way and that, we'll change the story to suit ourselves."

"But will we fool the chief?"

"My dear young fellow, it isn't a question of fooling the chief. He's no man to underestimate, but rest assured, when he goes to the movies he's simply another spectator who not only wants to be deceived, but who will ensure his own deception by suspending his disbelief and reacting to illusion. Which explains the immediacy of the cinema, you see, the wonderfully intense feeling of being present. Yes, when our spectator—in this case, Chief Broussard—submits to the world of film, his participation becomes a state of trance."

"Very interesting," Cameron said. "I happen to be wide awake, however, and full of disbelief."

The director gave a patient smile. "Tell me, d'you believe what happened?"

"What happened?" Cameron echoed. "What d'you mean?"

The director shrugged. "On the causeway yesterday. In the film we'll show the chief tomorrow. What's the difference? Which, in fact, is real?"

"Suppose you tell me."

"Art, my friend. Only art is real. Only art repeats itself. Yes, over and over. Endlessly."

Cameron shook his head. It's like talking to an oracle, he thought. "D'you always speak in riddles?" he said.

The director smiled again. "Strange," he murmured. "Your lack of curiosity. I was sure you were going to ask me about something else."

"What?" asked Cameron wearily.

"The stunt," Gottschalk replied. "The one you'll be performing on the pier tonight."

How different everything seemed! Cameron could scarcely believe it. Now, glancing at the bilingual sign that advertised the aquarium, he smiled to himself. Yes, less than a day later, the sign had lost its terrifying implications, and everything was changed. He had been granted a deferment, a whole new chance at life. Even Gottschalk seemed different. Or was it simply that he was seeing him for the first time in the harsh light of day? The director was wearing a full-length terrycloth beach robe and a pair of flapping sandals that smacked softly against the planks of the pier with each step. His pale, reflective face seemed even paler than usual in the sun—almost translucent—and carried its preoccupation sadly. He looks like a professor, Cameron thought. One of those legendary German professors who take the waters at the same spa town year after year . . .

"The sea," Gottschalk murmured. "It's always stimulating.

A mirror for mortality and meaninglessness, yet strangely restful because it tells time in a way we find acceptable. The way clocks do. With sound and movement. D'you know why I find the seashore the best location of all? Because it's where everything began, where man emerged dripping from the depths, and where I can live in the most precarious state, alone with my ideas, which are elusive phantoms, unformed and dangerous, yet full of beauty."

At this point, the director lapsed into silence and stood staring out across the water. Cameron began to wonder if, lulled by his own soliloquy, he had not lost himself in dream, but a moment later, Gottschalk took him by the arm and drew him to a bench beside the railing.

"D'you know what day it is?" he asked.

Cameron gave a shrug. "Tuesday?"

The director smiled. "Yes, Tuesday, June the twenty-sixth. According to a popular tradition among the early settlers in these parts, whoever stepped into the sea on June the twenty-sixth was cured of whatever diseases might be within him. The custom had its origins in the ancient Roman Fontinalia —the Festival of Waters—which was introduced into England and Ireland by legionaries in the first century before Christ. Having survived in druidic form, it was brought to these shores by Christian immigrants more than three hundred years ago. In the early days, the settlers visited the beach on June the twenty-fourth—St. John the Baptist's Day —but since the General Court of the colony sat once a year, on June the twenty-fifth, the date was changed so that people coming from far and wide to conduct legal business could take a holiday by the sea. Gradually, of course, the religious significance of the day was forgotten. Yet the tradition continues and the twenty-sixth is still considered the official start of the summer season here. Look at all the people on the beach! Far and away the largest crowd of the year. Why? How? What primitive influence, what residual tug still impels a farmer in some distant upland valley to leave his rocky fields and dairy barn, pack his wife and children into the family jalopy, and bring them to the beach on June the twenty-sixth? Can you explain it?"

"No," Cameron said. "I'm no good at riddles."

"How incurious you are! The sea, my friend. The sea explains it. The sea draws man as the moon pulls the tide. Yes, the sea beckons us with its incredible depth, its astonishing colors, and the immense force with which it is forever encroaching upon the continents."

Gottschalk removed his tinted glasses and gazed up at the sky. Cameron was amazed to see a look of anguish on his face, and his eyes glistening as if with tears.

"Are you all right?" he asked.

"I'm like Glaucus," the director replied. "D'you know the story? He ate a magical herb and leaped into the sea, where he was changed into a god and endowed with the gift of prophecy."

Cameron made no reply, but simply shook his head. More riddles, he was thinking.

"Glaucoma, my friend. I have glaucoma. An insidious affliction. Slow, progressive, and entirely painless. Sometimes it can be allayed by drops of pilocarpine. Other times it ends in loss of vision. The eyes atrophy. They become green and hard. Like emeralds in the sockets of an Incan sun god's head. Yes, eyes to emeralds—a haunting transformation. Try to imagine it. The terror. And I—I who, above all, must see!"

The director broke off and once again seemed lost in thought, but a moment later Cameron saw that he was studying the Ferris wheel in the amusement center, which was spinning in the clear blue sky.

"So many stories," he murmured. "So much simultaneity." Now, taking Cameron by the arm, he led him to the opposite side of the pier. "Right here should do. Now turn your head to the right and look up at the wheel. A bit higher, please. Yes, that's' it. D'you know what I see? I see the Ferris wheel superimposed on your eyes in the lenses of your sunglasses. Double-exposure has always been a trademark of mine. It'll make a perfect opening. Exactly what I've been looking for."

Riddles without end, Cameron thought. "The opening of what?" he said.

"My next film," replied the director, who had resumed his walk along the pier. "Which will be about the wife of the first astronaut lost in space. Lost and endlessly tumbling. An immortal mummy. Can you see it? An immortal mummy enshrined by accident amid the stars and in the hearts and minds of his countrymen. Ah, but the woman! She is what my film's about. This woman who is terrified of everything that spins. Must she remain forever faithful to her dead hero-husband? Must she not continue to live? Will she fall in love again? Yes, I've hit upon a perfect opening—the heroine staring, transfixed and haunted, at a Ferris wheel which the audience will see reflected in her sunglasses. No, first I'll show the Ferris wheel from a distance, then focus on it until it dissolves into the sunglasses, and, finally, pull away just enough to show her face. In that way, I'll create a mood of mystery and suspense."

They had reached the end of the pier and were starting over a porch that girdled the ramshackle dance casino. "Well," the director said. "What d'you think of it?"

"Sounds interesting," replied Cameron with a shrug.

The director fixed him with a reproachful look. "Interesting?" he echoed.

"The fact is, I'm only interested in one story at the moment."

"How fortunate to be able to concentrate on only one story."

"It keeps me busy," said Cameron dryly.

"I shouldn't wonder. Your story's quite intriguing. It begins with *trompe l'oreille,* proceeds to *trompe l'oeil,* and ends —well, who knows how it will end?"

Cameron gave a laugh. "With more tricks, I expect. Now how about this stunt you mentioned?"

"A simple matter," the director said. "The film we're presently shooting is an ordinary, straightforward little melodrama. The hero's a fugitive who, at the start of the sequence, is spotted by the police on the dance floor inside. He eludes them, however, and runs out to the porch. First he turns one way, and then the other, but his pursuers are coming from both directions. Finally, here at the corner, he realizes there is only one route of escape left to him."

"The sea," said Cameron, looking over the rail at the dark green water that welled against the pier.

"Exactly, which is where you, the stunt man, take over from the actor. You'll climb the railing, hesitate just a moment, and then . . ." The director gave a smile and a shrug to indicate the obvious.

"Dive into the water," Cameron said.

"We'll shoot your plunge with two cameras," Gottschalk went on. "One up here on the porch, the other in a boat below. After you leap from the railing, the police will rush up with drawn revolvers and begin firing into the water. The hero, however, will have . . ."

But Cameron was scarcely listening; instead, looking down into the water, he found himself thinking about the Fontinalia. Your turn to be baptized, he told himself. Ah, but what of that other immersion that had not been accompanied by any audible splash . . . ?

" . . . swum beneath the surface and come up under the pier, which will be illuminated by portable lights in the boat. Then he'll start making his way from piling to piling toward the shore."

"How about the splash?" Cameron asked.

"The splash?"

"When I hit the water."

The director smiled patiently. "Splashes are merely sound effects. There are whole libraries full of them. It's simply a matter of selecting the right ones and dubbing them in later."

Cameron nodded his head and, aware of a movement beside him, turned and saw his own reflection in a window. For a second, he was startled by the strange blond head; then, remembering his transformation at the hands of the make-up girl, he smiled to himself. Yes with a bit of pancake, anything was possible, including his own metamorphosis in this windowpane by the sea. And by dubbing in the splashes, did one not relegate them forever to the realm of afterthought? Only art is real, Gottschalk had said. Only art repeats itself. Over and over. Endlessly . . .

"The last part is difficult," the director was saying. "When the hero reaches the point at which the waves begin to break upon the shore, he swims out from beneath the pier so he won't be dashed to pieces against the pilings. Then he rides the surf onto the beach. At that point, the stunt ends, the actor takes over again, and the hero has escaped."

"Are you sure?" Cameron asked. "That he escapes?"

"Absolutely. Have faith, my friend."

"Faith," said Cameron with a harsh laugh. That baptism is a beginning and not an end, he thought.

"Besides, where could the hero be safer than with me?" the director went on. "In short, how better for a fugitive to go undetected than to be simultaneously an actor in and a spectator at the unfolding of his own story?"

"And does the hero always escape?" Cameron asked.

"Always," the director replied. "Over and over. From a whole series of breathtaking and hair-raising adventures. You seem dubious, my friend. How can I make you believe it?"

Cameron looked down at the water and gave an involuntary shudder. "I'll believe it," he replied, "when I see the film."

8

At suppertime, he ate sparingly and alone. Afterward, in his room, he lay upon the bed, clasped his hands behind his neck, and tried to conjure up some image of himself as he had been before. Where had he gone—the student who used to sit up all night in coffeehouses, talking of the future, and inveighing against the war? Over the hill, Cameron thought, a ridiculously short, yet irreversible journey during which, having first become Richard Jackson and then Arthur Coleman, he had ceased to exist. Ah, what would he not give to be standing at this very moment, tin tray in hand, in some endless chow line! Instead . . . Try not to think about it, he told himself. Try to get some rest. But now, as evening approached and the light faded from the sky beyond the window, he heard the surf pounding against the beach, and, closing his eyes, imagined himself soaring through the night, plunging into the cold water, and striking out for shore, a lone swimmer struggling in darkness. The reel ended with a brilliant flash upon the screen. Cameron opened his eyes. Night had fallen. Above the rising sea, like a condemned man waiting for his executioner, he listened to the sound of his own heart beating.

A knock summoned him to the door. He had been expecting it, but not the cameraman, whom he now saw, for the first time, close up and in full face. For a second, he could scarcely believe his eyes, which, filming over like a pair of blown fuses, faltered before a gaze of incredible malevolence that emanated from a countenance so ravaged by scars and pockmarks that it seemed to have been created not so much by disease as by a load of buckshot. The cameraman responded to the shock he had induced with a smile that disfigured him further by revealing a set of yellowish canine teeth.

"So you're the stunt man!" he exclaimed softly. "Allow me to introduce myself. I am Bruno da Fé."

"I know," Cameron said. "You've been pointed out to me."

"Speak louder, *caro*. Da Fé is slightly deaf."

"I said I've seen you before!"

"Yes, each has seen the other before. Permit me to tell you, I'm an admirer of your work."

"Very funny," Cameron said.

"Don't worry, *caro*. Everything that happened in the past is all forgotten. Everything is changed."

To protect the guilty? Cameron wondered. "Let's go," he said.

The town at night wore light in the manner of an outlandishly grotesque woman who uses make-up to mask unbearable defects and to affront the eyes that must behold her. The entire length of the avenue from which Cameron had first surveyed the waterfront was strung with incandescent bulbs that continued out along the pier to girdle the ramshackle façade of the casino, and the spinning, rocking, whirling components of the amusement center were illuminated in outline by colored lights that created a solid blur, as if motion were being churned beyond fluidity to the frozen state of one of those trick composite photos that are taken at night in Kodachrome. The cacophony emanating from this gaudy blaze had in upper register the shrieking of whip-ride passengers rotating in centrifugal terror, a bass section dominated by the reverberation of vehicles colliding on the plaza of a bumpmobile, and an intermediate range that mingled rock and roll, hurdy-gurdy, and barkers' voices, which, amplified by public-address systems and megaphones, had achieved an almost deafening pitch.

"*Son et lumière*," said the cameraman as they made their way through crowds of people jamming the various arcades. "How d'you feel, *caro*?"

"I'm all right," Cameron replied.

Da Fé was reading his lips. "You know what you're supposed to do?"

Cameron, who was keeping an eye out for the chief and the toll collector, nodded absently.

"Are you sure?"

"Yes, why d'you ask?"

"Well, there was no time to rehearse, so we may have to

improvise. After all, one never knows with stunts. When they start, they're out of control. It stands to reason, *caro*. Once the car is driven off the bridge, or the leap is made from the burning building . . ."

They had passed through the alley filled with pinball machines and reached the entrance to the pier—a picket gate manned by a pair of policemen. Here, da Fé produced a pass card that admitted them through the barricade; then he and Cameron started out toward the casino. Below them, bathed in the moonlight, a huge throng had gathered upon the beach.

"Look, *caro,* they've come to see the stunt man jump."

To see the stunt man jump, thought Cameron. Now, listening to the restless murmur of the crowd, he decided that it was probably the kind of crowd that waits with growing impatience for the suicide to depart his perch, or for the fugitive to take his last desperate gamble. For a moment, he was tempted to wave. Then, suddenly, he saw the toll collector. The toll collector was standing just below him on the sand, wearing a sports shirt and slacks, and scanning the crowd. You're looking in the wrong direction, Cameron thought. And for the wrong man . . .

"What's the matter?" asked the cameraman. "What do you see down there?"

"A comedy," Cameron replied.

Gottschalk was crouching behind a camera and tripod on the porch of the casino. He was wearing a white linen suit and a white yachtsman's cap that, tiped rakishly over one eye, gave him the appearance of a roguish sailor, and he was shouting instructions to several technicians who were adjusting a battery of floodlights that had been set up on the railing and the roof. Now, as Cameron and da Fé picked their way through a tangle of electrical cables, the director called for light and, bathed instantly in tremendous glare, bent down and peered through the lens of the camera. Then, straightening up, he saw Cameron and waved a greeting.

"Here you are," he said.

"Yes," Cameron replied. "Let's get on with it."

"Patience, my friend. First we'll give you a change of clothes." Now, leading Cameron into the casino by a side door, he handed him a pair of tennis sneakers, a pair of chino pants, and a white T-shirt.

Cameron changed in a men's room. When he emerged, a few moments later, he found the director talking to Lee Jordan, who was dressed exactly as he was, and recognized the blandly handsome face and disarmingly boyish grin of the hero of a weekly television series entitled *Hoedown*.

"Not a bad resemblance," said the actor, studying him in return. "Just so long as they don't use you in close-ups."

"He's standing in only for the stunt," the director replied.

"Well, best of luck. I'd try this one myself except I'm a lousy swimmer, and my agent doesn't like me to do dangerous things."

"That's the kind of agent I should have," Cameron answered.

The actor grinned and showed a mouthful of capped teeth. "Be brave. Think of my reputation for valor. Think of my fans."

"Don't worry," said Gottschalk. "We'll have your fans sitting on the edges of their seats."

"I knew I could count on you."

"Sure," Cameron said. "Just leave the diving to us."

The director stepped out on the porch. "The first part is easy," he said. "I want you to come through the door, glance quickly toward the camera, and then run toward the floodlights on the railing."

"I won't be able to see a thing!"

"Precisely the effect I'm after!" said the director cheerfully. "You're a fugitive filled with panic and fleeing blindly. By running from the foreground toward strong counter-illumination, it will appear that you're being swallowed up. Your shadow will stretch back grotesquely toward the spectator. A moment later, it will be overtaken by two policemen who are pursuing you, shooting their revolvers."

Cameron glanced in the direction of the camera and saw a pair of men who were dressed in the ice-cream-vendor uniforms of the town's police force. "They certainly look authentic," he said.

"They ought to," Gottschalk replied. "They're on loan from Chief Broussard. You're going to be chased by the real thing."

The real thing, Cameron thought. "And what will they be shooting?" he asked.

"Blanks. Fake ammunition supplied by the prop men. Actually, the sound of the shots, like that of the splash, will be dubbed in later. The blanks are simply for the immediate effect of making things seem real. And for the benefit of the crowd."

Cameron looked toward the shore, but the glare of the floodlights prevented him from seeing the spectators who had gathered upon the beach. An invisible audience, he thought, waiting to suspend its disbelief to the sound of dubbed-in splashes and fake ammunition. Now, remembering that the chief and the toll collector were searching for him out there, he smiled and shook his head.

"When you reach the railing, pause and look in the other direction," Gottschalk was saying. "You'll see two more policemen running toward you. Then climb up on the railing and wait until you hear the whistle blow to jump. Now, have you understood everything?"

Cameron nodded.

"You're certain?"

"Yes," Cameron said. "Everything."

But a few minutes later, as he raced toward the incredible brilliance of the floodlights, listening for the sound of feet pounding in pursuit, and waiting breathlessly for the reports of the revolvers, he realized that he understood nothing. Crazy, he thought. This is crazy. . . .

At the sound of the first shot, he stumbled and nearly fell. Crazy, he kept thinking. Crazy . . . Then he was standing on top of the railing, and looking down at the dark, heaving sea. Below him, he could see da Fé crouching behind a camera that had been set up on the foredeck of a small motor launch. The cameraman raised an arm. Lights flashed up at him, blinding him. Yes, Gottschalk was right. He had become both actor in and spectator at the unfolding of his own story. What a chance for drama! Cameron wondered if the toll collector was watching. Remember to jump, he told himself. You've got to jump. *Jump!*

When the whistle shrieked, he reacted instantly—a moonstruck Icarus sailing out into the night, where, for two or three splendid seconds, he saw himself bathed in light, as if through the eyes of the crowd that lined the beach.

The roaring was all in his ears as he struggled toward the surface. Then, emerging from darkness into the brilliance

of the floodlights, he took a huge gulp of air and thrashed
about to keep his head above water. There was a volley
of shots from above. Someone shouted at him to dive. Something made a splash in the water beside him. There was
another splash, and then another, and, taking a deep breath,
he went under again. When he surfaced a second time, he
found himself beneath the pier, surrounded by a maze of
pilings that rose into the gloom like trees in a deep woods.
When he grasped at the nearest trunk, however, he found
that it was coated with slime. For some moments, he clawed
for purchase; then the lights caught him again, and a heavy
swell tore him away and carried him farther into the gloomy
interior. The boat followed close behind, lighting the way.
Someone shouted at him to keep swimming. Exhausted, he
raised an arm toward the floodlights shining in his eyes, and
called for help; then, arms flailing, he sank beneath the surface. When he came up again, he was gagging on sea water.
A wave carried him against another piling, and, digging his
fingernails into the slippery wood, he hung on long enough
to call for help again. As he began to slip away, a shadowy
figure descended a ladder from the casino porch. Someone
in the boat ordered him to dive. There were several flashes
from the direction of the ladder, and then the sound of shots
echoed all around him. Helplessly, he lost his tenuous grip
and sank. They're going to let me drown, he thought as,
thrashing desperately, he came up for air. Again he shouted
for help, but though the boat was closer now, he could
scarcely hear the sound of his own voice above the thump of
the waves beating against the timbers and the rumble of the
casino floor vibrating overhead. He was giving way to panic
when, just above him in the shadows, he saw, reached up for,
and grasped a crossbar connecting two adjacent piles. For a
minute or two, he simply clung to the crossbar like a man
hanging from a tree limb; then, summoning up the last of his
strength, he hauled himself out of the water and draped
himself over it. The whistle blew. Someone shouted something from the boat, but, panting with exhaustion and relief,
he could not make it out. Besides, the crossbar was covered
with sharp barnacles that, cutting into the palms of his hands,
his knees, and his shins, soon made his resting place a rack
of pain. Now, as the boat drew alongside, he lifted his head,
blinked through tears of anguish, and found himself look-

ing up at the ravaged face of the cameraman, who was smiling down at him in triumph.

"It's going beautifully, *caro*. Beyond our wildest dreams."

"Help me," Cameron pleaded. "Help me."

Da Fé smiled hideously. "There's no time, *caro*. The tide is rising."

"Listen, I can't swim any more! I can't make it."

"Use the crossbars," da Fé replied, adjusting one of the floodlights to show a whole network of horizontal supports that, connecting one clump of pilings with the next, stretched ahead through the cavern beneath the casino like a vast obstacle course.

"Listen, Gottschalk said they'd be using blanks!"

"Absolutely, *caro*. Only blanks."

"But I saw splashes!"

The cameraman stepped into the light, extended his arm and hand, and, drawing back the elastic of a slingshot, sent a small projectile into the water by Cameron's foot. "D'you see, *Caro*? This is how we make the splashes. With a child's toy."

"Look, I'm bleeding," said Cameron, who was stalling desperately for time. "The barnacles are cutting me to ribbons."

"I'm sorry about the barnacles, *caro*. They're something we overlooked. Still, by adding another dimension to the terror of your escape, they prove effective. Now, when I blow the whistle again—"

"No!" Cameron shouted.

"—you'll hear more shots. Duck behind the timber beside you, and then start along the crossbars toward the pier. Go as quickly as you can. Are you ready?"

"Nothing doing," Cameron said.

"Positions, everyone!"

"*No!*"

But when the whistle shrieked and the sound of gunfire echoed through the gloom, he flinched automatically and cowered behind the piling until the reverberations died away; then, leaping to the next crossbar, teetering for balance with arms extended, and grasping at the timber ahead of him like a drunk clutching at a lamppost, he started toward shore. To begin with, his progress was slowed by his fear of falling into the water, but he soon found that by jumping to each crossbar when it was exposed in the trough of a wave, he could always reach the next pillar before the crest of the following wave overtook him. From then on, he proceeded without mishap, timing his leaps with the cessation of shooting and according to the rhythm of the sea, until, warmed by the exertion, confident of his technique, and exhilarated by his agility, he began to skip from crossbar to crossbar with the nimble aplomb of a child making his way through a jungle gym. When the whistle blew, some minutes later, he looked up and was amazed to find himself beneath the pier. I'm halfway there, he thought triumphantly. I'm going to make it. . . . But in the next instant, he heard the sound of the surf crashing down upon the beach, felt the timbers shudder, and turned anxiously to the boat that had drawn up beside him.

Da Fé was in a jubilant mood. "You've no idea, *caro!* The shadows upon the ceiling, the eerie light, the pilings stretching ahead, and the sea always moving beneath. It's incredible! It's like a man fleeing into a nightmare!"

"Listen to that surf," said Cameron between chattering teeth. "I don't like the sound of it."

Da Fé cupped a hand to his ear and shook his head.

"The surf!" Cameron shouted.

"Wait till we mix in the real sound, *caro*. The surf will roar. It will drown out everything. It will be truly terrifying."

"You're insane," Cameron replied. "D'you realize that? You're a goddam madman!"

But the cameraman was not listening. "At this point, *caro*, there's no turning back. Ahead, the waves are pounding against the pilings. Above, the police are running along the pier. Below, the tide is rising. Soon your perch becomes untenable. Your only chance is the sea. For a moment, you hesitate; then you dive into the water and swim away from the pier. We'll shoot you in moonlight as you ride into shore upon the surf."

"At least give me a life-preserver."

"But that would ruin the whole effect. Who would believe in a fugitive who manages to acquire a life-preserver?"

"Listen to that surf," Cameron said. "I'll get caught in the undertow."

"Don't fight the surf, *caro*. Ride with it. Now, listen carefully. When you hear the whistle blow, swim out fifteen· or twenty yards. Then head in for shore. It's not very far, and there will be a beam to guide you. Try to come straight in, for the beam will mark the spot where we wait to shoot you as you land upon the beach."

"Wait a minute. You're not going to leave me, are you?"

The cameraman bared his teeth in a grimace of mock distress. "Yes, *caro*, you must do this last part alone. From now on, you see, the stunt is out of control."

"Get me a piece of wood. A plank. Something to hold on to . . ."

"Remember the audience, *caro*. It is *they* who must experience your terror. If we provide them with something to hold on to—"

"Don't leave me!" Cameron cried. "Stay a minute longer."

But the boat was drifting away, and now, as its engine sputtered to life, da Fé raised his hand in a gesture of direful benediction. Cameron watched until the boat and the cameraman had disappeared in the gloom; then, glancing back over the route he had taken through the pilings, he saw that the tide had risen above the crossbars. Out of control, he thought, clutching the post beside him and listening to the surf like a man who, having reached the midway point of a trestle in the dark of night, suddenly feels the timbers trembling and, freezing in his tracks, knows that there is no sure way to turn.

When the whistle blew, he stayed on the crossbar that was now awash to his knees, and hugged the timber. The whistle blew again—insistent, shrill, commanding—and still he refused to leave his perch. But the tide was rising and the waves had begun to break heavily against the pilings, and now, looking up at the timber above him, he saw the highwater mark far above his head. It's no use, he told himself. All they have to do is wait you out. . . . The whistle continued to give out sharp, sporadic shrieks; then the blasts came steadily, as if keeping time with the tempo of the waves. Finally, the whistling ceased altogether. Cameron waited a moment longer; then he stepped off the crossbar and relinquished himself to the sea. The shock of cold water produced in him a strange feling of relief. The worst is over, he told himself, striking out from the pier with vigorous strokes. Then, treading water, he looked toward shore and made out a beam of light reaching toward him across the waves. The last leg, he thought. Just ride it in. . . .

For some minutes, he swam a steady course toward the light, but when he drew closer to the beach, he began to lose sight of it as he sank into valleys between the waves. Suddenly, a large crest overtook him, and, held high, he saw the light for one last instant; then the crest swept past, and a strong counter-current snatched at his legs and sucked him under. And now, caught between immense alternatives—flow and undertow that competed for possession of him—he began an aimless struggle to endure, gulping air as he came up in troughs between the breakers, and diving under as he was swept toward the next incoming wave. Finally, a crushing weight descended upon him and thrust him into a deep vortex, where, end over end, he tumbled endlessly. He held his breath as long as he could. Then, expelling it in a single gasp, he tried to hold back the sea. His head throbbed, his eyes ached, his lungs reached the point of bursting. When he gave up, the water entered all at once, filling him with darkness. Displaced, his spirit fled. His body swirled limply in the depths. For a moment, he remained divided, in suspense. Then, prayerfuly, as if through a zoom lens, he saw himself rejoined by an enormous comber that plucked him from the deep, lifted him high upon a curling crest of foam, and, hurtling him from the sea as if from a three-dimensional screen, deposited him within himself upon the beach. Now, face down, he lay inert upon the sand. Before him the screen was blank; the film was over. An imperceptible tremor of despair passed through him. There was nothing left. Even the illusion of the wave had passed. Over and forever ended— *trompe l'esprit* in the final moment of drowning, with everything dubbed in. And so he remained, half conscious and dimly convinced of his own death, until someone sat astride him and began pushing down rhythmically upon his back. Then, gurgling water, gagging on air, and retching a frothy combination of the two, he awakened slowly to pain. He tried to breathe, gave a cry of anguish, and vomited again. Someone thumped him between the shoulderblades. Choking, he lifted himself upon his hands and knees, and opened his eyes. For a second, he was blinded by a cruel glare; then, a few yards away, he saw a man dressed just like himself crawl from the sea on hands and knees, get to his feet, and run toward the light. Cameron stood and, staggering, tried to follow. A wave crashed down upon the beach. A sheet of water overtook him. Backwash swirled around his ankles. Horrified, he watched his footprints dissolve in bubbles before his eyes.

"Wait!" he shouted feebly, even as he fell. "Wait for me!"

9

The face in the mirror had changed. By removing the rough edges of exaggeration, the water had created a more subtle physiognomy in which, instead of being masked behind layers of pancake, the traces of his old self were now incorporated in perfect harmony. Turning from the mirror, Cameron peeled off his wet clothes, rubbed himself briskly with a towel, and pulled on a pair of dry pants and a clean shirt. Refreshed, confident, triumphant, he felt like singing. Had he not been returned from the sea, revived from drowning, and relieved of the terror of dying? Yes, his transformation was complete. It was as if he had been reborn. Looking into the mirror again, he experienced an exhilaration such as he had never known before.

In the lobby, a party was in full swing. As he came down the staircase, he heard himself hailed by the director, and, glancing over the upturned faces, saw Gottschalk standing in the center of the room with Nina Mabry. The actress was wearing the kind of brightly printed summer dress whose brevity compliments slender, tanned arms and legs, and, brushing back a strand of auburn hair, she regarded him with the quick look of appraisal with which beautiful women gauge the intensity of admiration flowing toward them. Cameron kept his eyes on her as he made his way across the lobby floor.

"A splendid performance!" cried the director, lifting his glass in salute. "Welcome back!"

"From the dead," said Cameron with a laugh that was improvised solely to bring a smile to her finely modeled mouth and somber face.

"But I told you! The hero always escapes."

"Over and over," Cameron said, scarcely hearing the sound of his own voice as he looked into her cool green eyes.

"We were worried about you," she told him gravely. "We thought you might have drowned."

"So did I," said Cameron, who detached his gaze from her like a diver withdrawing from the depths, and turned to Gottschalk with a grim smile. "I was lucky," he went on. "No thanks to your cameraman."

"Bruno gets carried away," the director replied. "He has a slight deficiency, you see—a one-track mind that's capable of believing only what he shoots with his camera and what he develops in the darkroom."

"Bruno's deficient, all right. He's a madman."

"But also a magician. Wait till you see the roughs of the stunt. You won't believe how real, how terrifying it will seem. I don't know how he manages to do it."

"Oh, I'll believe it," Cameron replied. "And we both know how he manages to do it. Since Bruno believes only in the reality of the darkroom, he can forget that the chances he takes with his magical camera are being taken for real by somebody else."

"The eternal question of what is real," said the director, smiling. "But one mustn't shrink from taking chances. Consider my own example. I was forgotten. Out of sight and mind. No one believed I would come back. No one had faith. I could have rested on my reputation, but I decided to show the world that I, Gottschalk, could still make films. A dream, you are thinking. Ah, but isn't it worth the chance? Yes, the gambler's chance."

The chance of a gambler who's going blind with glaucoma, Cameron thought, and, glancing at Nina Mabry, saw that she was hanging on the director's every word. "And you?" he inquired, vying for her attention. "D'you believe in second comings?"

Her immediate response to his banter was a smile that faded in the next instant. "I believe in him," she said. "And in his work."

Cameron wondered if this were the professional tribute of an actress, or the loyal affirmation of a mistress. "My own conversion may take some time," he replied. "Tonight was the first I've seen of it."

The director gave a tolerant laugh. "Mr. Coleman's come to us quite unexpectedly," he explained. "And not through the usual channels. The fact that he could step in on such short notice and perform so credibly is amazing. One could almost believe he was indeed a fugitive!"

Fear and fascination came into Nina Mabry's eyes. "Why?" she asked. "Why did you do it?"

"I took a gambler's chance," said Cameron, who looked hard at the director.

But Gottschalk no longer seemed to be aware of their presence; instead, head tilted back and eyes blinking behind the lenses of his tinted glasses, he appeared to focus upon some imaginary horizon far beyond the room. "At last," he murmured. "Everything has fallen into place. The film will open with a long forward-tracking shot from the helicopter. First, a missile base in all its phallic splendor, and then, just to the north along the same coast, in wonderful juxtaposition, a resort town and an amusement center full of towers and appendages. The camera will focus upon a Ferris wheel spinning in sunlight. Then, with a slow dissolve, the Ferris wheel will be seen to spin as a reflection of a pair of sunglasses worn by Margaret. The credit lines will be superimposed upon her face, which is deeply troubled. Then the camera will pull even farther back to show that she is not alone. She's with a space scientist, an associate of her dead, encapsuled husband—this astronaut who for months has been tumbling through the celestial void. The mission of the scientist is to persuade her that since her husband cannot be returned to earth, he must be intercepted and destroyed. His eerie presence overhead, you see, has proved unsettling to the public tranquillity and its need for equilibrium. As the dialogue begins, the heroine is watching the Ferris wheel and listening to the scientist, who is telling her that everything—everything from the planets in outer space to the bodies interred beneath the soil of earth—is in effect tumbling about in this eternally spinning universe of ours. He's trying to comfort her with a rational approach, but his metaphysical jargon and his astronomical vision of things merely unhinge her by destroying the most vital equilibrium of all—the illusion that we are firmly planted, that our surroundings are stationary, and that, by extension, our lives have meaning. D'you remember what I told you I wanted the film to demonstrate at the very outset?"

"I remember," the actress replied. "The sterility of cerebral explanations, of all solutions except that of human love."

"Exactly," the director said. "Later, perhaps that very day, she's standing with the scientist at the water's edge, watching the members of a religious sect preparing to baptize a child by immersing it in the sea. The scientist—this soulless, celestial mortician—points out the similarity of the Christian ritual to that of the pagan Fontinalia. To him it's simply superstition. To Margaret, however, it is a powerful and moving spectacle. Can this be the answer she's so desperately seeking? Now, holding the child in his arms, a lay minister wades out into the waves, and the camera pulls back to show some surfers kneeling on their boards in the background. The surfers are wearing those skin-tight black wet suits that, except for color, are similar to the apparel worn by astronauts. Protective suits reiterating the theme of hostile environments, and signaling the imminence of disaster. Now, as a large wave overtakes them, the surfers rise in unison upon their boards, and, nestled in a curling crest, skim swiftly and silently down upon the beach. Suddenly, one of them wipes out. The board continues, however, tumbling end over end in the breaker, and comes straight at the lay minister, who, in panic, loses his grip upon the child. A cry goes up. There is a frantic search in which everyone partakes."

Nina Mabry had placed the fingers of both hands against the temples of her head. "Will they save the child?"

The director came back from his distant horizon and gave a shrug. "Perhaps."

"Please," she said. "Let them save the child."

Cameron was staring at her. "Look," he muttered, "it's just a movie."

"Don't let the child die," she implored. "Let him live!"

"It's something I'll decide later," Gottschalk told her.

My God, Cameron thought. They act as if it's real! For a moment, he was tempted to intervene; then, aware that the director and the actress were caught up in a world from which he was excluded, he walked to the counter in the corner of the lobby, which had been set up as a bar. There, he poured himself a drink, leaned an elbow on the counter, and looked around the room. Behind him, the radio was playing softly. A news commentator was trying to explain a welter of rumor and counter-rumor about the war.

"At the same time, official sources, while denying that an invasion has taken place, have carefully avoided discounting the possibility that . . ."

Crazy, Cameron thought. The whole damn world's gone

crazy. . . . He had caught sight of Denise on the far side of the room and was about to go over to her, when he felt a hand upon his arm, and, turning, found himself looking into the piercing blue eyes of Chief of Police Broussard, who peered up at him from beneath his ice-cream vendor's cap.

"Got a minute, stunt man?"

"Sure," said Cameron.

"How did it go tonight?"

"It went fine. How about your end of things?"

"No luck," said the chief in his husky voice.

"Maybe your man isn't here after all. Maybe he took off for Bordeaux."

The chief gave a wan smile, and, striking a match against the counter behind him, applied its flame to the frayed stub of a cigar that was clenched between his teeth. "Maybe," he said, "but I don't think so. I think our man is holed up here in town. It's just that he's a little smarter than we figured."

"Well, like you said, sooner or later he's bound to show himself."

"That's right," the chief replied, chewing on the soggy end of his cigar and glancing about the room. "Tell me, Coleman, who're all these people?"

"What's he up to? Cameron wondered as, striving to keep calm, he too looked about the room. "Well, you know," he said. "Members of the cast, technicians, prop men . . ."

"Know most of them, do you?"

"As a matter of fact, I don't. You see, I just arrived. A few days ago."

"So you're new around here, hanh?"

"Yes," Cameron replied. What's he after? he thought, looking desperately around for the director. "If there's any way I can help," he said.

The chief gave him an appraising glance, and, in the manner of a falconer seeking to lull his bird, sent out a dense cloud of blue smoke that enveloped Cameron's head. "I was just wondering if it might be possible to slip somebody into the crew."

Cameron had been holding his breath. Now, letting it hiss through his teeth, he swallowed hard. "I don't follow you," he said.

"I mean, it's real good cover. See, if this fellow knows he's being hunted, he'll continue to play it cozy. But suppose I pull my men off the streets, keep the town sealed, put somebody who can identify him into the movie crew, and have him tail along wherever you're shooting. That way, we might make a catch, hanh?"

Cameron took a long pull at his drink, looked at the chief, and nodded. "Who've you got in mind?"

"The toll collector. Who else?"

"Well, you better ask Gottschalk."

"Yeah, but I don't see him."

"He was around a while ago," said Cameron. "Shall I go hunt him up for you?"

"No hurry," the chief replied. "I'd just as soon stay awhile. Besides, there's something I've been meaning to ask you. About that stunt . . ."

"Which stunt?" Cameron said, and felt his heart come into his throat.

"The one on the causeway," replied the chief, who spoke as if *his* throat were filled with sand. "How d'you do it? I mean, if you'd gone through with it."

Cameron shook his head. The room was reeling before his eyes. Was it an after-effect of his ordeal, the drink, or simply fear?

The chief was looking at him curiously. "Say you'd driven off the bridge and gone into the river. How would you have got yourself free of the car?"

"Ah!" said Gottschalk, who had appeared as if from nowhere and was leaning his elbows on the counter behind them. "Now that's a very interesting question, chief. As it happens, there are two schools of thought on the subject— both of them developed by the Dutch, who, because they're forever having to be fished out of some canal or other, have become the world's leading experts on the matter. The old school holds that one should keep the windows rolled up and wait until the pressure of the water pouring into the vehicle equals that of the air bubble inside before opening a door to make an exit. A newer school, however, refutes this technique by questioning its primary assumption. It maintains that because of the weight of the engine a vehicle invariably sinks vertically, and that the air bubble is usually forced out through the trunk before the occupants can utilize it for breathing. Moreover, the new school points out that because of the enormous pressure of the water, the roof of a sinking vehicle usually caves in to the very tops of the seats. For these reasons, our Dutch friends now recommend that when an unexpected skid or wrong turn has achieved aquatic consequences, the startled burger should temporarily close all windows and vents, then open them on both sides to keep pressure differences from building up and caving in the roof, and, finally, when the water has risen to the level of the windows, push open the doors and get out as quickly as possible. Assuming, of course, that he has the time, that he's not being harassed by a terrified wife, and that his wits haven't been anesthetized by alcohol—eh, Coleman?"

"Right," said Cameron, nodding in serious agreement and watching the stub of the chief's cigar, which had diminished during the director's discourse to the point where ash and saliva had achieved an equilibrium of their own.

The chief removed the cigar from his mouth, and, holding it between thumb and forefinger, aimed it like a dart in Cameron's direction. "Very interesting," he said. "And which technique d'you use, stunt man?"

"It all depends," Cameron replied.

"Depends on what?"

"On me," Gottschalk said. "Or, more precisely, on the requirements of the film. Suppose, for example, that the occupant of the vehicle is not, cinematically speaking, supposed to survive his accident. Then neither of the Dutch techniques can be employed, which means that the stunt man must wait until the vehicle is totally submerged before making his move."

"Well, which is it in this case?"

The director smiled and shrugged. "I can't answer that because I'm in the process of altering the script. With me, you see, a film is always in flux. Sometimes until the very last moment."

The chief dropped his cigar on the floor and ground it out with the toe of his shoe. Then, squinting at Cameron, he said, "Do they pay you well?"

"Yes," Cameron replied. "Besides, the hours are good and I like the freedom."

The chief screwed his face into a grimace of disbelief. "I wouldn't be in your shoes for anything," he growled.

"Nor I," said Gottschalk with a laugh. "But now you can understand more easily where Coleman lost his nerve yesterday, and perhaps forgive the defects in the rushes you'll see tomorrow night."

"Defects?" the chief echoed.

"Well, in addition to being the roughest sort of version, it's useless footage from our standpoint. The whole scene will have to be shot over."

"You mean Coleman here's really going to drive a car off that bridge?"

"Indeed he is. In fact, if I'm not mistaken, he's looking forward to the opportunity of vindicating himself, eh, Coleman?"

"Sure," said Cameron, but the word, sticking in his throat, came out like a croak.

"Well, I'd like to be on hand for that."

"Then we'll make a point of inviting you."

"Which reminds me," the chief went on. "I've got another request to make. How about letting the toll collector tag along with you for a few days? Pretend you've hired him or something, so he can keep an eye out for this fellow we're after."

"Certainly," Gottschalk replied. "We'll give him a beret to wear and stick him in with da Fé's camera crew."

"One thing I ought to tell you, he's got a record. He's a Peeping Tom. Been booked twice for it. Last time up, he got a suspended sentence."

"I'll warn da Fé," the director replied. "We'll keep an eye on him while he's keeping his eyes open for you."

"Much obliged," the chief replied. Now, turning to Cameron, who was pouring himself a second, stiffer drink, he said, "Tell me something, stunt man. How d'you practice for these capers?"

"Fearless fellows!" the director said cheerfully. "They learn by doing."

Denise was in a group that surrounded da Fé, who was being urged by a chorus of voices to describe his latest film. Cameron glanced at the faces around him and saw that they were filled with the kind of anticipation old friends reserve for the clown in their midst who never fails to entertain them. Then he noticed Nina Mabry standing just behind the cameraman. Smiling and gesticulating, the actress was engaged in animated conversation with a dapper little man he had not seen before. Cameron found himself wondering if she were always gayer away from Gottschalk, whose morbid concepts must surely remind her of the tragedy in her past.

"In my films there's never suspense," da Fé was saying. "It's not a question of will they or won't they, but of how and where. Motive is nothing. Everything is innovation. The camera is supreme. More than the eye, it is our deepest wish."

"To hell with cinematic technique, Bruno," someone cried. "Tell us the plot."

Eyes gleaming, the cameraman fixed his interrupter with a smile of infinite disdain. "But there is no plot," he said softly. "Haven't I told you before? Story, suspense, motive, character—they count for nothing in my films. That's why my work is true. Yes, pure!"

Da Fé waited for the laughter to subside; then, tilting his head back and closing his eyes as if to mimic the director, he continued in a voice that was hushed with the awe that attends a vision. "I open, as always, with a woman undressing. A young woman. She's looking ahead of her, smiling at what she sees. Looking in a mirror, perhaps, but it's difficult to tell. Something keeps getting in the way, which means we have only the most fleeting glimpses. A white dress, a foot, a thigh, a breast, a pair of crumpled panties on the floor. Now her eyes. Full of anticipation. But suddenly she's disappeared. What keeps getting in the way? It's maddening. There! She's in sight again. Her face. Completely open. Expectant. Eager. She's on a bed? The floor? No matter. Something's blurred the lens again. A man's body. How frustrating! And when the girl comes back into view, the angle of perspective has shifted. We see only her thighs and legs. Curve and taper. Constant motion. Bending, straightening, spreading, enveloping. Yes, as if impelled by the combination of her own pleasure and our deepest wish."

The cameraman opened his eyes and looked around him with a smile of triumph. "So how d'you like my little opening? D'you find it enticing? D'you want to know more? Yes, but above all you want to *see* more. What is this devilish obstruction? Ah, now we have it. The camera has pulled back to show a keyhole. Yes, we've been looking through a keyhole the whole time. Peering through a keyhole with the eye of a man. A rather silly-looking fellow. Fiftyish, perhaps. On his hands and knees. With his eye to the keyhole of a door that leads to an adjoining room. Yes, it's a hotel. A summer hotel. Old and wooden, but quite elegant. And this voyeur through whose eye, periodically blinded by trickles of perspiration, we've been staring—what's he like? None too virile-looking, hey? And tending a bit to flesh and flab. Well-to-do, though. One can tell from his clothes and the luggage in the room. And married. Yes, indeed. See the dresses on the bed, the lace underwear, and those expensive-looking shoes? They've obviously just arrived. Hardly unpacked. But where's the wife? Ah, there she is! In the bathroom taking a shower. My, what a woman! Exquisite. About thirty-five, I'd say. Here she comes with a large towel draped around her. Look at those lovely damp little feet and the delicate prints they make upon the tile floor as she pads over to the sink, and, looking into the mirror, sees the reflection of her husband in the other room. And what's he up to? Why, he's down on his hands and knees! Trying like the very devil to get a better look through that keyhole. Poor oaf. Squinting this way and that, wiping his forehead, rubbing at an errant eyelash. Now back to the wife. What's her reaction? There we have it. And we know all we need to know about the two of them. Look at her face. See the contempt? Yes, her face is positively dripping with it!"

Cameron was looking at Nina Mabry, whose gaze met his for just a second and then went past him. There was an immense reserve in her cool green eyes—a detachment that teetered on the edge of disdain.

"The rest is nothing," continued the cameraman with a shrug. "A cliché of towering proportions redeemed only by the beauty and elegance of the woman who plays the wife, and by the wonderfully imaginative lens—our own insatiable eye—that follows her now as she walks into the bedroom and surprises this husband who is groveling before the keyhole. Suddenly the miserable man is in motion, scrabbling about on all fours as he pretends to be looking for a cufflink. But it's no use. Her face tells everything. Still, she's a woman, and now, slowly, her contempt gives way to curiosity. Yes, she'll have a look. A quick one. Which, of course, produces another expression upon her lovely face. Well, surely it's easy enough to guess what happens next."

Nina Mabry was shaking her head. "Don't be modest,

Bruno. In pornography, nothing matters *except* what happens next. Otherwise, one would be tempted to ask why the woman would stay with such a man."

"*Cara, carissima,*" the cameraman murmured. "The answer to that is of no importance. Perhaps she's the dark side of one of our director's existentialist heroines. Who cares? Doesn't she stand before us now, torn between the delightful promise of the keyhole and the immediate privation of her most justifiable and deepest wish? No, *carissima*, if my stories are unbelievable, it's not because they lack motive, but because they have happy endings. I'm an incurable optimist, you see. I can't bear to have this woman dissatisfied. Look at her unhappy face as, a short time later, she and her husband are sitting at a bar in the dining room. What a miserable way to start a vacation! But wait. Who's the young man mixing her martini? And that full-breasted wench in the white uniform carrying a tray in from the kitchen? Who indeed? So the possibilities afforded by the keyhole are still intact! And now a dull but necessary bridge for the sake of continuity. Some animated coversation on all sides, some freely dispensed charm by the wife, a large tip proffered by the husband, and a jointly concurred-in suggestion that the four of them get together after the young folks finish work. Well, why not? Why not have a few drinks, a tour of the town, a ride or two on the bumpmobile, and then a nightcap in the room whose keyhole has ceased to be of interest? Surely you can imagine the rest. Simply a question of arithmetic. Ah, but the mathematics of the situation are of crucial importance. Four is not possible, you see. Four leads to an all too obvious division into pairs. Three is much better. Yes, three's a magic number, for it leads directly to that exquisite imbalance of two on one. So somebody must be cut from the roster. But how can it be done? Look at our lovely wife, all flirtation now, teasing her oafish spouse, spinning a regular web of wit around him. And of neckties, too. Isn't that hilarious? She's trussing him to a chair with his own garish cravats. Look at him laugh! And the younger couple. They're getting a kick out of it as well. Now what's she up to? Turned on the radio, kicked off her shoes, and begun to dance. Quite good, isn't she? A leggy pirouette, followed by a saucy can-can flip. Yes, all in fun. And Gulliver there, he's acting his part, too. See him strain at the neckties as, perch-

ing on his lap, she begins to tickle him? Oh, not there. That's
wicked. Ah, she's got him going! Laughing helplessly. What
sweet torment. Why it practically amounts to torture! The
lovely minx. Look at her dart around him. What'll she think
of next? No. Yes! She's taken off her stockings and draped
them over his ears. And there goes her blouse bandana-
style around his head. Goodness, how ludicrous he appears!
Like a float in a carnival. Now, silly thing, she's tied her
bra around his neck. Isn't this wild? Come on, everybody,
join the fun! Well, the other girl is game, isn't she? Look at
that. He's practically disappeared. And now what? No sense
tormenting a clothes rack, hey? But the girls are still chock-
full of good spirits. My gracious, what a pair! They simply
won't be denied, those two. They'll stop at nothing. Isn't that
something? The poor boy doesn't have a chance. Watch them
go at him. Look at him go under. Bold straddling hussies!
Sure of what they want and how to get it, too. They'll use
him up in no time. And look at them eyeing each other! Mark
my words, they're in a mood to try anything before this night
is through. Well, *cara,* can you guess what happens next?"

"Of course, Bruno. It's what makes these little sequences
of yours so boring."

"No, that's the fault of the actors, *cara.* A badly trained
lot. Forever mechanical, always wooden, utterly incapable
of playing their roles with the proper abandon."

"That's because they're not actors but performers, who
haven't the slightest concept of dignity or the need for pri-
vacy."

"But I offer them something better! The chance of exposure without risk. The opportunity to inflict and be inflicted
with every desire, and yet remain anonymous. In my films
one can live every fantasy without fear."

"Or self-respect."

"Self-respect," the cameraman said softly, "is a barrier
people erect against the possibility of having to recognize
the true self."

"What a wicked idea!" said the actress. "You're an evil
man, Bruno."

"Not at all," da Fé replied. "I simply know what people
dream about. So I make it possible for them. With a touch
of pancake, a wig, and some eye-shadow, one can play in
my films without fear of detection."

"And what of blackmail?"

"*Carissima*, how can you suggest such a thing? That I of all people . . . Hasn't our great director said over and over that Bruno cares only for what he can capture on celluloid? No, believe me, I have no desire for that kind of power. Besides, it's not blackmail people fear. What they fear is the chance I afford them to recognize and affirm their deepest wish."

"Are you trying to goad us, Bruno?"

"Believe me, *carissima*, I'm simply trying to enlist your help. I need someone to play the husband and someone to play the wife."

"Well, I have no suggestions."

"Will you at least think about it?"

"Perhaps," she replied, and walked away.

The cameraman smiled. "The wife especially," he called after her. "That role is crucial. The others less important. Practically any oaf will do for the huband, and as for the younger pair. I've already got them in mind." (Here, da Fé turned and grinned at Denise and Cameron.) "In fact, the opening—the scene through the keyhole—has already been shot. This morning . . ."

Cameron stared at the contemptuous, grotesquely pitted face before him, and a second later struck it. The blow, a roundhouse swing, landed on the side of da Fé's head, but instead of knocking the cameraman backward or down, it simply propelled Cameron into his arms, which closed around him like a vise. For some moments, the two men swayed back and forth, locked in awkward embrace, like a pair of clumsy dancers. Then the cameraman began to tighten his grip. Cameron continued to struggle until, all of a sudden, he felt himself lifted off the floor and realized that it was no use. Now, caught in a grasp that was like that of the sea, his struggling grew feeble. The breath was being crushed out of him, the room swirled before his eyes, everything began to grow dark. He was at the point of losing consciousness, when the cameraman simply opened his arms and allowed him to drop, like a crumpled paper bag, upon the floor. Gasping for breath, Cameron looked up expecting to receive a blow, and saw Gottschalk standing above him.

"What's the matter here?" the director demanded.

"Listen, he's making a film and—"

"Bruno's forever making films."

"—I'm in it!"

"You?" exclaimed Gottschalk with a weary smile. "My dear young man, who are you? Or should I say, which you? You're like the pictures in a roll of film that never gets turned. Each time the shutter clicks, there's another image of you superimposed on the one that was before. D'you know what I'm talking about?"

"No," said Cameron. "What *are* you talking about?"

"Double-exposure," the director replied.

10

The morning was swollen with impending heat. Beyond the window, a gray, indolent sea stretched like a slab of slate toward the horizon that was obscured by mist. A few gulls stood sentinel upon the roof of the casino, which had melted into its own reflection, and the uppermost rim of the Ferris wheel was shining in the rising sun. It's going to be another scorcher, Cameron thought, and wondered if the toll collector would show up for his new job with a jug of lemonade.

As soon as he had dressed, Denise knocked on the door and came in with her make-up kit. "Good God!" she exclaimed. "Don't tell me you slept in all that gunk!"

At first, he failed to understand; then he remembered his new face, and smiled. "I forgot," he said.

"Well, take if off at night or it'll ruin your skin. Besides, that face is awful. It isn't you." .

"Oh, I don't know," he replied. "I've gotten used to it."

Denise gave a laugh and shook her head. "You're a strange one," she said. "Come on, sit down so I can do you over."

"Can't you just touch me up?"

"With all those whiskers sprouting through?"

Cameron sat in a chair beside the sink and tilted his head back while Denise swabbed away at him to remove the make-up. Yes, he had forgotten all about the necessity of shaving, which meant that she would see him every day. How fortunate, then, their encounter on the linen pile.

"Okay, now you can shave,"' she announced. "Remind me to give you some lotion. Otherwise, you're liable to crack and peel like an old painting."

Cameron stood up and, looking into the mirror, lathered his beard and took up his razor. For a moment, he stared at himself with the dismaying realization that each morning he would have to shave, and that this face—the face he so desperately wished to efface—would be there to evoke the past. Now, stretching his neck back, he applied the razor to the skin beneath his chin, and, gazing into his own eyes as if they belonged to someone else, reminded himself that he had been seen. First by the toll collector, then by Gottschalk, and now by Denise . . .

She was watching him with amusement. "What a bore," she said. "To have to shave every day."

A terrible bore, Cameron decided, pulling at the corners of his mouth and passing the razor over his upper lip. And dangerous, too, for was it not a time of vulnerability? The toll collector, Gottschalk, Denise, and who else? he wondered as, shaving gently, he uncovered the scab that had formed over the abrasion on his cheekbone. Who else? As usual, he had managed to nick himself, and now, staring at the tiny trickle of blood that was turning the lather pink, he remembered. Then, finishing up quickly, he pulled the drain plug and watched the soapy water disappear from the sink with a rush and a froth of bubbles. Afterward, he splashed himself vigorously with cold water, mopped his face with a towel, and turned around.

"That's better," said Denise. "That's the real you."

The real me, thought Cameron, who was remembering the bubbles as he sat down in the chair again and closed his eyes.

Denise began to apply the first layer of make-up. "About last night," she said. "Everybody thinks it was just a joke that got out of hand."

"Some joke," Cameron muttered.

"Well, you were crazy to pick a fight with him. He's strong enough to break a phone pole."

"I mean the film he took of us."

"Oh, that," she said with a laugh. "Don't worry about that. Bruno's bluffing. He may've been watching us through the keyhole, but that doesn't mean he's got it on film. Not unless he has some kind of camera I've never heard of."

"What was he doing there to begin with?"

"He probably came back to look in on the chambermaid. She's his latest protégée. A local number who thinks he's going to turn her into a sex goddess. Good old Bruno. Can you imagine what he must be teaching her?"

"Good old Bruno," said Cameron grimly. "One of these days, I'll have to even the count with him."

"Why not leave well enough alone and stay in one piece?"

Cameron stood up and looked into the mirror. "Okay," he

said, pleased with the beach boy's face that was once again grinning back at him. "But next time let's not wind up drawing at Bruno's box office."

Denise gave a mischievous smile. "Not even for kicks?"

"Not even for kicks," said Cameron. "I like my home movies in private."

At breakfast, he sat opposite the dapper little man with whom Nina Mabry had been talking the night before. The little man wore horn-rimmed glasses and a mournful countenance that was accentuated by a pair of drooping mustaches. The Brechtian face goes better with brawn, Cameron reflected. Otherwise, it lacks authority. . . . "Hello," he said. "I'm Arthur Coleman."

"The stunt man."

"Yes."

"I'm Dalton Roth." Now, wagged by a smile of self-deprecation that accompanied this declaration, the mustaches flared briefly; then, twitching, they subsided once again into melancholy. "The screen writer."

Cameron buttered a piece of toast and stirred some sugar into his coffee. "Does that mean you work on the script?" he asked.

"It would ordinarily," Roth replied, "but on this job I'm just a glorified secretary. A stenographic extension of genius. In other words, I jot down the great man's inspirations. There isn't any script, you know. Mr. G's improvising everything."

Cameron nodded and spread his toast with marmalade. "But you must have some idea of the story. Of what happens next, I mean."

Roth gave a harsh laugh. "When you've been here longer, you'll begin to realize that our director's methods create an entirely new concept of continuity."

"I don't get you."

"Simply that there are half a dozen films rattling around in his head, and that it's impossible to tell at any given moment which one he's talking about, working on, or even shooting."

"Well, as far as I know, I'm doubling for Jordan in the one that's supposed to be about a fugitive."

The screen writer took a sip of coffee; then, replacing cup in its saucer, he pursed his lips, wiped his mustaches a napkin, and regarded Cameron morosely. "What is it want to know?" he asked.

"I was just wondering if you might have any idea my next stunt will be."

"You don't suppose they shoot them in order, do y said Roth with a shrug.

Cameron grinned. "Isn't there a schedule?"

"Certainly," the screen writer replied, tapping a forefi against the temple. "But, like everything else around it's in the director's head."

"Okay, what's the next stunt in the story?"

"Another chase scene," Roth said wearily. "The hero trapped in an amusement center and jumps on the F wheel. Our director has a thing for Ferris wheels, you ki They appear in most of his films. You might say they' kind of trademark with him."

"I understood his trademark was double-exposure."

"Double-exposure's simply a technical phenomenon," explained. "It's a device used to express two levels of re —the objective physical world and the subjective worl dream or thought. Mr. G's use of Ferris wheels is somet else. They're a recurring theme. On the primary level, signify the common desire of people to escape from car thrill or sensation. But circling is also revoultion, and, th fore, futility. Thus the Ferris wheel becomes the whee chance. In the final analysis, it symbolizes the universe thre which all of us are spinning endlessly. In fact, in the ope scene of his next film—"

"I've heard about that," said Cameron impatiently. interested in the Ferris wheel on its primary level." This sounds like a graduate student reading a term paper, he thinking.

"The primary level is always melodrama," said the sc writer with a sigh.

"That's my thing," Cameron replied. "I'm the stunt man

"I'm afraid I've bored you," said Roth with a smile.

"Not at all," Cameron protested. You're talking to a p he told himself. Try not to offend his heightened sens aesthetics. . . .

The screen writer was nodding in sympathy. "All

jumping and crashing about," he murmured. "It must be trying on the nerves."

"I'll tell the world," replied Cameron. "That's why I asked you about the next stunt. I kind of like to prepare myself, you know?"

"Well, prepare yourself to take a flying leap," said Roth cheerfully.

"A flying leap?"

"Off the Ferris wheel at twelve o'clock and onto the whip ride."

Cameron had been chewing on a piece of toast. Now, swallowing hard, he shook his head and said, "You're kidding."

"Scout's honor," Roth declared.

Cameron took a deep breath. "When you said 'all that jumping and crashing about,'" he asked, "what did you mean? About the crashing part?"

"Oh, that," Roth replied. "I'm supposed to be doing a preliminary treatment right now. It comes at the end of the film when the hero goes off a bridge and into the river in his car."

Cameron found that he was holding his breath. "Does he survive the crash? In the story, I mean."

"Gottschalk hasn't made up his mind about that," said Roth with his mournful smile. "I don't see how he could, though. He's going to drive through a guard rail and into thirty feet of water!"

"Through a guard rail," Cameron echoed.

"It's the kind of problem prop men solve in no time. They'll construct the guard rail out of wood. Balsa maybe. Or papier-mâché. You'll go through it like cheese. The sound track'll take care of the rest by giving out an ear-splitting crash, followed by a spine-tingling scream of tearing metal, and ending with a whopping big splash."

"Don't you think the splash might be overdoing things?" said Cameron. No one's going to believe the splash, he thought. Least of all the fugitive . . .

"But there's got to be a splash!" Roth replied. "To go with the geyser."

"Then don't forget the bubbles," Cameron told him grimly.

"Bubbles?"

"From the sinking car."

The screen writer whipped a notebook out of his breast pocket, and, flipping it open, began to scribble furiously in it with a pen. "You know, you've really got something there!" he said. "I'll put it on the list of pick-up shots. A whole bunch of bubbles bursting upon the surface. It'll make a swell soft-focus fade-out."

In the lobby, the quiet, professionally crisis-stricken voice of a newscaster was describing a mistake in which planes had bombed the wrong village. "Medical corpsmen have been rushed to the scene to render aid, and the military authorities are conducting an investigation to ascertain—"

Reaching behind him, Gottschalk turned off the radio; then he looked toward the members of the company, who had gathered around the counter. "Today's schedule will be as follows," he announced. "This morning we'll shoot the motel scene in which the fugitive wakes up to find himself in bed with the waitress. Remember, Jordan, you come bolt upright, eyes wild and full of the terror of the previous night. Then you look down at the sleeping woman who has sheltered you. She's in her middle forties and a bit dowdy. A faded beauty. Not your cup of tea, but no matter. She's saved you from the police. When she awakens to find you looking at her, each of you is suddenly aware of what the other is thinking. Yes, both of you are grateful to each other. It's in this mood—of resignation and momentary respose—that you make love."

"But tenderly," said Nina Mabry, who was standing by a window. "We make love tenderly, do we not?"

"Tenderly," the director replied. "Yet, above all, aware of the realities."

"The best way," she murmured.

Looking at her, Cameron saw that Denise had made her up with a lot of white powder and without lipstick or eyeshadow. She's just right, he thought. She looks like one of those aging girls who pour endless cups of coffee in bus-terminal cafeterias. . . .

"After lunch, I'll be in the cutting room," the director continued. "The rest of you can take the afternoon off. Except for Jordan and Coleman, who're going to rehearse the escape scene in the amusement center. Have you made arrangements for that, Bruno?"

The cameraman nodded. "Everything's ready, Mr. G. The Ferris wheel will be shut down between two and three o'clock, and the fire department's been cooperating nicely. The trampolines and nets are being set up this morning, and a hook and ladder will lift the whip ride to the proper level."

"Are you sure we can fake the rest?"

"Easily," da Fé replied. "A matter of shooting from the right angle."

"Remember the budget, Bruno. We've been straining it."

"Count on us, Mr. G. Everything will go letter perfect when we shoot tonight."

The director got to his feet, and glanced at his watch. "It's eight-thirty," he said. "All crews leave immediately for the set. I want everyone else there by nine. We'll start at ten. Oh, and one other thing, Bruno. You have a new assistant. . . ."

The lighting and camera crews had already begun to head for the door, but now there was a hesitation in the general movement, which was accompanied by a soft ripple of laughter.

Cameron could scarcely believe his eyes, for the toll collector, who was smiling uneasily across the room, was wearing an ornately flowered sports shirt, slacks, and sandals, and a pair of white-rimmed sunglasses that smothered his eyes like the outstretched wings of a giant butterfly. It's either the chief's notion of a disguise or a fool's idea of Hollywood, he thought, and, shaking his head, suppressed a smile.

Watching her in the soft throes of love, Cameron felt himself trembling as, with eyes tight shut, she turned her head from side to side and blew gently through half-pursed lips toward a flame she wished neither to kindle nor to extinguish. For some moments, she appeared to maintain herself upon the knife edge of an equilibrum too exquisite to bear; then, flinging her head to one side, she opened her eyes with a sigh, and looked up at the ceiling.

"Cut," said Gottschalk softly, and stepped before the camera. At this point, the room came to life. Da Fé and his crew swung the camera to one side on its dolly; the mike man drew the sound boom out of the way; a mixer in headphones flipped a series of switches on the panel of his console; and the electricians shut off several of the brightest lights.

Now, as Denise came in carrying a large puff and a can of powder, Jordan raised himself upon his knees, swung his legs over the side of the bed, and accepted a lighted cigarette from one of the prop men. Only Nina Mabry remained in position, lying exactly as she had in his embrace, with one arm flung up over her head, the other dangling, a knee slightly raised. For a second longer, she held the pose; then she sat up, tugging at the edges of panties that swathed her hips, and submitted her face to the powder puff.

The director was pacing back and forth, wearing a scowl of concentration. "Better," he said. "The best yet. But I could still catch glimpses of your profile, Jordan, whereas all I want to see of you is shoulders and back. Nothing else, d'you understand? In the act of love, the man is nothing. Everything is the woman and *her* face. Everything!"

"I get it," the actor said. "Let's take a break, though. This is rough on the old elbows."

Gottschalk glanced at him with impatience. "If you'll follow instructions, the next take will be the last."

"Well, let's hope so. No offense, Nina."

"None taken," she replied coolly. "The old elbows, as you put it, shouldn't be abused. In fact, why not strengthen them with exercise? A few push-ups each morning and the old amatory technique could be vastly improved."

"Hell, Nina, I was only kidding. Why carry on?"

"Because it pleases me, and you do not."

"Enough," commanded Gottschalk absently. Now, sitting on a corner of the bed, he stared at the screen of a television set on the far side of the room as if lost in thought; then, with a smile of elation, he called for Roth.

Notepad in one hand, pencil in the other, the screen writer bounded into the room.

The director held up a hand for silence. "Get this down on paper," he said. "It's for the scene where Margaret's seduced by the space scientist. Technology has failed to soothe her. Religion has proved a disaster. She grasps in desperation at physical love. But the trauma of it—her guilt—is too much to bear. Even as she approaches ecstasy, she sees a television set on the far side of the room whose blank screen in her mind's eye and ours shows a missile poised on its pad for launching. Now she hears the voice of the mission control officer calling countdown. *'Five, four, three, two, one . . .*

Lift-off!' Yes, at the very moment of orgasm, the rocket explodes into the sky. And, once again, she is devastated. Nothing can assuage this woman. She will always be alone. Forever terrified. Because of the awful vision that is constantly before her . . ."

When the director finished speaking, the set came alive as the floodlamps were turned on and the camera was wheeled back into place. Jordan stubbed his cigarette in an ash tray, Nina Mabry lay back on the bed, and Bruno da Fé, his ravaged face frozen into a mask of concentration, crouched behind the lens.

For a moment, there was complete stillness in the room; then the cameraman raised his head and looked inquiringly at Gottschalk, who was still staring at the television screen.

Turning slowly, the director looked around him blankly; then his face assumed an expression of monumental indifference. Shaking his head, he gave a weary shrug. "That's enough," he said. "The last take will do. Make it for printing."

There was a rush for the doorway, and, turning to get out of the way, Cameron found himself face to face with the toll collector, who had lifted the lepidopterous sunglasses over his forehead for a better look.

"Aren't they going to do it again?" he asked.

Cameron started to reply, but, afraid that his voice might give him away, he thought better of it and simply shook his head.

"Damn," the toll collector muttered. "I thought she was going to have to do it again."

Cameron pushed past him and, walking out on a balcony, pretended to look at the sea. Then he saw Gottschalk striding along the beach toward the hotel, followed by Roth, who was scribbling away on his notepad and struggling to keep up. Maybe they're discussing that imaginary geyser. Cameron thought. Yes, what could be more imaginary than a geyser preceded by no splash, yet followed by endless bubbles . . . ? Now, turning away from the railing of the balcony, he nearly bumped into Nina Mabry, who came out of the motel room wearing a brightly printed shift. For a moment, he simply stood before her, gaping. Then he gave his head a tiny shake of awe. "Excuse me," he said. "It's just that you . . . look so different."

"Different," she repeated, gazing directly at him and passing the fingertips of both hands over her hair, which had been brushed straight back and fastened with a large ribbon behind her neck. "D'you mean now that I'm dressed?"

"Oh, no," he protested. "I meant without make-up. And with your hair brushed back."

She gave a smile that acknowledged his embarrassment. "You like it?"

He drew a deep breath that nearly strangled him. "I like it," he said huskily, "because it emphasizes the structure and the beauty of your face."

"What lovely compliments you pay. You should have more confidence in them."

He smiled bleakly at her as she walked past him to the railing. Then, joining her, leaning on his elbows, and feeling immeasurably relieved that they were no longer standing opposite one another, he said, as if in explanation, "I didn't expect to see you."

"All the better," she replied. "For paying compliments that are uncontrived."

Now, groping for the plane to which she had shifted them, and suddenly afraid of seeming glib, he launched into an explanation that evolved into an aimless retraction, which, awkwardly expressed, provoked her to laughter.

"So you watched the take. What did you think of it?"

"I thought you were wonderful," he replied. "Perfect."

"Is that all?"

"No."

"Something else?"

"Yes."

"Tell me," she demanded. "An actress always wants to know. What was your real reaction? How did you feel?"

"Deprived," he said instantly, and looked at her as if for the first time.

"Deprived," she murmured. "Yes, the best compliments of all are those with which men give women pleasure."

Amazed at his own boldness and surprised by her reply, he found himself tongue-tied once again, and thinking that never again could he hope to pay a compliment that would derive the same response. Never . . . The idea was suffocating. The heat of the sun unbearable. A trickle of perspiration found its way into his eye. Half blind, he rubbed at it with his knuckles. Say something, he told himself. Say something. . . .

At this point, mercifully, someone called up to her from below. "Hey, Nina! Nina, look!"

It was Jordan who, spread-eagled upon the sand, had begun to perform a series of push-ups. For a while, the actor raised and lowered himself with vigorous determined strokes. Then, weakening, his rhythm grew ragged. Finally, flushed with exertion, he subsided upon the sand, elbows up, a limp grasshopper. "Twenty," he groaned. "I'll raise it ten a day. By the end of the week—ah, Nina, to what lengths would I not go to please you!"

"To please me?" she said with a laugh. "Or to prove yourself?"

Jordan rolled over and sat up. "Nina, my dear, by the end of the week, I'll have elbows of sufficient strength to astonish you."

"How convenient," she replied. "To astonish by brawn alone."

"Be kinder," Cameron whispered. "He's only trying to retrieve himself."

"Ah, so you sympathize with him! D'you feel a common bond, perhaps?"

Cameron looked down at Jordan, who had got to his feet and was gazing up at them with a puzzled smile. She goes right to the point, he thought. "Not with him," he said softly, "but his predicament."

"The same thing," she answered. "Men are so alike. Only the bodies and faces have been changed. To protect the adolescent."

"Speak up, Nina," Jordan called. "I can't hear you."

"I was saying that you never fail to amuse me. So boyish. So full of antics. Always charming."

The actor beamed. "Nina, let's have lunch."

"Shall I continue to be kind?" she whispered.

"What's there to lose?" Cameron replied.

"Lunch together."

"Be cruel," he said.

She gave a soft, triumphant laugh, and, leaning over the railing, smiled gently down at Jordan. "Too late, my dear. I'm already taken for lunch today."

"With him?" exclaimed the actor, staring up at Cameron.

"With him," she answered.

"My double," Jordan said with a grimace that slowly became a grin. "My very own double."

At least he's making the best of it, Cameron thought. "I'll behave accordingly," he announced with mock solemnity.

"That's what I'm afraid of," Jordan replied. "Take care, Nina."

"I shall. I'll treat him as if he were your very own alter ego."

"Then don't trust him."

"Not for a single moment."

The actor saluted them with a smile and a wave, and turned away. Cameron watched him as, trying to look unconcerned, he loped across the sand. A television cowboy, he thought. Saving face with badinage and swagger. "So men are all alike," he said. "Fools doubling for one another."

"Don't exaggerate," she replied. "Perhaps the male fraternity is not as solid as I thought."

"It can be fractured," Cameron remarked dryly. "Because the bond is fragile."

She glanced at him with cool appraisal. "You have a ruthless streak."

"Only when fencing," he said.

"Remember, when fencing, that no one should win or lose."

"You approve of fixed matches?"

"The best matches are always fixed," she replied. "By adversaries who duel for pleasure."

11

⤙⤙✦⤙⤙

Her car, a white convertible, was parked in the street behind the motel. She insisted that he drive, and now, holding the door for her as she climbed inside, it seemed to him that the spell under which they had been operating was broken. All at once, everything seemed practical and real. He slid in behind the wheel, and, following her directions, set off along the road which paralleled the beach.

"Straight to the end," she told him. "Until you come to the river."

Glancing sideways, he saw her tip her head back to catch the breeze. Yes, she was suddenly too real—a woman riding in an open car in summertime. In this mood, he withdrew into a private theater where the windshield before his face became a screen upon which he found himself watching a series of disconnected shots that revealed her in flashback. Now, as if through a view-finder, he saw the Ferris wheel reflected in her sunglasses, her face rigid with horror as the surfing board came tumbling down upon the beach, her half-naked body lying in Jordan's embrace, and, finally, a lascivious dance in which, tossing her auburn tresses, she removed her garments with taunting grace and flung them gleefully toward the lens of da Fé's camera. Then he noticed sand dunes streaming past him on either side, and, feeling the disorientation of someone who has walked out of a film into the bright light of day, gave his head a shake. "I ought to let you take the wheel," he said. "I'm a terrible driver."

"You!" she laughed. "A stunt man?"

"That's the trouble. I don't always stop at rivers. I have a tendency to drive off bridges, over cliffs, and in front of loco-motives."

She laughed again.

"Why hit people," he went on, half-singing it in the manner of Ray Bolger, "when you can pull your punches? Or walk downstairs when you can tumble?"

They had come to the end of the road, where a row of shabby cottages and tilting shanties formed a barricade along the river bank. Here he pulled up before a roadside stand with a screen-windowed take-out counter beneath a sign that read, FRIED CLAMS. On one side of the stand, a warped porch that was evolving into debris continued out over the water on stilts to a small wharf that was piled with lobster pots. On the other side, an immense jetty channeled the river out to sea.

"Is this the place?" he asked.

She nodded soberly. "They make good lobster rolls."

"How many can you eat?"

"Two, please."

For a moment, he continued to sit behind the wheel, staring at the river. Relax, he told himself. It's just a river—a river that keeps its secrets at all stages of the tide. Were they not all alike, these murky tidal rivers? Old refrigerators, bedsprings, rubber tires—what, including ancient cars, did not eventually find its way into them? And as for the car in question, did it exist except on celluloid which, even now, was being edited by the director? Yes, Gottschalk was right. What's the difference? Which is real? And who—no matter if the car was discarded into the river or simply deleted with a snip of the scissors and dropped into a convenient wastebasket—would ever know?

Inside, he ordered three lobster rolls and two bottles of beer from an elderly counterman whose face was wrinkled like one of those inshore sandbars that have been corrugated by the sea.

"To go?" the old man asked. "Or d'you want to eat 'em here?"

Cameron glanced at a pair of tables that stood next to a flyspecked window overlooking the river. "To go," he said. Now, looking through the window, he saw that the river mouth was stitched with weirs which cast intricate shadows upon the surface of the water. "What d'you catch here?" he asked.

"Nothing since they built the causeway," the counterman replied. "Don't hardly bother to haul these days."

Cameron thought of the river fighting for supremacy with the tide each day, and wondered what it might carry to the sea. He imagined the old man hauling his nets to discover

—ah, but what could those nets possibly hold except a soggy newspaper whose unintelligible headline no longer posed a threat to anyone? After all, by this time the newspaper had disintegrated, and even the war it had so belligerently celebrated seemed as blurred and indistinct as the toll collector's muffled shouts. A make-believe conflict. He had scarcely thought about it since crossing the bridge—the bridge that would once again become a movie set. . . .

The counterman handed him his order in a boxtop.

Cameron paid and started toward the door.

"Caught me an arm once," the old man called after him.

Frowning, Cameron turned around. "In an accident?"

"In my nets," the old man said. "An arm and elbow. From a train wreck upriver. But that was years ago."

Cameron stepped outside, took a deep breath, and saw Nina smiling at him through the windshield.

Fifteen minutes later, as they clambered out across the jetty, jumping from one vast tilting slab of granite to the next, he turned to give her his hand, and, looking back, saw that they had come nearly a quarter of a mile out to sea.

"Far enough," he said.

"We're only halfway," she replied. "Let's go to the end."

Cameron glanced into a small chasm that separated them and heard the sea washing back and forth in the bowels of the jetty. "What if the tide starts coming in?"

"We'll run back ahead of it."

"Why take the chance?"

"Why walk downstairs when you can tumble?"

"This isn't a movie," he told her.

She was standing on a slightly higher rock whose plane sloped another way from his. Now, stepping across to his side, she touched his shoulder to steady herself and looked up at him with somber eyes. "It doesn't matter," she said. "We can eat here just as well."

"No, we'll go to the end," he replied. "I guess I'm jittery. It's because of last night."

"But you're right, you know. The tide does come in over the rocks."

"We'll run back ahead of it," he told her with a smile.

They ate beside a beacon whose triangular base was an-

chored in concrete that had been poured around some
slabs at the tip of the jetty. For a while, he watched
addressing herself greedily to her lobster roll; then he f
himself studying a rock at the waterline that had been
covered by the ebbing tide. When the water rises over it,
start back, he told himself, and imagined them hurryir
keep ahead of the sea. "It's nice out here," he said.
from everything."

"I know. That's why I wanted to come back."

He paused, not wishing to appear inquisitive. "You've
here before?"

She munched tentatively at her sandwich and gave a s
"I flew over once. In the helicopter. The waves were brea
against the beacon and there was foam and turmoil e
where. It was breathtaking,"

Cameron said nothing.

"We came out here to see what it would be like," she
tinued. "At that time, he was thinking of using the jetty i
film."

"Which film?"

"The one we're shooting. He was considering it for a
ternative ending. The fugitive was going to flee out he
night, but no one could follow because of the tide. The
the morning, there was going to be nothing. Just the day
breaking and the sea washing against the rocks."

Cameron got to his feet. "And what was supposed to
pen to the fugitive?"

She gave a shrug. "It was going to be left up in the
she said. "The kind of ending that's endless."

Endless . . . the word churned through his brain, conj
up for him the maelstrom in which he had tumbled endl
until, extracted from the sea and expelled upon the san
had come alive in spite of his despair that all was over
forever ended. Only art is real. Gottschalk had said.
art repeats itself. Over and over. Endlessly . . . He had
gotten that the director avoided endings.

Nina was looking up at him, still and open-eyed, an
knew that if he should dare to kiss her now, the stil
would remain in reserve, untouched by the confrontatic
their lips, like the sea that was waiting to arbitrate its str
with the river. Her stillness was engulfing—an ocean
which, having committed himself by stages, he would b

quired to embark without a backward look. In this mood, he hesitated, a swimmer testing the water before venturing farther out. Or was it simply that he had glanced again at the rock whose submergence would signal their return to shore? No matter. There was still time, and they were alone. But were they alone at the end of this jetty that, like the bridge, might also become a movie set? The thought lapped at him like the water against the rock, and, suddenly, the granite blocks that surrounded them seemed false, as if fabricated from cardboard—fragile props that would not acquire the semblance of solidity until light was passed through a strip of celluloid.

Now, as if on cue, a large wave broke over the rocks and traveled along the ragged wall of the jetty toward the shore. The sea and its sound effects are real, Cameron thought. "We're alone," he said, and imagined that he felt her tremble.

"So is Margaret," she murmured. "A woman who derives no confidence from science, no comfort from religion, and no solace from love."

"That's just a film," he told her.

"But her terror is constant, and since I must constantly try to imagine it . . ."

"We're alone," he repeated softly.

"So is she."

"We're real. Margaret's a character. Someone he dreamed up. An exaggeration."

"Real?" she said, smiling up at him. "And isn't Margaret real? Yes, because she's truly alone. And because we fear it so."

"Listen, it's just a film," he told her again, and stole a glance at the rock. "Not even that. It's a series of fragments that haven't been pieced together. An improvisation. Anyway, there aren't any cameras here. We're between takes."

"Between takes," she murmured. "Is that how you think of it?"

"My work is disconnected. All I do is stunts. In place of Jordan."

"Then you have no curiosity about the film?"

"Which film?" he answered with a laugh.

"How convenient to be detached. But d'you like your work?"

"I haven't been at it long enough to tell."

"It must be difficult. You must have to practice."

"Practice!" he exclaimed: "You forget how arbitrary his methods are."

"Remember, it's only a film," she told him gently.

"Only a film," he repeated, as if tracing the flight of a boomerang. She had brought his exhortation back to him, and now, struck by the echo, he saw them standing alone in a land of make-believe, casting no shadows beneath harsh lights as, between takes, they waited to resume acting out a story in which, trapped on jetties, swept beneath the sea, and lost in space, they seemed doomed to languish in isolation, for *in extremis*, without hope of direction. Then he imagined himself clinging through the night to the rusting spars of the beacon, shouting his defiance as the tide rose higher toward a camera made invisible by a blinding red light that had been illuminated by the mindless collusion of darkness and a photo-electric cell. Suddenly, he felt invincible, as if he would be able to perform any stunt!

He gave his head a shake. "We're going in circles," he said. "Margaret's afraid to live, the fugitive's afraid to die. D'you suppose they'll come together?"

"In the next reel," she replied with a laugh.

"Too long to wait," he whispered. "Can't we speed up the projector?"

"That might spoil the picture. One scene must build to another. Otherwise, we take away from our characters the pleasure of anticipation."

"But do they have time to waste, those two?"

"They must be allowed to think so."

For a moment, he gazed steadily at her; then, looking down at his feet, he saw the level of the sea had risen ever so slightly on the rock. "The tide's turned," he said.

"Do you have to go?"

"Not yet," he replied, and, taking her head between his hands, his thumbs at her temples, drew her face to his.

12

~~~

When they drove up to the amusement center, he pulled the car to the curb, climbed out, and watched her slide across the seat behind the wheel. How gracefully she accomplished even the most ordinary movements! Now, leaning against the door, he looked down at her with wonder. For the first time since he had crossed the causeway, it seemed possible that he might resume his life. I'm in love with her, he thought. I've fallen in love. . . . "I'll be through in an hour or so," he said. "What will you be doing the rest of the afternoon?"

She released the hand brake. "It depends," she answered. "He may want me to rehearse, too."

"Not today," Cameron told her. "He's busy putting together the rushes for a special screening tonight."

Nina regarded him soberly. "What are you saying?"

"That we don't have to worry," he replied, amazed at his boldness. "Will you be in your room?"

"Perhaps."

Smiling, he bent down to the level of the window. "Wait there for me. I'll come as soon as I can."

"You'll come between takes," she answered coolly, and put the car into gear.

He shook his head with dismay and started to protest, but the car was already moving away and he was standing in the space it had vacated, slightly off-balance, like a man who, having made a futile grab for a wind-snatched hat, hesitates between the impulse to pursue and the necessity to be on his way.

A few moments later, as he walked through the amusement center, he passed a house of mirrors, and, seeing his reflection in its glittering entranceway, was reminded that she had never seen him without his movie face. Would she find the other disappointing? Now, oppressed by the idea and by the sounds and smells that came belching from the labyrinth of arcades, he struggled to keep his vision of her intact. But she was already receding before him like some-one conjured up from a magical lamp, and, suddenly, he found it difficult to believe that he had ever kissed her. It was as if he had embraced a cloud that had been shaped in her image.

Da Fé stood waiting for him at the base of the Ferris wheel. The cameraman was wearing a scarlet jersey, and wolfing down in huge mouthfuls a honey-dip doughnut pur-chased from a nearby stand. Now, licking his fingertips, he raised his canine head aand grinned. "You've discovered my weakness, *caro*. A sweet tooth. But doesn't everyone have some secret vice?"

Cameron watched da Fé bite ravenously into another doughnut; then, recoiling from the sight, he looked at the Ferris wheel, from which the last passengers were debarking, and allowed his eyes to travel clockwise around its dial. A flying leap from twelve o'clock . . . But a quick glance at the cables supporting the chairs of the adjacent whip ride told him it was impossible. They're not long enough to reach, he thought.

The cameraman spoke through a stuffed mouth. "What's the matter, *caro*? Afraid of heights?"

Never show fear before a dog, Cameron told himself. "I was wondering how close the whip chairs come to the Ferris wheel," he said.

"About fifteen feet," da Fé replied. "That's at top speed, of course, when they're almost flat out with the centrifugal force."

"What d'you think I am? A flying squirrel?"

The cameraman laughed and, because he was in the midst of swallowing, began to choke. Then, recovering, he shook his head with suppressed mirth. "Believe me, *caro,* your mortality's been taken into account. Which is to say that the cable of the whip chair you're going to ride has been length-ened sufficiently so that all you'll have to do is reach out and grab it."

"Just like that."

"Yes, *caro,* just like that. Everything will be faked to ensure your safety. The chair will be stationary, you see, held in place by a slender wire supported by the tower ladder of the fire department's hook-and-ladder truck. As for the leap, the sheer flight through space, we can shoot that any time and almost any place. In fact, the porch railing at the hotel will do nicely. A mere five-foot flop upon the sand, but with the proper grimace and the correct camera angle, no one'll know the difference."

"And how're you going to give the illusion that the whip ride is in motion?"

"Simply by having you whirled around on it at arm's length a few times, and then splicing it into the sequence at the proper place."

They had been joined by Lee Jordan, who was listening intently. "A lead-pipe cinch," he said, grinning at Cameron. "I'd do it myself except I'm scared of heights. A nine-hand horse is my absolute limit."

"After you've made a couple of circuits, the whip ride will slow down and you can let go above the trampolines," da Fé went on. "That'll be the only difficult part. You want to be very relaxed when you hit the canvas or—"

"Hey, I thought I was going to do that!" Jordan protested.

"Who else, *caro?* The stunt man leaves the film when the fugitive lets go the whip ride and is flying through the air. You come into it in close-up when he lands on the trampoline bounces everybody out of it, and makes his escape through the arcades in the resulting confusion. But we'll shoot that part later."

"Crazy," the actor said. "It'll be a great bit of slapstick, bouncing them out of the trampoline like that."

"Just like falling off a horse," Cameron told him. Crazy, he was thinking. But perfect, too. Who else should perform slapstick in close-up but Jordan, who, by playing the leading role, ensures that his double remains obscure—a shadow performing high-altitude tricks in the background . . . ?

But half an hour later, as he sat in brilliant sunshine at high noon on the Ferris wheel, he was once again overwhelmed by the absurdity of his situation. Far below, a thin cordon of policemen held a growing crowd at bay; just above his chair, da Fé sat in a basket at the end of the fire department's tower ladder, studying him through a view-finder. From his gently rocking vantage point, Cameron could see the entire crescent of the beach and an immense expanse of sea. Everything else—the hotels, cottages, and the pier, but espe-

cially the people on the ground—seemed incredibly minuscule.
Now, squinting at the piano wire that supported the whip-ride
chair, which lay just beyond arm's reach, he suddenly became apprehensive. He tried not to look down, but he could
not prevent himself from stealing furtive glances. *Terra firma.*
The phrase took on new meaning. Wistfully, he imagined himself running through an obstacle course in basic training.
Child's play. What would he not give at this moment to have
two combat-booted feet upon the ground? Acrophobia, he
told himself, tearing his eyes from the ground. Don't give
way to it. . . .

With his face hidden behind the view-finder, and his
enormous torso leaning out over the edge of the basket, the
cameraman looked like a baboon preparing to swing down
from a treetop. Now, lowering the view-finder, he grinned at
Cameron. "So, *caro,* up to this point everything will be shot
with Jordan, who, in blind panic, has jumped on the wheel,
seeking to escape his pursuers. But they've seen him, the
police, and instructed the operator to remove the passengers.
In this way, tick by inexorable tock, the fugitive'll soon be
delivered into their hands at six o'clock. No way to avoid
it. Ah, but suddenly the whip-ride chairs come whizzing past.
Tantalizingly close. It it worth the chance? No, it's impossible.
But think of what awaits below! So why not give it a try?
After all, there's nothing to lose."

"You must be kidding," said Cameron. "Who the hell's
going to believe that anyone could grab hold of a whip ride
that way? Why, even a circus performer—"

"But he *does* it, *caro!* It'll be on film. In black and white.
And, therefore, utterly believable. Besides, we're going to
make it look good. No accomplished acrobat, our fugitive.
Just a young fellow full of desperation, who's going to be
unaccountably lucky. Think of him crouching, waiting, trying
to time his leap with the approach of the chairs, and thus
ensure the exact split-second synchronization by which his
fingers must grasp . . ."

Cameron was staring at the whip-ride chair five feet away;
then, in spite of himself, he looked down at the ground again.
Oh, God, he thought. What if I miss? "Listen," he said,
"what's the point in rehearsing? It's too damn dangerous."

"Practice makes perfect, *caro.* In everything. Believe me,
you'll feel infiinitely more confident tonight if you've done it

before. Besides, it's not as hard as it looks. Forget the height.
Pretend you're on the ground. Just reach out and take it."

"And then what?"

"Then I'll have the firemen reel us in, and we'll go on to
the next phase."

"When d'you want me to do it?"

"Whenever you're ready, *caro*."

Cameron stood up on the arm rest of his seat and, edging
out gingerly across a supporting bar, grasped the outermost
rim of the Ferris wheel, which, searing hot from the sun,
began to burn his hands. Now, crouching, he riveted his eyes
on the arm rest of the whip-ride chair. Do it, he told himself. Do it now before—

"Now!" the cameraman said.

He reached out, hands clawing for nothing, and pushed
off with his feet; then he was dangling, legs kicking and
fingers coiled for dear life around the arm rest of the whip-
ride chair. His heart was pumping madly. Looking up, he
tried to locate da Fé, but found himself gazing directly into
the sun. Blinded, he shut his eyes. Below, the crowd gave a
throaty murmur that, pierced by a woman's scream, welled
into a roar. Afterward, eyes tight shut and stomach sinking,
he felt himself being lowered. When his feet touched the
ground, he opened his eyes, took a deep breath, and, lurching away on unsteady legs, leaned against the doughnut counter, whose sickly sweet odor filled him with nausea. A moment later, he bent over and retched upon the ground.

Munching another honey-dip, da Fé eyed him calmly and
watched until he was through. "Splendid, *caro*. Do it that
way tonight and we'll finish in a single take. How d'you
feel?"

"How d'you *think* I feel?" Cameron gasped, looking at
him through eyes that were filled with tears.

"It'll pass," the cameraman replied, and glanced at his
watch. "Remember, we've only an hour to rehearse. Less
than twenty minutes left."

Cameron swallowed and made a face at the acrid taste.
"Please," he said. "That doughnut."

Da Fé pushed the last of the honey-dip into his mouth.
"Sweet things soothe the nerves, *caro*. You should try them."

Turning his head, Cameron saw Lee Jordan leaning over
a snow-fence barricade that had been erected by the police

to seal off the area. The actor was shaking his hands and signing autographs. Then, on the other side of the Ferris wheel, he caught sight of the toll collector, who was standing watch near the entrance to the fun house, where a hidden air vent tickled the legs and raised the skirts of unsuspecting girls. Keeping his eyes peeled, Cameron thought, and smiled in spite of himself. "Okay, now what?" he said.

"A little spin on the whip ride, *caro*. To give the illusion that it's in motion when you make your leap from the Ferris wheel. According to the operator, it'll be easier and safer if you start out hanging and just let yourself be dragged along until things get airborne. One or two times around and the whip will have accelerated to top speed, at which point you'll be flat out—an extension of the cable itself. We'll shoot two full revolutions of this. Then we'll take your fall into the trampolines. Naturally, the whip will be slowed down for that part. Otherwise you'd go flying out into space."

"In hammer-throw style," Cameron said.

"What's that, *caro?*"

"A track-and-field event."

"Ah, so you're an athlete!"

"A replacement from the junior varsity," Cameron said. "A second-stringer brought up for the big meet because of injuries."

The cameraman frowned. "You're making jokes with Bruno."

"It means I'm happy in my work. But how'll I know when to let go of the whip ride?"

Da Fé pointed to a row of trampolines that had been set up before the bumpmobile plaza. "Simple, *caro*. When you feel the machine slow down, wait until you swing past the funny-looking automobiles, and then release your grip. Remember to keep relaxed. It's possible to injure oneself on the canvas if the muscles are tense."

"Your concern is touching," Cameron said dryly.

The cameraman screwed his scarred face into a grimace of mock distress. "Let's agree to let bygones be bygones, *caro*. Believe it or not, your safety is not only a personal concern to me, but also a professional necessity. In other words, there are more stunts to come."

More stunts to come, Cameron was thinking a few minutes later as he was plucked gently off a loading platform and swung in a lazy circle that, as the whip ride accelerated, carried him higher and higher into the air. Now, on the second revolution, he felt his hands and wrists straining against the centrifugal force and his body streaming out behind him like a pennant. More stunts to come, he told himself as the machine achieved top speed and, spinning like a slingstone whirling in its strap, he imagined himself propelled into space, where, end over end, he would tumble endlessly like the immortal mummy of Gottschalk's film. No, he thought, closing his eyes . . . No . . . tightening his grip . . . No . . . fighting for breath against the tearing wind . . . No . . . trying to dispel the awful dizziness . . . No opening his eyes again . . . No . . . as the whip slowed with a sickening lurch . . . No . . . and he began his attendant descent toward . . . Not yet . . . and now abreast of the bumpmobile plaza . . . Yes . . . with its absurd little cars . . . Now . . . where he let go as if the seat had come loose in his hands, and . . . Oh . . . falling, open-mouthed, thought even again . . . *No* . . . when, bouncing high off the trampoline . . . *there are* . . . and somersaulting at the apex . . . *more* . . . and bouncing again . . . *stunts* . . . and again, and still again . . . *to come!*

Chief of Police Broussard was staring down at him along the barrel of a cigar to whose end he was applying the flame of a match. "Tell me something" . . . puff . . . "stunt man" . . . puff . . . "how old're you?"

"Twenty-six," said Cameron, who was sitting on the ground and trying to get his breath back.

"Twenty-six," Broussard muttered. "Same as the fellow we're looking for. But you know something? In the long run, his chances which don't amount to a straw in a bonfire are a helluva lot better than yours."

"What d'you mean?"

"What do I mean? What for Chrissakes d'you think I mean? You looking to get yourself killed or something?"

"Please," said the cameraman, shaking his head. "Don't say such things. It's bad luck."

The chief looked at da Fé and gave a soft curse of exclaim and wonder. "Who the hell're you to tell me what to say?"

"Believe me, *caro mio,* all the necessary precautions have been taken."

Broussard blew a mammoth cloud of smoke in the cameraman's direction. "Speak English when you talk to me," he growled.

Da Fé backed down with a smile that in no way altered the malevolent glitter in his eyes. "Of course," he murmured, "any recommendations you wish to make will be carried out. But if the stunt man isn't worried . . ."

The chief glanced tolerantly at Cameron, who was still sitting on the ground. "Maybe the stunt man hasn't got sense enough to worry."

Cameron got to his feet. Things can't be going too well, he thought. "How's the man hunt?" he asked.

Broussard made an unhappy grimace. "Today we got the military police on our necks. Who knows what tomorrow?"

"Isn't it a bit unusual? I mean, all this hullabaloo for an A.W.O.L.?"

"They must be looking to make an example," said the chief, chewing reflectively on the end of his cigar. "Want to keep the other young conscripts in line, I expect."

Da Fé was all cordiality and helpfulness. "I ought to tell you, chief, this fellow you've inserted into my crew isn't exactly—how shall I say?—tending to business. . . ."

"Lemme know if he steps too far out of line," Broussard replied grimly. "Meanwhile, he's the only witness I got."

The cameraman smiled at Cameron. "You mean he's the only one who can identify the fugitive?"

"Only one I got," the chief repeated in his rasping voice. "I hear the M.P.'s have imported their own."

Cameron was desperately trying to think of a way to phrase the question that had suddenly occupied his mind.

"So you're closing in," da Fé said softly. "The net is getting tighter."

"The M.P.'s," Cameron began, but he had nowhere to go. "Sound like they mean business," he added lamely.

Broussard gave a shrug. "That's what they get paid for, hanh?"

"But even if they want to make an example—I mean, why this particular fellow when there must be hundreds?"

"How should I know? But don't waste your time feeling

sorry for him. Feel sorry for the guy who's got to be his replacement."

Cameron was still trying to figure out a way to ask the chief who the military police had brought along to look for him. It must be the sergeant, he decided. Yes, it could only be the sergeant. . . . "Did you say 'replacement'?" he asked.

Broussard puffed on his cigar and nodded sagely. "Look at it this way. No matter what you think about the war, the monthly draft quota's got to be filled. It's the law. So if somebody decides to bug out or go over the hill, somebody else has got to fill the empty slot. Simple arithmetic, hanh?"

Cameron glanced toward the snow fence where Jordan, all smiles and banter, was cutting a caper for a dozen youthful fans. The chief has a point, he thought with a grim smile. In fact, he has no idea . . . "Yes," he replied, "no one should have to take risks for somebody else."

Broussard looked at him and shook his head. "Just for laughs sometime, I ought to introduce you to my insurance agent."

"I'd insist on a double-indemnity clause," Cameron said.

The chief barked with laughter, and spat the cigar from his mouth. "Hell, that's for accidents!" he exclaimed. "This is different. You hang in tight tonight, young fella. I got enough to worry about without you committing suicide in public."

As he was leaving the amusement center, a few minutes later, Cameron glanced into the window of a gallery that advertised pastel portraits, and saw superimposed upon a display of uniformly pink countenances the reflection of Jordan in the crowd behind him. For a moment, he was annoyed at the idea that the actor should be following him; then, remembering how much they looked alike, he was amused. We'll be taken for twins, he thought. Now, strolling away at a pace that was calculated to appear unconcerned, he crossed a promenade leading to the ocean pier, stepped upon a miniature escalator that carried him over a stagnant moat surrounding the fun house and the tunnel of love, and, ducking around a corner, waited by a ticket booth. Seconds later, dished up and delivered electronically, as if on a platter, the actor was deposited at his side.

"Welcome to playland," Cameron said.

Jordan manufactured a quick grin. "Hey, I thought I saw you come in here! Mind if I join up?"

Ruling out the fun house because of his stomach, Cameron bought a pair of tickets for the tunnel of love, and the two men stepped into a boat that carried them off into a dank and gloomy cavern.

"You were great up there," Jordan told him. "Really great."

"Thanks," said Cameron, who was wondering what was on the actor's mind.

"I just wanted to tell you because I know how you must feel."

"How's that?"

"You know, me getting the credit and you taking the chances."

"It's part of the game," Cameron replied with a shrug. The boat had glided into a dimly lit opening in the tunnel where some awkwardly animated prehistoric monsters loomed up and roared at them over an unconvincing sound track.

"Well, at least I did you one good turn," Jordan said. "I mean, I really heated her up for you, hey?"

Cameron glanced quickly at him, but the boat had rounded a bend, and all at once they were enveloped in darkness.

"Listen, no hard feelings," the actor went on, "but you know why she put me down and took up with you that way?"

"No," said Cameron. "Why?"

"Because I really got to her on the set this morning, that's why. I can always tell. There's a tiny bead of sweat they get on their upper lips, and a lovely little smell that comes out of their ears."

Cameron was tempted to silence the actor with the back of his hand, but the boat had rounded another bend, where several stuffed savages in loincloths shrieked war cries and threatened them with spears, and he was suddenly disarmed by the appearance of his companion, who was grinning at him like a fellow conspirator.

"Listen, old double, I really had her ready to go. I mean, my knee was starting a fire in her pants, my little finger was in her ear, and my tongue was halfway down her throat. Christ, was she mad! But her tits got hard anyway. She just couldn't help it, you know? Those lovely tits were pushing up through the hair on my chest like flowers in a forest. It's amazing how they can't help it even when they hate your guts. I mean, for Chrissakes, it's in*vol*untary!"

They had entered another darkened stretch of the tunnel, and choking down a reply, Cameron made an immense secondary effort to control himself.

"Another two or three minutes and I could've laid her. Right in front of the whole crew. Including him! Wouldn't that've been something for the camera?"

"Yes," said Cameron, who found himself wondering if the water in the tunnel of love was sufficiently deep to drown someone in.

"So how did *you* make out?"

"Me?" Cameron said. "I didn't."

"No kidding."

"No kidding."

Jordan gave a pleased laugh. "You missed the chance of a lifetime, old double. Believe me, she was all set up."

Cameron made no reply. Ahead of him, he could see daylight at the end of the tunnel of love.

"All set up and waiting for it."

"All right," Cameron said. "I believe you."

"Well, don't feel bad. I mean, it was sort of risky, you know? Fooling around with her like that right under his eyes. On the other hand, he's probably too busy to notice these days. He's been leaving her alone a lot, and now that we've started shooting . . ."

The boat had emerged from the tunnel and come into the glare of the sun. Cameron climbed out of it quickly and felt a wave of dizziness and nausea pass over him.

"So she got away from us this time, hey?" said the actor, clapping him on the back.

Cameron started off.

"Don't worry," Jordan called after him. "There'll be another time. Once you plant the notion in their heads, it starts working at the other end."

Cameron turned and looked at him with loathing, but the actor, who was wearing his irrepressible cap-toothed grin, seemed to mistake it for a grimace of incredulity. "Sure," he cried. "You get them thinking about it and you're halfway there!"

When he returned to the hotel, he showered, changed his clothes, and contemplated the knock with which he would announce his presence at her door. But just as he was about to leave the room, he looked into the mirror above the washstand, which, instead of reflecting the happy, confident narcissism of a man anticipating love and anxious to please, reproached him with the mask that guaranteed his anonymity by casting him as Jordan's double. For a moment, he stared at this face, in which lust stood surrogate for love, as if he were confronting the actor himself. I ought to wash it off, he thought. But did he dare reveal himself to her at this point? No, it was too soon. Yet how else could he resume his life? Cameron hesitated before the mirror as if searching for some memory of himself beneath the bold beach boy's countenance that mocked him with the brutal promise of Jordan's final dictum; then, quickly, he turned away, went out into the corridor, and started down the staircase to her room.

She came to the door in bare feet from her bath, wearing a terrycloth jacket, a towel piled high like a turban upon her head, and a grave expression upon her face. His first impulse was to apologize for intruding, but his feet had already carried him past her. He waited until she closed the door behind him; then he turned to her with a smile.

"Didn't you think I'd come?" he said.

"Yes," she answered. "I thought you would come."

There was neither expectation or acceptance in her voice. "Is something the matter?" he asked.

She shook her head and looked away.

He wondered if she were afraid of being found with him, but a glance at her eyes told him that she was suffering not from fear of discovery but from despair. "What's the matter?" he said gently.

"I'm no good," she whispered.

"No good!" he echoed.

"You'll see."

"No good," he repeated, as if dumfounded.

"I haven't been for a long time. In fact, ever since—" She broke off short of the word and the sound of its harsh and hissing consonants.

He scarcely knew what to say, for he had naïvely supposed that she was passing not a sexual but a moral judgment upon herself. Now, untangling himself from his false assumption, he realized that she must have been dating a great part of her life from the time of the assassination from whose aftermath she had been excluded by the tacit consent of everyone, including herself. Small wonder, then, that the part of Margaret should frighten her. Could Gottschalk be so blind as not to know that she would suffer in this film of his? Or had the director deliberately cast her in the role of wife to a dead hero as some kind of drastic therapy? No matter. Nothing mattered now. He would supplant all her lovers past and present. He waited until her eyes met his again; then he took her in his arms.

"I love you, Nina," he said.

"Take me with you," she told him. "When you go, take me, too."

"Yes."

"Soon."

"Yes."

"Now."

Once again, she had gone far ahead of him. He felt as if he were hesitating at the edge of an abyss on the far side of which she stood offering him the possibility of resuming his life. Should he tell her who he really was? Or would his own past only serve to frighten her? "I can't leave now," he said desperately. "I have to stay and finish the stunts."

"Are they that important?"

"They're necessary," he told her. "Please believe me. I'll explain everything later."

She had been holding him tightly, but now he felt her go limp in his arms as if she were transferring all hope for herself to him. He wanted to say something soft and reassuring, but he could find no words; instead, undoing the belt that tied her jacket, he led her to the bed, where, all erogenous mouth and tongue, he undertook to replace her submissiveness with ardor. At first, she gave a series of tiny cries that seemed as much engendered by satisfaction derived from the swiftness of her response as by the mode of his address; then, whimpering, she began to writhe in rhythm to the movement of his tongue; and, finally, no longer able to endure the slowness of his measure, she skipped far ahead of him with sharp convulsive shudders and a deep groan of pleasure.

Moments later, when he raised himself above her, he saw that they had traveled up along the bed, and that her head, flung backward, was hanging over the edge. The turban had fallen away and her damp auburn hair was touching the floor. Looking down at her, he watched a tiny pulse throbbing in her throat, heard her panting in the heat, and was filled with tenderness and a sense of triumph. I'm going to take her away from him, he thought. "Was I dreaming?" he asked with a gentle, mocking smile. "Or did I hear you say you weren't any good?"

She tried to answer, but the blood had rushed to her face, and her voice was choked.

"No good," he murmured, and, cupping the nape of her neck in one hand, lifted her head, guided himself into her with the other hand, and watched the effect of his entry mirrored in her eyes. "No good," he repeated.

"Don't go away," she whispered.

He smiled and shook his head.

"Don't come too soon."

"I won't," he told her.

"Take me when you go."

"Yes."

"Take me with you."

"I promise."

"Come now."

"All right."

"Come with me now!"

"Yes," he gasped, no longer sure of or even caring what she meant. "Yes!"

13

At suppertime, he sat with Roth, who looked more harassed than ever. "Rough day?" he said.

The screen writer pursed his lips and inserted his soup spoon between them in a way that avoided using his mustaches as strainers; then, replacing the spoon beside his bowl, he gave his head a weary shake. "I don't know whether I'm coming or going," he complained. "This morning I was working on one film; this afternoon I've been shifted to another."

"I guess it takes some getting used to," Cameron replied.

"Tell you what," said Roth, leaning forward and lowering his voice. "I think our director's slipping. In the old days, there was a strong sense of narrative in even the most surrealistic of his films. Now his work's becoming formless. Personally, I think it's his eyes. His fear of going blind."

"He told me he avoids stories with a beginning, middle, and end," Cameron said. "He claims the interesting thing for him is fragments and the order in which he chooses to arrange them."

"That's all well and good," Roth replied. "But there's got to be *some* dramatic narrative." At this point, the screen writer raised a forefinger as if to hold the attention of a class of students. "D'you know what dramatic narrative is? It's an action from which, once involved, the protagonist can't withdraw until things have run their course. Thus, in the case of the fugitive, he either escapes or is caught."

"Seems to me the fugitive's escaping all over the place," said Cameron with a laugh.

Roth shook his head mysteriously. "Our director's having trouble with this character. He keeps changing his mind about him. To begin with, we had a simple, straightforward opening in which the fugitive, having been wrongly accused and convicted, escapes from a police wagon that's taking him away from court. Now, as of yesterday, Gottschalk wants him to be a deserter from the army. The first idea was to show him pulling guard duty on the periphery of some military camp, and suddenly taking off in the middle of the night. But then Mr. G decided he should escape from a truck or bus in which he's being transported to the camp from civilian life."

Cameron looked warily at the screen writer. "I like the first version better,' he said. "The other depends too much upon the chance of mechanical failure, which is less convincing."

Roth was chewing on a piece of pot roast; now, swallowing, he looked across the table at Cameron and frowned. "Who said anything about mechanical failure?"

"Well, I just assumed," Cameron began, and faltered. You're getting overconfident, he thought. You'd better watch your step. . . .

"As a matter of fact, the bus stops at a rest station, and the fugitive goes through the window of a washroom and into the woods. I'm supposed to be writing a treatment now."

"And what've you done about the end?" Cameron asked. "When he drives off the bridge?"

"First things first," said Roth with a smile. "We'll cross that bridge when we come to it."

Preoccupied with the screen writer's revelations, Cameron was toying with his food. All at once, Nina's face floated before him in the gravy of the pot roast as if in the waters of a dream. Then the image dissolved and he saw her grave profile superimposed upon the pages of a script that Gottschalk was leafing through. Once again he found himself wondering why the director had cast her as the wife of a dead hero. How curious that Gottschalk seemed to be putting each of them into his own story! But what did it mean? Cameron struggled to unravel the insight that he felt he was verging upon, but the threads were elusive and the pages of the script were turning endlessly. If only I could get a look, he was thinking. Just to keep a scene ahead . . .

"What's on your mind?" Roth asked.

"Huh?" said Cameron, gazing at him blankly. "Oh, I was wondering how you came to work for him."

"Simple enough," the screen writer replied. "I'd been on the blacklist. Out of work for years. Then I heard he was making a come-back, so I applied to him on blind chance and he accepted me. Out of the blue."

"Out of the blue." Cameron murmured. "And what was your first assignment?"

Roth closed his eyes and tipped his head back. "Let me think. It was either about the population-control expert who loses his child in an accident, or the one about a man who's falsely accused and blackballed from a club that's crucial to his business. The reason I find it difficult to remember is that neither of them ever got into production."

"It doesn't matter," said Cameron, who was remembering Gottschalk's description of him as an actor in and a spectator at the unfolding of his own story.

"Listen, there's something I'd like your advice about," Roth went on. "It's about the make-up girl. You know, Denise. I've kind of had my eye on her, but she won't give me the time of day, and I was just wondering . . . well, if you'd noticed her with anybody else."

Cameron wiped his mouth with his napkin and shook his head. "No, I haven't noticed," he said. One false step and you're going to lose an ally, he was thinking.

Roth shook his head. "I've thought of giving her a copy of my book, but now I don't know. I mean, I don't know if it would do any good, and the book's out of print. I guess I never told you, but I published a book once. A collection of short stories."

Which explains the Brechtian face, Cameron thought. It's a leftover from literary aspirations. . . . "I'd like to read it sometime," he said, and, excusing himself, got up from the table and went out into the lobby. As usual, the radio was tuned in to the twenty-four-hour news. An investigating group had just determined that nearly a fifth of the embattled country had been defoliated; whether or not the resulting alteration of its ecology was irreversible was of little consequence compared to the fact that, deprived of cover and natural camouflage, large numbers of the enemy were being slaughtered.

Half an hour later, he was sitting comfortably tipped back in one of the folding chairs that had been arranged in rows in a corner of the lobby, and looking at a portable screen in front of him with the calm expectation of an inveterate movie-goer about to savor a film he has seen often enough to know by heart. Yes, he could afford to relax, for what could possibly surprise him in a picture through which he had sat so many times? Certainly not the appearance of a river that keeps its secrets at all stages of the tide, he thought. No, the alarming twists in this little documentary would have been edited out by Gottschalk, so he could settle back and watch it in the manner of those esoteric critics who, asserting technical expertise by writing about the fine points of camera angle, focus, and montage, end up by examining not so much the film they have seen as their own exquisitely heightened awareness of what its director was about.

Now, lowering his line of sight, Cameron studied the Chief of Police, who was sitting in the front row beside a tall man in a three-button summer suit. The chief had crossed his legs and hung his white peaked cap upon his knee, and, with arms akimbo, was staring straight ahead. Cameron detected a certain grim forbearance in the tilt of the grizzled head. That must be an F.B.I. man he's with, he told himself. Perhaps it's the one who initiated the wildgoose chase that missed its quarry by a continent. . . .

The lobby was filling up. Behind him, Gottschalk was giving instructions to the projectionist, who was threading film through the wheels of his machine. On the far side of the room, da Fé was engaged in animated conversation with the toll collector. Nearby, Denise and Nina Mabry were discussing hair styles, and Roth was hovering beside them as if waiting for an opportunity to intervene. Let's hope nobody starts comparing notes, Cameron thought grimly, and, looking back at the screen, was relieved to hear the director call for quiet and lights out.

At this point, the room was plunged into darkness, and there was a burst of light upon the screen followed by waves breaking silently upon a beach—a whole series of waves cresting, breaking, and receding each into the next—which constituted a lullaby of such easy rhythm that Cameron soon felt his eyelids growing heavy. After a few minutes, however, there was a change in the angle of the camera that, as the shoreline lengthened, he realized had become airborne. Then he was looking down upon the jetty, whose entire length was being battered by combers and whose tip was submerged in boiling foam. It seemed impossible that only a few hours ago the scene of such turbulence had been a quiet picnic spot, a

trysting place where, between takes . . . Cameron started to
look around for Nina, but thought better of it when he saw
that the director, who was standing just behind him, his
gaunt face lit by a beam of light that escaped from an aperture
in the side of the projection machine, was perfectly positioned
to intercept the slightest sign of recognition or acknowledg-
ment. In which case, eyes front, Cameron told himself. But
why was Gottschalk showing the jetty? Was it coincidence, or
did he suspect something? Now, suddenly uncomfortable,
Cameron shifted in his chair. It's just a movie, he thought.
Try to remember it's just a movie. . . .

The camera had left the jetty and was sweeping along in
a slow, panoramic tracking shot to show the beach and the
town behind it; then it focused upon the amusement center,
and, finally, closed in upon the Ferris wheel spinning in sunlight. At this point, there was an abrupt break in continuity,
followed by a series of white flashes upon the screen, which
marked the end of the sequence. When the film resumed, it
showed an aerial view of the salt marshes behind the town.
Cameron sat up in his chair as the camera followed the river
meandering through a vast tract of grass and mud flats and
swept quickly over the bridge where he had crouched beside
the air compressor. Then, suddenly, he found himself looking
down upon the car with its high hump-backed trunk and oval-
shaped rear window, which was speeding over the causeway
toward the bridge, where, because his mind was racing ahead
of the film, he was no longer crouching beside the air compressor. But just when he should have appeared—an in-
explicable figure in the background—there was a merciful break
in the reel, which was accompanied by a clatter in the projector and a murmur of disappointment from some of the
spectators.

Cameron slumped in his chair as the lights came on.

Behind him, the projectionist worked feverishly to splice
the broken film.

When the director called for quiet and darkness again, the
film resumed with the car still racing along the causeway, but
beyond the bridge.

So far so good, Cameron thought, looking at the outline
of Chief Broussard's grizzled head. But will he swallow it if
the film breaks twice?

Now, having made the turn at the far end of the causeway, the car was shown speeding back toward the bridge in a side-view shot, and, leaning forward in his seat, Cameron found himself once again racing ahead of the vehicle toward a suspenseful future that was already part of an excruciating past. But this time, as the car began to veer toward the bridge, its movement seemed to be matched by an erratic maneuver of the helicopter; then, in the next instant, the car was shown circling in the road. Why, he's cut out everything! Cameron thought, but no sooner had the idea crossed his mind than the right-hand door of the vehicle flew open, and the body of a man came somersaulting out of it. Now the car headed toward the edge of the bridge and drove out of the frame, and the helicopter made a violent turn that, in turn, turned the whole scene on its side. When the picture got back on an even keel, Cameron saw himself lying face down upon the apron of the bridge.

Chief Broussard was on his feet, standing in the beam of light that came out of the projection machine, and casting an eerie shadow upon the screen. "Can we have that again?" he said. "That last part with the car. But this time in slow motion, hanh?"

There was a short delay while the reel was reversed, and then the car was shown weaving at is approached the bridge, turning slowly in the roadway, and then heading back toward the edge above the water as its door came open in stages, followed by the head, shoulders, arms, and legs of a man whose incremental appearance merely accentuated the gymnastic grace of a breathtaking flight.

As soon as the picture turned on end, the chief was on his feet again, stabbing at the screen with the butt end of a cigar that he held scissor-fashion between his forefinger and index finger. "Once more," he said. "The part where the stunt man jumps out . . . Yeah, right there, where he's in mid-air . . . Now what's that, hanh? What's that coming out after him? It looks like a bag!"

Mind reeling, breath held tight, Cameron groped desperately for an explanation, and, almost instantly, was rescued by the calm voice of the director.

"Why, that's a pillow! To bolster the stunt man against the shock of hitting the water—that is, if he had gone through with the stunt and into the water . . ."

The lights came on to show the chief looking puzzled. "A

pillow," he muttered to the man accompanying him, who stood up and whispered something in his ear. "Yeah, that's a good point," Broussard continued. "How come you jumped out of the car on the passenger's side, stunt man? Isn't that kind of an ass-backward way to go about it?"

Cameron was still thinking about the duffel bag, which he had afterward given to the chambermaid. Now, interrupting his train of thought to focus upon the chief's question, he heard himself say, as if following Gottschalk's calm example, "The door had flown open. I had to close it before going into the water, but by the time I reached across the seat, I knew it was going to be too late, so . . ." Shrugging to indicate that the rest of his answer must be obvious, Cameron resumed his earlier preoccupation with the duffel bag. How could he have forgotten that the chambermaid to whom he had given it to be laundered on the very first day had also seen his face?

The chief placed his hands upon his hips, gave his head a quizzical shake, and, shunting the cigar from one side of his mouth to the other, turned to Gottschalk. "You mind telling me something?" he said. "You got this young fella driving off a bridge, jumping off a pier, and swinging by his fingernails forty feet off the ground. What's it add up to anyway? What's this film of yours about?"

"Why, I thought you knew!" the director exclaimed softly. "It's about a fugitive, a young man seeking to elude the police and escape arrest."

"Well, I'll be damned," the chief growled with unconcealed amazement.

"But life is forever imitating art, you see."

Scowling, the chief put on the cap that, except for lack of a vending cart, would have made him instantly and joyfully recognizable to any child. "I suppose that's why movie fugitives always get away and movie cops always look dumb."

"Films exaggerate to compensate for human error," the director replied. "Indeed, if it were not for human error, truth would probably never be stranger than fiction. Take, for example, the story of that other fugitive—the one who managed to flee to France . . ."

The chief permitted himself a fleeting grin; then his eyes veiled over as if with a new idea. "Okay," he said, "let's assume the movies have all the answers. How does this character of yours manage to keep getting away?"

"People help him," replied Gottschalk with a shrug.

"What sort of people?"

"The people he meets."

"For example."

"Well, take the dance-hall scene. There he's helped by the members of a rock-and-roll band. When he runs into them, his predicament is desperate. The police are hot on his heels. In fact, they've got him trapped out at the end of a dead-end amusement pier. The hippies hide him by giving him a funny hat to wear and an extra guitar to strum."

"So he just happens to be a guitar player, hanh?"

"No, he's never touched one before, but the guitar isn't plugged in. Incidentally, that's how he's discovered. One ear-splitting number ends with such stunning abruptness that our would-be musician, intent upon mastering his newly acquired instrument, goes right on playing but without making a sound, which, by the time it seems odd to him, has also struck a suspicious note with one of his pursuers."

"And what happens then?"

"You've seen it," the director replied with a smile. "That's the stunt we shot on the pier last night."

The chief was puffing reflectively on his cigar. "You know, you may have something there," he said. "We've been looking for a college-educated fella, figuring he might try to find work as a waiter or bartender or something like that. But maybe he's like the character in your motion picture. Maybe he's doing something he's never done before. Right under our noses, hanh?"

"Anything is possible," the director said softly, and glanced at the chief's companion, who was talking to the projectionist.

The chief grinned. "That's Mr. Concannon of the F.B.I. He's come down from the city to help us country boys solve another case. Speaking of which, I think he wants to show a picture of his own on your machine. It's a photo of the man we're after, and young Mr. Concannon is hoping it'll work like one of those wanted-by-the-authorities posters you see in the post office. Idea is to enlist the support of the public, but if your movie theory is correct—I mean, if the fugitive's being helped by the people he meets—then the whole plan could backfire, hanh?"

"Perhaps you should tell Mr. Concannon."

Chief Broussard shook his head, which caused a length of

dead ash to dribble down over his shirt front. "I don't try to tell Mr. Concannon anything," he growled. "Mr. Concannon's a college man, a lawyer, and a graduate of the Bureau's crime-detection school. He's an expert on geography and a very smart operator."

Hearing his name mentioned, the F.B.I. agent looked up from the projection machine. "All set here," he said. "D'you want to make the announcement?"

Chewing on the end of his cigar, the chief glanced at Gotts-chalk and shrugged. Then, facing toward the lobby, he removed the cigar from his mouth. "Ladies and gentlemen," he intoned. "We're going to show you the picture of a man wanted by the military authorities. Anyone with knowledge of this person or his whereabouts should contact the local police."

The announcement was followed by a moment of stunned silence, then by a ripple of suppressed laughter, and, finally, when someone on the far side of the room muttered, "Fink!", by a wave of immoderate glee that turned into loud applause as Cameron's picture was flashed upon the screen.

Ignoring his detractors, the chief turned to Concannon, who was wearing a puzzled frown. "Turn the damn thing off," he said wearily. "Can't you tell whose side they're on?"

Cameron had been vastly relieved to see that the photograph was simply a blow-up of the passport-size version the chief had shown him on the previous day. But just as he was reassuring himself that no one could possibly recognize him from that sullen countenance, he remembered the make-up girl, and, wheeling around, saw that Denise's face was rigid with surprise and disbelief. A moment later, however, her expression softened into a dreamy grin of intrigue, which the screen writer standing at her side appeared to assume was meant for him. Cameron was just about to raise a warning forefinger to his lips when he noticed Nina Mabry smiling at him, and, looking quickly away, pretended to be engrossed in the room. Suddenly, he found himself trying to keep track of everyone and to think of everything at once. Da Fé was nowhere in sight, and the toll collector had also disappeared. He could count himself lucky for that. But where was the chambermaid, whom he had not seen since the moment he had handed her his duffel bag? How on earth could he have forgotten the chambermaid? Now, tired of trying to get his eye, Denise came over to him. Didn't she realize that Roth would tumble onto things in no time? No, she could have no idea. "I can't talk now," he whispered. "Come to my room later." As he spoke, he glanced at Nina, who, obviously puzzled by his neglect, was standing beside the director, who was smiling at Chief Broussard, whom he imagined saying in jest that the best and most obvious place for the fugitive to hide was with the film company. Dimly, he heard Gottschalk reply that anything was possible. Yes, the director was up to something. Why else would he have given out such hints? He's baiting me, Cameron thought. He's setting me up. . . . His head was positively reeling from the sheer effort to fathom the multiple reactions around him, which seemed to close around his skull like the jaws of a trap. He had an almost uncontrollable desire to make a break for it. Instead, in an agony of suspense and doubt, he froze in place.

Only when he was spinning through the night sky, an hour later, did he feel free again, for there was not only freedom but immense exhilaration in this absurd performance in which, tethered to the centrifugal force of the whip ride by his fingertips, he saw lights and stars flashing past him as if the r.p.m. of the universe had suddenly been accelerated to the pitch of Doomsday. For a few seconds, he transcended himself. He was no longer just a stunt man. Half of him was an astronaut floating weightless in space; the other half was Ixion, who, screaming defiance, had been chained to a fiery wheel that whirled him perpetually through the sky. "I'm Cameron!" he shouted. "I'm the one you want! *Look at me!*" But below him the crowd was roaring, and the sound of his voice was lost in the wind that tore at his face, and who would have believed him anyway?

14

When he left his exuberant orbit, he fell back to earth, landed on his back, and, bouncing high off the trampoline, came down upon his hands and knees. For a few seconds, he remained on all fours, forehead touching the canvas, teeth rattling, and lungs gasping for air in the manner of a prizefighter knocked down by a combination to the head and solar plexus. Then, revived by a smatter of applause from the crowd, he crawled to the edge of the trampoline and dropped to the ground. It was only a short drop—a matter of four or five feet—but, already dazed and disoriented, he landed awkwardly and turned an ankle. Stupid, he thought, and, hobbling around to shake off the stiffness, found himself near one of the snow-barricade fences that had been erected to keep the crowd at bay. He was bending over to massage the ankle when a small boy thrust a sugar-candy paper cone over the fence and asked him for his autograph. Cameron straightened up and, using a pen lent by an onlooker, held the cone against his thigh and wrote "Arthur Coleman" on it. Then he handed it back. Smiling, the child dashed off through the crowd to join some friends. Cameron watched him as, holding the cone aloft, he darted around the adults in his way. And suddenly it occurred to him that he had signed the alias in his own handwriting. Stupid, he thought again. What a stupid thing to do . . . For a moment, he was tempted to go after the boy and retrieve his mistake; then, thinking that he might encounter resistance, he imagined himself pursuing the child through the dark alleyways and arcades of the amusement center. He was about to reach out for the tiny collar, when someone leaned over the fence and touched his arm.

"My pen," a man's voice said.

"Hunh?" replied Cameron, who was still chasing the child.

"Gimme the pen!"

"Sorry," said Cameron, who returned the pen to its owner

and limped away. Imagine going after a child, he thought. What's come over me?

The cameraman intercepted him near the trampolines. "What's the matter, *caro?*"

"Nothing," Cameron replied. "I've twisted an ankle is all. How did it look?"

"Magnificent! Unbelievable! When all the pieces are stitched together, they'll think you're the greatest acrobat of our time. A regular human fly!"

"A human fly," Cameron murmured.

Believe me, *caro*, everyone was tremendously impressed. And Mr. G above all, I'll bet. He was in the helicopter, you know. Can you imagine how it must have seemed from up there?"

Cameron shook his head. So he had not been in the ascendancy after all, but simply a satellite observed from above by the director, who, as usual, dominated everything. Now, grimly, he found himself wondering if Nina had gone along for the ride, if she too had looked down upon him swinging helplessly by his fingertips like another gaudy appendage in this garish and cheaply lit amusement center. As if on cue, a calliope started up on the merry-go-round. "Funny," he said. "I never heard the helicopter."

Da Fé gave a laugh. "How could you with everything else going on? But why be so gloomy, *caro?* This is a time of triumph. We should celebrate!"

"Celebrate!" Cameron echoed.

"Life is short. One must learn to celebrate each moment as it comes."

Philosophy from a pornographer, Cameron thought, and bent over to rub his throbbing ankle.

"Tonight I'm going to celebrate a brainstorm," the cameraman went on. "It came to me in a flash. The perfect husband for my film. A perfect oaf with a perfect pander's face."

Cameron tested the ankle gingerly, and winced. "Who's that?" he asked.

"Who else but the toll collector? Staring me in the face the whole day! Now all I need is someone to play the wife." Da Fé smiled and, reaching into a grease-stained paper bag, pulled out and bit ravenously into a sugar-coated doughnut. "Guess who, *caro?*"

"You're sick," Cameron told him.

"But I understand this woman! She's an existentialist heroine torn between the world of flesh and the cerebral terror of our director's esoteric concepts. In short, she's guilty and wants to be punished. Therefore, she'll betray her mentor. Believe me, in the end she'll submit to my plot as she would inflict herself with pain."

"And what if Gottschalk finds out?"

The cameraman munched thoughtfully on his doughnut. "In its most minuscule form, the balance of terror exists in the equilibrium of secrets between people," he replied. "For example, the secret you've been keeping from Chief Broussard, and the one you and Miss Mabry are keeping from our director."

Cameron feigned a look of puzzlement.

"Don't worry, *caro*, I haven't been spying on you. In this case, it was simply a matter of putting one and one together. Or, more precisely, of interpreting a bit of overheard conversation. In short, the unhappy reaction of Miss Mabry's leading man, who, quite understandably, doesn't relish the prospect of you standing in for him with regard to his deepest wish."

Cameron shifted his weight to relieve the pressure on his ankle, and studied da Fé carefully. The cameraman's put one and one together, but there's no answer to the equation unless you're dumb enough to tell him, he thought. "What is it you want from me?" he said.

"You continually misunderstand, *caro*. That's because you're always on guard. Would you believe that I want nothing from you? Or, rather, that what I want will happen anyway? I'm a realist, you see. I describe the way things are and plan for what I know will be."

"Buzz off," Cameron said. "You bore me."

The cameraman stuffed the rest of the doughnut into his mouth and shook his head as if in sorrow. "I'm also a patient man, *caro*. I can wait. It's just that I'd hoped in this moment of mutual accomplishment we might bury our differences and celebrate our success with some entertainment. You see, I'm planning a little spectacular tonight. I'm going to start shooting my new film and I thought you might like to be on hand."

"Thanks all the same," Cameron replied.

"You disappoint me, *caro*. But, as I've indicated, I'm a patient man."

"Don't hold your breath," Cameron told him, and hobbled away.

He returned to the hotel by way of the beach—a solitary path that provided a cushion for his ankle—and soon put the harsh illumination of the amusement center behind him. Above a calm, deceptive sea, the moon drifted behind a thin veil of clouds; ahead of him, a string of incandescent street-lamps delineated the contour of the crescent beach that stretched away to the north, toward Canada. He imagined himself continuing up the coast, first along the sand and then over cliffs and rocks that buttressed the land against the tides. Keeping the water on his right, he would swim the smaller estuaries and skirt the vast, roundabout indentations of the larger bays and rivers. The whole journey lay before him as if he were looking down upon a map of the continent, and for a moment he considered the prospect; then, turning inland, he saw that he had drawn abreast of the hotel, where lights were coming on in the sporadic manner of the building whose façade provides the opening title shot for the late-night tele-vision movie. On the second floor, the windows of the direc-tor's suite were ablaze, but the helicopter was nowhere to be seen, and, suddenly overtaken by a wave of doubt and jealousy, Cameron imagined it hovering somewhere far out over the ocean, its plexiglass canopy illuminated by the light of the moon, and Nina's cries of delight smothered by the whirring of the rotor blades as Gottschalk directed her toward the climax of a scene in which she no longer felt herself to be inadequate. Now, all at once, a chill wind blew in from the sea and made him shiver. How vulnerable he was! How complicated everything seemed! Once again, Cameron looked up at the rectangles of light in the façade of the ramshackle edifice that towered above him; then, crossing the sand, he climbed the front veranda, and went inside.

The lobby was empty. The projector, the screen, and the folding chairs had been taken away, and nothing remained of the tense scene that had accompanied the showing of the rushes except the wariness that now impelled him slowly up the stairs. When he reached Nina's room, he knocked upon the door, got no answer, and continued on up to his own room, which seemed strange and unfamiliar. He tried to read, but it was no use. His spirit was miles away, soaring like a night bird above the sea as it carried him on a dark journey out to the moonlit horizon, where, having set the helicopter on automatic pilot, the director was orchestrating the frail song of her ecstasy above the engine's roar. . . .

When he heard a knock upon the door, some minutes later, he was filled with a wild and sudden hope. But it was only Denise carrying her make-up kit.

"For appearance's sake," she told him with a smile.

Cameron laughed to hide his disappointment. "Now you know why I'm so fond of the new face you've given me."

"Listen, I nearly went through the floor when I realized. You ought to take it off at night, though. This gunk'll ruin your skin."

"I can always grow a new layer," he told her.

"But I like your own face. It goes with the real you."

"Let's try to forget the real me."

Denise was smiling a conspiratorial smile. "Why're you doing it? I mean, why're you taking the risk?"

"They needed a new stunt man," replied Cameron with a shrug. "And I needed a job and another face." My God, how easy to say! But hadn't the director absolved him? Hadn't Gottschalk himself described it as a perfectly honest and, under the circumstances, natural mistake? Now, as he saw another question forming in Denise's eyes, he intervened before her lips could give it sound and shape. "Be careful with Roth," he told her. "It wouldn't do for him to find out about us."

"Why does it matter?" she replied. "Dalton's sweet but hopeless. Would you believe he wants to improve my mind? He's even given me a reading list."

Cameron shook his head. "Try to understand. Roth is my one way out of this bind. He knows what's in store for me— I mean, what the script's about." Now, seeing the frown that creased her forehead, he realized there was no use trying to explain. For that matter, was there any explanation? "It's very complicated," he told her. "Just remember that it's important for Roth to be kept in the dark."

Denise teased him with a smirk. "D'you want me to make up to him?"

"I want to keep him on my side."

"How about me?" she asked with a mock pout. "Don't y
want to keep me on your side?"

"Of course," he answered, and thought of Nina.

"Then do it," said Denise.

Cameron made no reply, for he was standing once aga
at the tip of the jetty, holding her head between his han
and drawing her face to his. Was it possible he had ev
kissed her? Or was he only imagining the tender elation
that moment?

"I can tell what you're thinking," Denise said softly. "Yo
eyes are full of it."

He took a deep breath. "Listen, there's something I wa
you to try and understand."

"You were sensational," she murmured. "Dalton and
watched the whole thing. God, it was thrilling!"

What's the use? he thought. I'll only antagonize her f
nothing. "I'm tired," he said. "I've turned an ankle."

"Lie down," she told him. "I'll fix your face."

He shook his head. "Somebody might come barging in."

"Then come along," Denise replied, and started for t
door. "In our director's house are many mansions."

Cameron limped after her. "Listen, this ankle's stiffeni
up. I've got to get off it."

Placing a forefinger to her lips, Denise led him a sh
way down the corridor and opened the door next to t
chambermaid's room.

Cameron leaned on her shoulder to steady himself. "A
you out of your mind?" he exclaimed.

"Be quiet," she whispered, and, supporting him arou
the waist, drew him into the room.

Cameron looked around him, half expecting to find som
one lurking in the shadows, but the room was empty exce
for several racks of costumes, a box of skin-diving equi
ment, and a cot. Then Denise closed the door and plung
them into darkness. "Crazy," he whispered. "This is crazy."

Without reply, she pushed past him, crossed the floor, a
raised a window blind. For a moment, Cameron studied h
face in the light of the moon; then he hobbled to the cot a
sat down upon it.

Denise came up behind him and began to massage t
back of his neck. "Try to relax," she said. "You're awful
tense."

"Relax," he muttered. "D'you know where we are?"

She gave a soft laugh. "We're in the wardrobe room. But don't worry, Bruno's going to be much too busy to bother us."

Cameron glanced toward the door that adjoined the chambermaid's room. "You know about it?" he said. "The film?"

"By invitation, which I declined. He begged me to let him watch us again, but I told him it was our turn now."

"*Our* turn!"

"To watch *him*," said Denise, who reached into her make-up kit and took out a jar of cold cream and a box of Kleenex.

"D'you mean he knows we're here?"

"More or less."

"But why on earth did you tell him?"

"I told you. Turnabout's fair play."

"You really are crazy, aren't you?"

"Don't you want to see it?"

"Not especially."

"Bruno's promised quite a show. First, he's going to let the toll collector have the girl. Then he's going to have each of them separately. And afterward he claims he's going to have each of them while they're having each other."

"That's a lot of having," Cameron said.

"Not for Bruno."

"Well, it would be for me."

"You have to be in the mood," replied Denise, who reached down and then unzipped, unsheathed, and took him in her hand.

"You're crazy," he said thickly.

As if in silent answer, she began to stroke him.

"Crazy," he said again.

"But nice?"

"Yes."

"Better?"

"Lovely."

"Say when."

"Not yet."

"Hold still," she commanded, and, ensuring his immobility with one hand, began wiping the make-up from his forehead with the other.

"That's enough," he told her, but without conviction.

"I think you're getting there," she murmured, continuing

her escalation of him as she removed the cosmetic from his face.

"Soon," he said.

"Tell me when," she whispered.

"Now," he gasped.

"Ah!" she exclaimed, and, bending over him, applied lips and tongue as if to the mouthpiece of a woodwind in an embouchure of exquisitely subtle variation, which soon played the sound of the crescendo to which he had been building.

Strange how Nina kept coming to mind—a sweet torment that filled him at the same time with nostalgia and a sense of perversity. Yes, to think of her now seemed truly blasphemous. For a while, he lay perfectly still and tried to exorcise her from his memory; then, aware that Denise was no longer beside him, he sat up and looked about the room until a slight movement of her head betrayed her presence before the door to the chambermaid's quarters by revealing the aperture that was admitting light to the camera obscura of her deepest wish.

Cameron got up from the cot, approached on bare and silent feet, and stood behind her, admiring the symmetry of her flanks. Then, kneeling down, he began to administer a caress of reciprocation that, like a switch in a two-way electrical conduit, set her trembling with conductivity. Finally, as if overloaded, Denise withdrew her face from the keyhole and touched her forehead to the floor. Raising himself above her, Cameron placed a hand upon either of her hips, and studied a tiny pattern of light that, distorted in passage by the angle of the keyhole, had fallen upon her back. The keyhole itself was at eye level, inches away, and for a second he withstood its challenge as he might have stared at the barrel of a gun. Then, mounting Denise, he looked through it, and, as if watching the rerun of yet another film, saw a silent tableau in which the chambermaid, kneeling on the floor, was gorging herself upon the toll collector, who, bound hand and foot to a straightbacked chair, was in turn being gorged with brutal leverage by da Fé, who stood before him. Denise had begun stirring to the rhythm of her pleasure, which provoked Cameron to increase the measure of his own until, as if camera and screen had become interchangeable, and her body a prism refracting the fierce desire which the cameraman insisted was everyone's deepest wish, he heard a soft, muffled cry that, repeated over and over, echoed deep inside him with accusation, in acclimation, and as an aphrodisiac.

"Stunt man," she whispered hoarsely. "Stunt man. *Stunt man!*"

15

The radio in the dining room was playing a symphony of words that seemed designed to dampen any doubt that it might be losing ground in its non-stop coverage of the news. The third bombing pause in as many months was being announced over and over again—a recurring theme above background reaction from various foreign capitals, which was provided by a stringed section of correspondents who managed to produce tones of identically hushed solemnity. The nation was embarking upon a phase of excruciatingly delicate negotiations. The dialogue would be repetitive and endless. It would be a time of testing, according to the President, who urged the public to be patient in its resolve for peace even as he warned the enemy not to mistake this resolve for weakness. A masquerade of threats and counter-threats, thought Cameron, nodding at Dalton Roth, who lowered his breakfast tray upon the table and himself into a chair behind it as if the tray were attached by invisible strands to the drooping mustaches that framed his mouth.

"What's new?" he asked.

The screen writer shook his head. "Nothing," he muttered. "Listen, d'you have any idea where she might be?"

"If you mean Denise, she just made me up."

"She makes you up and she makes me look foolish. Last night, for example, just when I thought we were getting on, she up and vanished."

"You don't say," said Cameron, cracking an egg over his toast.

"We were looking for you, as a matter of fact. To offer congratulations. My God, you were fantastic up there! I never saw anything like it!"

Cameron reached for the salt shaker. "I took a walk," he said. "Along the beach."

"Everybody pulled a disappearing act," replied Roth with a morose smile. "After hunting for her high and low, I came back here and knocked on her door. She wasn't in her room the whole night. I guess you know what that means."

Cameron shrugged without reply, and avoided looking at the screen writer by studiously sprinkling his egg with pepper.

"Women," Roth went on. "They're a puzzle, aren't they?"

"Yes," Cameron replied. "Especially at night."

"All around the clock if you ask me. And, speaking of puzzles, I've just been handed a dandy by our director. He's decided that the fugitive's got to do something at the very outset to make his flight irrevocable."

"What might that be?"

"He's going to kill someone. In self-defense, of course. To ensure audience sympathy."

Cameron was holding his breath. "Kill someone?" he said. "Who's he going to kill?"

The screen writer looked with distaste at a bowl of oatmeal, and gave a shrug. "I suggested a cop, but Mr. G, as usual, has a more complicated idea. He thinks it shouldn't be a cop but someone the fugitive thinks *might* be a cop."

"Sounds complicated, all right," Cameron observed, but he scarcely heard his own words, for he was listening to something deep within him, a soft whisper that accompanied the opening of a final door which revealed the ultimate insight. So delicate was this sound and so fragile the vision attending it that for some moments he closed his eyes in an attempt to imprint it upon his memory. But new thoughts and old memories were already displacing it and pushing it back into a dark region from which he would not, in spite of his fierce concentration, be able to evoke it by sheer volition. Now, as if in a trance, he found himself remembering how gratefully he had relinquished himself to Gottschalk on the very first day. Yes, even then it had been evident that there could be all manner of endings to his story, and that the director, with his extraordinary tendency toward complications and his penchant for putting fragments together, was the one who should assume full responsibility for the finished script. Cameron opened his eyes and saw Roth studying him intently. Only art repeats itself, he was thinking. Over and over. Endlessly . . . "So the hero won't survive the crash," he murmured.

"Huh?" exclaimed the screen writer. "I thought we were talking about who he's going to kill."

"I'm getting ahead of myself," Cameron replied, and got to his feet.

"Well, you've lost me."

Cameron stacked some empty dishes on his tray and picked it up. Then, looking down at Roth, he forced a smile. "The oldest cinematic cliché of all," he said. "If the fugitive kills someone at the beginning, he's got to die at the end, doesn't he?"

In the lobby, he came upon Gottschalk and Nina sitting side by side on a couch before the front windows, whose curtains had been opened to admit the morning light. Now's the time, he told himself. Get it out in the open and over with. . . . But there was something in the inclination of the director's head and in the intensity of expression upon the actress' face that forbade interruption. Instead, he sank into an easy chair behind them, and tried to organize his thoughts.

"How frustrating for him!" Nina murmured. "To have to work out of context and within a continuity you never wholly share with him."

"My dear, if he were to know my intentions, he would feel impelled to try to improve upon them. That's why I tell him only what he needs to know for each individual scene. By keeping him in the dark, I make certain that he'll devote his energy to details—in this case, to composing dialogue. Mind you, I don't tell him how to do what I want done. I simply describe the effect I want from a given sequence, and switch him to my train of thought, which frees him to write from his own experience."

"And also prevents him from becoming a rival."

"I prefer to think that I use Roth to best advantage. That I am, in fact, putting him in focus."

"As you do everyone," she said softly.

"Not you, my dear. The others are technicians whom I use in place of tools. You are central in my whole conception. Everything in this film will flow from me through you, and be altered during passage."

"Woman is central, then, because her function is gestation."

The director smiled. "Have you been considering what we discussed yesterday?"

"Oh, yes," she replied with a laugh. "Yes indeed."

"I thought of it merely as a method of putting you in the proper frame of mind."

"But I didn't find it disturbing to contemplate the universe and space. I found it—rather restful."

"Perhaps because you unconsciously substituted the sea."

"Perhaps."

"Still, that very substitution expresses the movement of the film. By flinching from the horror of space, the heroine is compelled to relinquish herself to another hostile environment —the sea."

"So that part remains the same. She'll be a suicide."

"Regrettable but necessary."

"Tell me, have you ever made a film without death?"

"Once, in my early days."

"But one without the fear of death?"

"Never."

"D'you think it impossible?"

"Nothing is impossible."

"Implausible, then?" said Cameron, getting to his feet.

"Yes," replied the director, who greeted the interruption without surprise.

"I'm on to you," Cameron told him. "I know what you're up to."

"You do?" said Gottschalk calmly.

"And you're not going to make it."

The director's face assumed a pained expression. "D'you mean the audience won't suspend its disbelief?"

"Come off it," Cameron answered. "You know what I mean. The fugitive's not going to survive the crash, is he?"

The director erased his frown with a smile and then a laugh. "My dear young man, here you come breaking in without so much as a 'by your leave,' and now you insist upon compounding the discourtesy by bringing up irrelevant matters. If your performance last night were not so remarkable, I'd have cause to be angry."

"How about answering the question?" Cameron said.

"How can I possibly answer such a question without first reminding you that you've got a most uncanny knack for making wrong assumptions?"

"Not this time," Cameron replied.

"Yes, this time as always. The fact is, whether the fugitive survives or not depends upon a number of factors that have

yet to be decided. And today I'm involved in other wo
Something infinitely more important."

"There's no point trying to con me any longer," Camer
said. "I've got you figured out."

The director glanced at Nina Mabry, and gave a reass
ing smile. "Try to understand, my dear. A certain amou
of audacity is essential to his work."

Cameron studied her face in vain for some sign of adm
sion of what had taken place between them yesterday, t
Nina's expression betrayed nothing except a faint trace
puzzlement. She's been subdued, he thought. He's dragg
her back into his goddam film. "Let's skip the obfuscatio
he told Gottschalk coldly. "I can predict your whole lo
scheme. It's plain as day."

"Plain as day," the director repeated. "But even dayli
has its mysteries. For example, look out at the beach a
tell me what you see there."

"Sand and water," Cameron answered shortly.

"Is that all?"

"Light."

"What kind of light?"

"Brilliant light."

"Yes, brilliant light," Gottschalk murmured. "But I
more than that. I see a multi-colored halo in the window.
an incredibly beautiful side-effect of my affliction. These ha
ening lenses of mine, you see, transform light into perpet
rainbows. Now, what else d'you see?"

"Nothing," replied Cameron.

"Nothing," Gottschalk repeated. "How myopic of you."

"All right, since you have super vision, tell us what *you* see.

"I see a scene of terror," the director whispered. "I se
woman, surfers, a lay minister, and a child. I see it all
clearly as I will one hour from now, when you will see
too."

Cameron looked directly into Nina's eyes, and shook
head in silent warning. But it was no use. She doesn't reali
he thought. I'll have to make her understand. . . .

Gottschalk was staring out to sea. Now, without turni
his head, he addressed Cameron with the gentle and pater
voice of a trusted family doctor. "You've been under strai
he said. "You're tired. It's only natural. Take the day o
Go swimming. Amuse yourself."

"I want to know what I'm in for," Cameron replied. "I want to know what's going to happen to me."

"But it has been my intention to tell you all along."

Cameron waited for several moments. "Well?" he said finally.

"On top of my desk," the director continued, "you'll find a manual on the escape techniques perfected by the Dutch. Read it. Commit it to memory. Practice it in your mind. Dream about it in your sleep. . . ."

"And then?"

The director shrugged. "We shall see," he said.

The manual, which had been translated from the Dutch by someone whose working knowledge of English was less than fluent, consisted of a series of awkwardly described experiments performed by two members of the Fire Brigade in the Hague named R. Janssen and T. Bakker, who had set out to prove that the old method of escaping from submerged vehicles was obsolete because it had been formulated in tanks with test capsules that, although they were constructed to simulate the chassis of cars, made no provision for the propensity of the engine to cause vertical sinking, or for the tendency of the roof to cave in under pressure. De Heren Janssen en Bakker had marshaled their evidence with stolid logic, and, lying on his bed, Cameron studied their findings with considerable interest until he reached the point where, using a real car, the two Dutchmen were preparing to drive off a pier and into a real canal. Here, he came across a sentence that read, "Now Janssen and Bakker insert the air hoses into their mouths and, with a gallant wave to the assembled spectators, launch themselves into the murky waters of the Koninginnegracht. . . ." So the Dutch equip their stunt men with aqualungs! he thought with a smile, and tossed the manual on the floor.

Now, getting to his feet, he went to the sink, looked into the mirror, and saw a slight frown upon the face to which he had so recently grown accustomed. What objection could they have to letting me wear an air tank? he wondered. But even as the idea crossed his mind, he remembered the cameraman's refusal to give him a life-preserver when he had been floundering beneath the pier. Yes, they would probably ob-

ject on the grounds that an aqualung would ruin the effect
of reality. On the other hand, da Fé would surely be shooting
close-ups of the accident with Jordan, which invalidated the
argument. If they refuse to let you wear an air tank, it'll mean
just one thing, Cameron told himself. It'll mean you're ex-
pendable.

When Cameron glanced into the mirror again, he saw
that his new face had absorbed this conclusion without a
trace of apprehension. Watch out for that face, he told himself. It's going to make you overconfident. . . . And now—
was it his memory of what had taken place on the causeway
or what he had seen in the rushes the night before?—he
imagined the car weaving toward him again, its door having
been shut by the very hand that had shoved him out upon
the pavement. But there was still no concrete evidence that
the rock he had thrown had anything to do with what came
next, for was it not an absurdly dangerous stunt to begin with?
Cameron picked up the manual from the floor and put it on
the bed. Yes, an absurdly dangerous stunt. So risky, in fact,
that his predecessor had lost his nerve, and the Dutchmen had
prudently thought to equip themselves with aqualungs. . . .

Now, like a lazy shark, the car swam toward him, and,
moving to the window, Cameron saw the director and his
assemblage setting up the Fontinalia scene down at the water's
edge. ". . . d'you believe what happened?" Gottschalk had
asked him once. "On the causeway . . . in the film. What's
the difference? Which, in fact, is real?"

The car, Cameron thought, remembering his desperate
dance upon the edge of the bridge. The car was real. . . . But
now, making montage of memory, he deleted the next sequence—the throwing of the rock—and found himself looking down upon the scene as if through the plexiglass canopy
of the helicopter. Below him on the sand, Gottschalk in his
terrycloth robe was standing between Nina, who wore a bikini,
and a man who held a child in his arms. Nearby, barefoot
at the edge of the sea, Bruno da Fé was peering through the
lens of a camera mounted upon a tripod, toward a surfer who
sat waiting upon his board. A wave broke in foam upon the
beach. . . .

Bubbles—a horrifying effervescence—since Cameron no
longer imagined them welling up to a surface that was below

him, but exploding all around him as air hissed out of the car and was replaced by jets of water. The vehicle was sinking nose first, as if in one of those wartime photographs of torpedoed tankers that tilt desperately toward the sky in a final salute to visibility before plunging into the eternal darkness of the sea. . . .

Down on the beach, the director pointed toward the water, the man who held the child in his arms waded out into the breakers, and the surfers turned to gauge the arrival of a large wave that had begun to curl the surface of the ocean. Within the sinking car, the last bubbles of air had fled, and there was only blackness. Desperately, Cameron tried to extricate himself. Dimly, he heard the old man say, "Caught me an arm once." Now, kneeling on his board, the surfer caught the crest of the wave that overtook him, and, standing, rode it in toward shore. Cameron watched him extend his arms and teeter as he tried to keep his balance; then he saw him fall backward, feet in the air, into the water. The board came on, tumbling in the foam, and, flinching, the man who held the child let go. There was an immediate commotion among the extras, some of whom ran into the surf. Cameron tore himself away from the window, burst from his room, and rushed madly along the corridor. The fools! he thought. They've lost the child!'

Hand skimming the banister rail and feet just barely keeping up with his body's headlong flight, he went down the stairs two at a time. At the bottom, he turned and raced across the smooth tiles of the lobby floor, flung open the screen door to the porch, and, vaulting the rail, leaped to the sand below. Then, regaining his balance and cursing the stiffness in his ankle, he dashed pell-mell toward the sea. Ahead of him, he saw that the extras had come out of the water and were standing in a group near Gottschalk, who was gesticulating toward the waves. He looked for the child in vain. Oh, my God! he thought. They've given up! "Don't give up!" he shouted as he galloped past them and plunged into the surf. "Don't give up!"

When he came to the surface, he felt the tug of a strong lateral current sweeping him toward the pier, and, reasoning that the child must also be caught up in it, struck out with strong strokes in its direction. But he was full of despair. How hopeless it seemed! How could he possibly find such a

tiny thing as a child in this boiling foam? Now, swallowing a
mouthful of salt water, he dove beneath a breaker, and, all
at once, his despair gave way to murderous hatred. The
bastard, he thought. To take a chance with the life of a
child . . .

He was about to give up when he saw something tossing
in the inshore foam. Was it a tiny arm and hand raised helplessly toward the sky? Fighting the undertow, he swam toward
it, trying desperately to make it out through eyes that were
smarting with salt water and tears of outrage. Yes, an arm!
He saw it again, absurdly buoyant in the incredible turbulence,
and floating toward him on the backwash that came off the
shelf of the beach and into the next incoming wave. Now,
expending the rest of his strength, Cameron swam the few remaining yards that would position him to make an intercep-
tion. He would have just one chance before the breaker arrived. Oh, God, if I'm not too late . . . Treading water, he
waited, pushing against the wash that was carrying the child
in his direction, and sensing with dread the immense force
of the comber building behind him. Then he reached out,
missed, reached out again, and grabbed. The wave broke over
his head. Don't let go, he told himself as, sucked under and
pummeled, he felt himself hurtling toward the shore. Don't
let go. . . .

He hit the beach as if he had been slammed upon it by an
immense blow. For a moment, he clawed at sand that
streamed away beneath his fingers; then the backwash began
to drag him out, and, touching bottom, he made a desperate
forward lurch. The current was pulling at the body of the
child and tearing at his legs and thighs. And, suddenly, it
was behind him, and he was running up the shelf that, because of his numbing fatigue, seemed incredibly steep. If only
I'm not too late, he thought, clutching the cold wet body of
the child to his chest, and stumbling toward the assemblage
that was gathered at the hightide mark. "Do something," he
gasped. "Hurry!"

Now, thrusting the child toward the nearest man, he found
himself looking into a face that was blank with stupefaction;
then, and only then, did it dawn on him that he was holding
a doll—a doll whose cherubic pink plastic countenance and
absurdly long-lashed eyes gazed back at him with soft and
touching gratitude. Before him stood the director, regal in his

white robe, a look of concern upon his face. Nina was beside him, a hand to either cheek, her eyes streaming tears. Cameron simply stared at them, openmouthed, gasping for breath, unable to speak. Then, holding the doll beneath its shoulderblades and its thighs, he knelt down and placed it gently upon the sand.

Da Fé appeared as if from nowhere, pushing through the crowd until he stood in front of Cameron, who, looking up, saw a grin on the ravaged face that seemed to be a combination of joy and anguish.

"Caro," said the cameraman softly. "Why didn't you tell us? If I'd only known, I could've reloaded in time. As it is, we've missed the whole thing. All of it. For nothing . . ."

For a moment, Cameron gazed blankly at the hideous face above him; then, scooping up a handful of sand, he lifted himself to his feet and flung it into da Fé's eyes.

Clasping his hands to his face, the cameraman screamed in pain and sank to his knees. Beyond him, Gottschalk never moved a muscle or changed the expression on his face. Cameron studied the maddening serenity in the pale, aquiline features; then, glancing at the doll, he said in an almost inaudible whisper, "Another wrong assumption."

"Yes," the director replied.

16

≈≋≈

Humiliation, fear, and an excruciating sense of futility stalked him all the way back to the hotel. What a fool he had been! A fool twice over. To have jumped to conclusions about the child, however, was one thing; to have attacked da Fé was another—the height of folly. An irretrievable mistake, thought Cameron, who realized that it was high time to take French leave and head for Canada. When he reached his room, he stripped off his wet clothes, pulled on a dry pair of pants and a shirt, and began to collect his belongings in a pile upon the bed. Then, suddenly, he thought of Nina and gave his head a shake. Could he save himself and abandon her to a script that promised to end no less terrifyingly than his own? No, he would have to make her understand so they could go together. But there was no question of seeing her now, and she would probably be working for the rest of the day. He would wait until night, then, when he could go to her room and talk to her alone. At this point, he looked out the window, and, studying the peaks and valleys of the rooftop, decided that it would make a perfect hiding place. All he had to do was keep out of sight until darkness. The rest would be a cinch. The easiest stunt of all . . .

Now, full of plans and preparations, he looked around for something in which to carry his possessions; then, remembering his duffel bag, he went next door and knocked upon the door to the chambermaid's room. The girl who answered was no one he could remember having seen before. Yet he had seen her twice—once through eyes swollen with tears of hilarity and relief, and another time through a keyhole that framed her within the focus which the cameraman insisted was everyone's deepest wish. Astonished that he could have seen her twice and have absolutely no recollection of the sullen, sleepy face that peered out at him through a crack in the door, he found himself groping for words. "My duffel," he mumbled. "I was wondering if you'd—"

"What?" she exclaimed. "Your what?"

"Don't you remember? A white duffel bag. I gave it to you a couple of days ago."

The chambermaid opened the door a bit wider, and brushed a strand of dark hair from her brow. "Yeah, I remember. A duffel bag. Look, I'll have to hunt for it. Can you come back later?"

"Sure," Cameron said. "I'm just next door." She's probably with somebody, he thought. Yet he continued to stand there, watching her finger the third button from the top of a man's shirt which she had obviously pulled on just before coming to the door. He was about to turn away when he heard a suppressed exclamation—was it one of surprise or protest?—from behind her. Glancing at the girl, whose eyes had suddenly veiled over, he asked, "Is everything okay?" and, without waiting for a reply, pushed past her and entered the room, where he found the toll collector strapped to the chair with a length of clothesline wrapped around his chest. For a second, Cameron studied the rolling eyes of recognition that looked up at him above a mouth that wore a strip of adhesive tap; then, turning to the chambermaid, who, having shut the door, was now leaning demurely against it, he said, "What's going on?"

The girl shrugged. "It wasn't my idea."

"Well it's your room, isn't it?" said Cameron, who glanced again at the toll collector and saw that the clothesline, which had been doubled loosely around his torso, could not possibly be holding him in the chair against his will. But if the man was reveling in a captive voyeur's paradise, what need of adhesive tape? "Who gagged him?" he asked.

"I did," the chambermaid replied with a soubrettish giggle. "He talks too much."

Cameron looked down at the toll collector, who, with eyes still rolling, was pretending to struggle against the ropes. The toll collector talks too much, he thought. Even with his eyes . . .

"I mean he's a real bore," said the girl, who walked across the room, and, curling her legs beneath her, sat upon the bed. "All he wants to do is watch."

Cameron found himself watching her as if she were performing in the preview of da Fé's film he had seen the night before, as if she were still without any other dimensions than

those defined by the shape of the keyhole in which she ⌐
appeared before him as a trained response to fantasy. `
even as he took a tentative step in her direction, he could
help wondering what secret urge had impelled her to sub
to the toll collector. But to submit to a prisoner, was that
also to inflict? Yes, she was the protégée of a master wh
place and prerogatives he could now usurp with impunity-
prospect that repelled him even as it filled him with the
archy of lust. In this mood, the girl waited before him
only as an object of desire, but also as a threat to be ov
come. For a second longer, Cameron hesitated; then
turned away. What's the matter with me? he thought. `
toll collector had ceased his simulated struggling against
ropes, and was staring up with eyes that bulged in antici
tion. Cameron reached down and, with a savage swipe, t
the adhesive tape from his mouth.

The toll collector winced in pain. "You!" he gasped. "Ri
here! All the time!"

"Hey," the chambermaid whispered. "You know e
other?"

"Only on location," said Cameron with a grim smile.

The toll collector nodded weakly. "Just having a bit
fun," he muttered. "You won't say anything about it,
course."

"Of course," Cameron replied, but he had no confide
in the bargain, for was he not looking down at another
the protégés whom da Fé had enslaved to his concept of
universal wish? Now he suddenly understood why murde
killed to cover up their tracks. But that's crazy, he thou
I'm not a murderer. I simply made a mistake. In self
fense . . .

Restless, the chambermaid had got up from the bed
gone to the window. "Hey, look down there!" she cr
"Something's happened to Bruno!"

"He's got something in his eyes," Cameron told her.

"But he was supposed to come back," replied the girl v
a glance at the toll collector. "I mean, what'll I do with *hir*

"Amuse him," Cameron said, and, reaching down, secu
the knots of the rope that held the toll collector to the cha

"Now, look, there's no need for that," the toll collector ↑
him nervously. "We've got an understanding, haven't we?"

"Yes," Cameron replied. "But the ties between friends need constant tightening."

The chambermaid laughed and stepped away from the window. "Let's have some fun with him."

"Let's find my duffel bag," Cameron said.

The girl gave him a look of reproach; then, opening a closet door, she rummaged through a pile of laundry and brought out the bag. "Why hurry off?"

"Bruno'll be back," he told her soothingly. "In the meantime, keep your guest occupied."

The chambermaid screwed her sullen face into a grimace of augmented displeasure. "God, what a bore! What'll I do?"

"You'll think of something," Cameron said.

"Now look," the toll collector protested. "Fun is fun, but—"

"Bonne chance," said Cameron as he went out the door. *"Et bonne continuation."*

Back in his room, he stuffed his books, shaving articles, and soggy clothes into the duffel bag; then, impelled by the idea that he had been exposed to the most potential betrayer of all, he glanced into the mirror above the sink. Some disguise, he thought grimly. You should have saved it for Halloween. . . . At this rate, there would soon be no one left to fool. And to think he had unmasked himself for a laundered duffel bag that had no more tales to tell, and a collection of personal odds and ends that could have been replaced for next to nothing! Now, looking at the bag that sat, bulging, upon the bed, he realized that he was about to compound the error with still another. After all, if they were to find the room bare, would they not instantly deduce that he had flown the coop? "Stupid," he muttered. "Stupid." Yes, in the space of half an hour, he had become a fool not twice but four times over. Shaking his head, Cameron unpacked the duffel bag and replaced his effects in scattered profusion about the room; then he folded the bag carefully and tucked it in beneath the mattress of the bed. I should have left it on the bus with her letter, he thought. Then it couldn't have come back to haunt me. . . . Now he took a last look about the room and climbed up on the windowsill. He was halfway outside when someone knocked softly upon the door. Cameron froze in place. Perhaps it was Denise. On the other hand it might be da Fé or Chief of Police Broussard. In any event, it had to be someone from a world he was determined to depart. It's time to leave the cast, he told himself, and, crawling out upon the roof, pulled the window, like a curtain, down behind him.

For several minutes, he crouched beside the dormer and studied the topography; then, on all fours, he scrambled up a steep pitch to the roof peak and, straddling it, surveyed the town. From one side, he could look down upon the pier and the dance casino; from the other, he could see the Victorian police station perched incongruously upon its hill. Ahead of him, at eye level, was the uppermost rim of the Ferris wheel, through whose spokes he could make out the distant outline of the jetty where he and Nina had picnicked on the day before. As he took in the view, however, he realized that he ought to relinquish a vantage point which left him exposed to the upward glance of any of the minuscule figures walking far below. No one's going to mistake you for a weathervane up here, he thought, and started down the incline on the other side.

But he had not bargained on the heat that, even though the sun had not yet reached the meridian, was rebounding off the shingles of the roof with incredible ferocity, and he found himself descending into a V-shaped cut formed by two steep slopes that were bisected by a strip of green copper flashing, which, too hot to touch, flowed between them like a stream of molten metal. It was an untenable ravine where, though sheltered from sight, he could scarcely breathe. Finally, unable to stand the heat any longer, he clambered up the opposite face in search of shade. But except for thin slivers cast by a row of dormer windows that lined the oceanfront side, everything was bathed in light. Now, grabbing hold of a lightning rod, he crawled over the peak of the roof, and slid down to the nearest dormer. The scant protection it afforded would rapidly diminish, however, for even as he sat against it, he realized that the sun, rising toward its noonday zenith, was cutting down the angle of the shadow. Soon, in fact, there would be none except the one he was casting himself. Cameron watched the shadow of his head creeping in beneath his foot, and remembered reading somewhere that it was considered a sign of doom by primitive men, for whom the noontime hour was one of dread. But even as he smiled at the ancient superstition, he found himself recalling his flight across the causeway. The symmetry was unmistakable. Had he not walked unwittingly into the director's world by venturing across an asphalt pavement whose searing reflection of the sun had made him the victim of *trompe l'oreille* and then of *trompe l'oeil?* And was he not leaving it via this parched desert of a roof whose asphalt shingles threatened to produce a similar ordeal by fire? But that was equally superstitious—nothing but nonsense—for now, glancing overhead, Cameron realized that the notion that he was leaving the director's world was simply, like the apparent daily motion of the sun, another illusion. You're not going anywhere on this roof, he told himself grimly. You've just come from the frying pan into the fire. . . .

But the fact that his departure was no less a figment of imagination than the arc the sun was supposed to describe in the sky was also comforting, for it took his mind off the unbearable heat. Now, as if reciting long-forgotten school lessons, he reminded himself that it was the earth spinning on its axis in the opposite direction that gave the sun its apparent course. I'm more in Gottschalk's world than ever, he thought dazedly, and closed his eyes. How far was it to the sun? Ninety-three million miles . . . an impossible distance to imagine unless one converted it in terms of a beam of light, which, traveling at one hundred and eighty-six thousand miles a second, takes eight minutes to reach earth. Eight minutes, Cameron thought, opening his eyes and wincing in the merciless glare. So even if there were an eclipse, I'd have to endure the heat for eight more minutes. . . . Glancing at his watch, he saw that it was exactly noon. Which meant eight hours to go until dusk. I'll never last that long, he told himself. Never in a million light-years . . . But even as he imagined himself crawling back to his room, he thought of the possibility that da Fé might be waiting for him there. On the other hand, if he stayed put, he might faint. And if he fainted, might he not slide off the edge of the roof? From the frying pan into the fire, he told himself again. Suddenly, from somewhere behind him, he could hear peals of laughter. Was he hallucinating already? No, the laughter was coming from the amusement center, where the Ferris wheel and the whip ride were spinning endlessly. Endlessly . . . The heat was getting to him. He tried to concentrate. Was it apparent or real, the motion of the Ferris wheel and the whip ride? Had he really leaped from one to the other and, whirling through the night sky, made good his escape? Or was it simply another illusion that would merely gain the semblance of reality through the director's genius for montage? Was it only a brief moment of time, then, in which he had been a shooting star in Gottschalk's galaxy? What an idea! First a stunt man, then a shooting star, and now, in this incredible heat, a victim of sunstroke . . .

Ah, but it turned out to be an exquisitely slow broil! A regular cookout. An agony that was augmented every once in a while by a delicate waft from the sea, the merest fringe of a breeze that, piping hot from passing over the sand, seared him like basting from the bottom of a pan. He was cooking like a cutlet in a skillet. Yet was he not the chef of his own cuisine? In spite of his torment, the idea amused him. He even tried to improvise a tune to go with it, but the lyrics that came through his parched lips were hoarse. "If you can't stand the heat," he croaked, "stay out of the kitchen."

And to think he had decided that it would be the easiest stunt of all! Now there was the ultimately wrong assumption; the consummate joke. It kept him going for a whole hour. So he was a fool five times over. And it was only two o'clock. Keep it up, he told himself numbly. You'll set a world record. . . .

He was dozing in a foetal position, with his knees drawn up, his back against the dormer, and his head cradled upon his hands, when he heard the sound of scratching, and, opening his eyes, gazed along the surface of the roof, which was shimmering in the heat. For a few moments, he strained to listen above the cries that came from the amusement center; then, lifting his head, he peered around the dormer. The roof was empty in both directions, but now there was a new sound—a measured cadence like that of footfalls. Cameron pressed his ear against a shingle, and listened to the soft vibrations. Someone was approaching from the other side. It must be da Fé, he thought. Who else could it be except da Fé?

The idea filled him with dread. Yet the dread gave him strength, and now, raising himself upon his hands and knees, he backed slowly along the side of the dormer toward the edge of the roof. Don't look down, he told himself as, reaching around, he gripped the window sash between thumb and forefinger and tried to raise it. The window, however, refused to budge. He tried again, this time butting against the frame with the heel of his palm. It was locked. He considered crawling along the gutter to the next dormer, but in the end he decided against it. Too far. And he would be out in the open. Helpless. If worse comes to worst, I can always smash the pane with my fist, he thought, and peered anxiously toward the peak of the roof, where the sound of footsteps continued to reverberate from the other side. His hands and knees were trembling uncontrollably. No soldier ever cowered in a trench with more trepidation, or stared with eyes more fixed in terror toward the parapet above him than did Cameron, who, listening to the sound of footsteps, and waiting, waiting, still waiting, saw, unaccountably, a solitary seagull, an incredibly ungainly seagull picking its way over the crest of the roof with the gait of an old man negotiating unaccustomed ground. For a second, he was too numb to react; then, heaving a sigh of relief, he collapsed once again upon the shingles. Surprised, the gull took off with a squawk, and, shaking with laughter, Cameron watched it flap away to the north. Another wrong assumption. Which made him a fool six times over. Was there no end to his gullibility? Wait and see, he told himself. It's not even three o'clock. . . .

How far to Canada as the gull flies? An intriguing combination of question and dream which he was still contemplating, some minutes later, when he heard the unmistakable clatter of the helicopter. But the appearance of the seagull had diminished his capacity to be surprised, and he found himself listening to the roar of the approaching machine as if it were the most natural of sound effects. Yes, it was only fitting that the helicopter should make this scene, for was it not another example of art reiterating itself? Or was it more a question of history, which, as the philosophers said, those who forgot were doomed to repeat? In any case, the script is a cinch from here on out, Cameron thought. All that's lacking on this godforsaken roof is another young fellow on the lam who will draw a mistaken conclusion to match my wrong assumption, which, having set us to grappling, ends with my going over the edge, whereupon the astonished fugitive will meet a director who listens to his tale, unravels its mysteries, and, after explaining some obscure points, offers him sanctuary by recruiting him on the spot to fill a vacuum. Yes, a perfect script, with a classic case of mistaken identity.

Now the helicopter was hovering just off the edge of the roof, and, buffeted by the wash from its rotor blades, Cameron found himself giving way once again to fear. Hang on, he told himself as the machine descended out of sight and settled upon the sand below. You can always say you're out here building up a suntan. Or keeping in trim for the next stunt . . . But no one came to pose the questions he imagined answering, and a few minutes later the helicopter rose into the sky and flew off to the north, in the same direction as the gull. Cameron barely had enough strength to turn his head and watch it go. Perhaps they've set off to look for me, he thought dimly. If so, they ought to ask the gull. Yes, they should ask the gull, for who could know the whereabouts of one gull better than another?

He awoke shivering, and found the sky dark. Was it evening already? No, a storm was coming and black, billowing thunderheads had covered the sun. Thank God, Cameron thought. The worst is over. . . . As he waited for the rain, he glanced along the roof and planned his approach to Nina's room. At the far end, he would climb down a drainpipe that would afford him access to one of the iron fire escapes that stitched the façade of the building. The rest would be easy. But even as he reassured himself, the storm broke with a flash of lightning followed by a tremendous clap of thunder. A moment later, the valleys and ravines of the roof became a watershed, its gutters overflowed with run-off, and Cameron found himself clinging to the shingles as he might have clung to the slippery shale of a stream bed. No sooner had he begun to worry about being swept away, however, than another flash of lightning lit the sky, and, tossed into the air by the ear-splitting reverberation that accompanied it, he saw the lightning rod on the roof peak giving off a strange blue glow. For a second, he could scarcely believe his eyes; then, realizing his peril, he pushed his face against the shingles. One bolt would do it. Just a tiny part of one bolt, which, splitting off from the lightning rod and conducted by the sheet of water streaming down from the peak . . .

Now, rigid as a condemned man awaiting the current, he found himself thinking of Nina, conjuring up her face, and clinging to his vision of her as fiercely as he clung to the shingles. Only she could save him now. And only he could save her. We've got to save each other, he thought. We've got to get away from here and make a new start. . . . The storm was growing in intensity all around him. Then, as suddenly as they had come, the clouds passed out to sea. Long after the deluge ceased, however, Cameron lay cold and shivering against the roof. Finally, when he summoned up the strength to lift his head, he saw that dusk was falling. Time to go, he told himself. Time to go before something else happens. . . . With an immense effort, he got to his hands and knees, and started crawling toward the far end of the roof, but by the time he reached the drainpipe, it was nearly dark. Cameron sat on the edge of the roof, and rubbed his hands together to get back the circulation. Then, grasping the curve of the pipe, he went down the side of the building like a mountain climber descending a steep face, until he drew abreast of the fire escape, and, reaching for it, swung himself to safety. Afterward, he climbed down the steps until he came to the window of Nina's room, where he could see her sitting before a dresser. Her presence seemed such a miracle that he suddenly felt cold and weak. He tapped feebly upon the pane, but she did not stir. Then, struggling to make a fist, he rapped upon it with his knuckles. The face she turned was filled with alarm, and, pressing his own face to the glass, he tried to smile, and saw in reflection a hideous grin. Now, realizing that she was frightened, he lifted the window, leaned in, and, through chattering teeth, said, "Don't be afraid, it's" . . . as, pitching forward, he fell . . . "only" . . . over the sill and onto the floor . . . "me."

17

He opened his eyes to find her sponging his face with a wet towel, and, remembering his make-up, sat bolt upright and snatched it from her hands. Too late. The rough pile was coated with flesh tint. Cameron got to his feet, went to the dresser, and peered into its mirror. Most of the cosmetic was gone from the left side of his face. The effect was strange. Almost crooked. Two differently shaped eyes peered back at him, and one corner of his mouth was markedly unlike the other. Turning from the mirror, he looked at Nina, who, still kneeling on the floor, was gazing up at him.

"It's only me," he said again.

"I just realized I've never really seen you," she told him.

Unconsciously, he raised a hand and touched his fingertips to the cheekbone that no longer wore make-up. But it's not me, he thought. Only half is me. Now, shivering in the onslaught of another chill, he sat heavily in a chair.

Getting to her feet, Nina went to the dresser, poured half a tumbler of whiskey, and handed it to him. "You look awful," she said. "Where on earth have you been?"

"On the roof," he answered with a weak grin, and, gulping down the liquor, saw through tears that flooded his eyes a puzzled, painful frown come over her face. Suddenly, he realized how difficult his task was going to be. Could he possibly hope to convince her without revealing the other half of his face, and, therefore, the whole of his story? "You look as if you don't recognize me," he said.

She sat down beside him and gave her head a tiny shake. "Between last night, this morning, and now, I hardly know what to think."

"Last night?" Cameron said. "What about last night?"

"Watching you," she murmured. "So helpless."

"You mean the stunt. That was nothing. Believe me, the stunts are the least of my worries."

"That's what he said."

"So you were up in the helicopter."

"Yes."

Cameron suppressed the first question that came to mind, and asked another. "How did it look from up there? What did you think of it?"

"I was afraid," she said.

"Afraid," he repeated. "For me?"

"And for myself, too. He kept telling me that if I could imagine how I would feel if I cared for you, I would truly be able to imagine the role of the astronaut's wife."

"D'you think he knows about us?"

"No, but it was frightening that he should come so close to knowing simply through his preoccupation with his work."

"Yes, it's uncanny, isn't it?" said Cameron dryly. Now, sipping some more of the whiskey, he remembered Roth telling him that the director was going to change the fugitive into a deserter, and the refinement of insight which had come that very morning, when the screen writer had explained that, in order to make the fugitive's flight irrevocable, he would have to kill someone in self-defense. Yes, it was uncanny, all right, but it was becoming less and less of a mystery. The pieces are falling, Cameron thought. It's just a question of putting them together. . . . "Our good director was trying to frighten you with his marvelous artistic intuition. But suppose it isn't really intuition. Suppose it's part of a plan."

"I don't understand," she replied. "What kind of plan?"

"D'you remember my telling him this morning that I knew what he was up to?"

"Yes."

"And how careful he was not to answer the question of whether the fugitive is going to survive the crash?"

"Yes."

"Well, don't you see? The fugitive's not going to survive. He's not *supposed* to survive. In fact, he's supposed to die. In fiction and in fact."

She was smiling at him gently. "Yesterday, on the jetty, you kept telling me it was just a film."

"I was wrong," he replied harshly. "It's a bad movie. A bad movie we can't get up and walk out of."

She was still smiling, but her eyes had filled with tears that moved and chastened him. After all, if the stories were true, and she had been deprived of one lover by an assassin's bullet, might she not tend to feel protective toward the director who had saved her from subsequent despair and brought her back into the world? Yes, he would have to be circumspect about the manner in which he brought her to the point of judging her benefactor. But now, as he watched her weeping, he remembered her face that morning, when he had staggered from the surf, holding the body of a child who, in the next instant, would become a plastic doll. And, suddenly, realizing that she was crying, as she had then, because of him, he was struck by successive waves of awe, tenderness, and desperation. She'll never believe me, he thought helplessly. "Look, I know what's bothering you," he said. "It's that business about the doll. But that's the point he's brought us to, can't you see?"

She gave her head a tiny, almost infinitesimal shake.

"D'you remember asking him if he was going to save the child, and what his answer was?"

She shook her head again, but this time as if to ward off his reply.

"He said, 'I don't know yet.' And then you said, 'Save the child. Don't let him die. Let him live.' And he said, 'It's something I'll have to decide later.' D'you remember that?"

"Yes," she whispered.

"Well, don't you see? What's real? he's always asking. Only art is real, he keeps answering. Only art repeats itself. Over and over. Endlessly . . . It's as if he were programming us to believe in ourselves by showing us in film. But it's more complicated than that. Listen, he even told me once that there was no better way for a fugitive to go undected than to be simultaneously an actor in and a spectator at the unfolding of his own story!"

"What d'you mean?" she asked. "What does being a fugitive have to do with it?"

Cameron took a deep breath and raised his glass to his lips; then, swallowing the rest of the whiskey, he tried to think of how to go on. I can clinch it now, he told himself. By telling her everything . . . For a second longer, he hesitated, but the moment had passed. "Listen, there's something I want to get straight," he said. "This morning, when you and he were talking in the lobby, didn't you ask him if the heroine would be a suicide?"

"Yes."

"And didn't he say she would?"

"He said it was regrettable but necessary."

"How does she commit suicide?"

"He said by relinquishing herself to the sea."

"In other words, by drowning."

Nina gave a faint smile. "I suppose so."

"But you haven't seen the script."

"Script?"

"Script, scenario, treatment—whatever it is that Roth writes and Gottschalk shows you before you do a scene."

"No, I haven't."

"You won't either," said Cameron heavily.

"It may not have been written yet. It's probably one of those scenes he'll improvise."

"Oh, he'll improvise it, all right. It'll be the most arbitrary little fragment of all."

"You've changed since yesterday," said Nina sadly. "I scarcely feel I know you now."

"Yesterday you asked me to take you away," he reminded her. "You said you wanted me to take you with me."

"I remember."

"D'you still want to go with me?"

"I don't know. At this point, I'm . . . confused."

"What's happened to change your mind?"

"What's happened to change you?"

"I've been piecing things together," Cameron told her. "It's called montage."

"But you may have blinded Bruno! Why did you do that?"

"Because I suddenly realized what he and Gottschalk were doing to us."

"They took him off to a hospital in the helicopter, you know."

Cameron gave a short, harsh laugh. So the helicopter that had failed to frighten him was carrying the cameraman whose footfalls had turned out to be those of a seagull. His terror had been for nothing. The whole agonizing day a waste. Wrong assumptions piled upon wrong assumptions. *Trompe l'oreille* reverberating in an echo chamber. He felt a wave of dizziness descend upon him; then, with an act of will, he squeezed the thoughts from his mind as if suppressing the memory of a nightmare, and looked again at Nina. "Good old Bruno," he said. "Is he really blind?"

"They don't know," she answered. "He's being held for observation."

"Don't worry," he told her. "Bruno's indestructible. That one-track mind of his will pull him through. Remember, he's got to shoot the rest of the film—the one in which he expects you to star as the embodiment of our deepest wish."

"Why d'you say a thing like that?"

"He said it. He said you were truly Margaret, a heroine torn between the world of flesh and the terror of your director's cerebral concepts. He said that you were guilty, and that you would betray Gottschalk and submit to the plot of his film in order to punish yourself."

"And d'you believe him?"

"I'm like you," he told her wearily. "Between last night, this morning, and now, I don't know what to think. All I know is that Gottschalk's trying to make you into Margaret, and she's the kind of woman who's desperate enough to try anything."

"But we're real," said Nina. "Margaret's a character. Someone he dreamed up. An exaggeration."

"Yes, I said that," Cameron replied. "Yesterday on the jetty. But since then, things have changed."

"We're still between takes," she murmured. "Between takes in a bad movie we can't get up and walk out of."

For some moments, he made no reply, for he realized that her intelligence was a barricade behind which she had taken refuge. Then, leaning forward, he smiled at her. "D'you really think I've changed? Truly changed? Or d'you think it's because you're seeing me with only half my movie face?"

"I don't understand."

Cameron got to his feet and, gazing down at her, brought his fingers to his left cheek. "This half is someone you've never seen," he whispered. "The other half is the stunt man. No wonder you don't recognize me."

"But it's more than that. Something's happened *inside* of you!"

"Wait," said Cameron, who walked to the dresser, picked up the towel, and began to rub briskly at the right side of his face. When he turned around, a few moments later, she

was staring at him as if he had just committed a crime.
"Now," he said softly. "Now you know."

She was still looking at him as if she had just seen him
perform some barbarous act, but there was also a strange
fascination in her face, as if some deep longing had been
accorded a sudden and surprising gratification. As he went
on to fill in the details of what had happened, however, he
sensed that she was not listening to his story as much as
backtracking over her own. Was she aware, then, of the
similarity between them, and, by extension, of the crazy
symmetry in the director's design? Or was she simply thinking of the future with the insatiable curiosity of an actress
for each new role? Tangled in the uncertainties of his own
thinking, Cameron ended his narrative abruptly, and studied
her in silence. Then, unable to fathom her expression, he
found himself comparing her reaction with that of Denise,
whose disbelief had given way so quickly to desire. Strange
how both of them had wanted to see his real face, and how
necessary its revelation to enlist their aid and thus ensure the
continuation of his freedom. But who could pretend to have
found freedom in Gottschalk's world? No, he had been a
prisoner of his film face every bit as much as he was now a
prisoner of his real face—a delicate poise of physiognomy
in which his terror of the stunts was precisely balanced by his
fear of apprehension. Cameron thought furiously to figure
a way out of the corner into which he had painted himself
by removing his make-up. "I want you to help me," he told
her finally. "Go to the wardrobe room. You'll find a wet suit,
a pair of flippers, and a face mask there. Bring them with you
and meet me at your car in ten minutes."

"What are you going to do?"

"We," he corrected gently. "We are going to get the hell
out of here."

"But the roads are blocked! They're stopping everyone
and searching all the cars."

"We'll go out over the causeway. I'll be wearing the suit
and mask. If we're stopped, I'll tell them I've got to practice
for the stunt."

"And then what?"

"If we get through, we'll just keep on going."

"Keep going?" Nina said.

"To Canada," he told her.

"Canada . . ."

"It's our only chance. We can break away from him now."
She gave a tiny shrug. "What will we do in Canada?"

He started to answer, but thought better of it. He would
persuade her later. Once across the causeway and past the
toll gate on the other side . . . "There's not much time," he
said. "Will you meet me at the car?"

"Yes, but how will you get there without being seen?"

It was out of the question to chance the stairs and the
lobby. On the other hand, if he went out the window and
down the fire escape, he risked the possibility of being recognized by someone on the porch. He considered climbing back up to the roof, crossing it, and going down a fire
escape at the back of the building, but the idea of venturing
out over that treacherous terrain at night filled him with
misgiving. Then he remembered the dumb-waiter in the
hallway by the staircase landing. Yes, the dumb-waiter was
his best chance, for it would surely take him down to the
kitchen, where he could easily make his way outside.

Only when he went out into the corridor did it occur to
him that the dumb-waiter could not possibly take him to the
kitchen, which was located at the rear of the hotel, but that
it led to the lobby directly below. It must be for luggage, he
decided, until, yanking at the door to the shaft, which had
been painted over innumerable times, he realized that the
dumb-waiter had not been used for years. When he finally
got the door open, he looked into the shaft and saw that the
rope was still there, and that the walls were made of brick.
Thank God it's brick, he thought. That means it has to go
down to the basement. Now, pulling on the rope, he brought
an ancient cab up the shaft, past the opening, and on up
toward the floor above. Then he gave several sharp tugs on
the rope to test its strength.

Nina was staring at him breathlessly. "Don't do it," she
said. "There must be a better way."

He smiled to reassure her. "With luck it'll be the last
stunt of all," he replied. "Remember to bring the skin-diving stuff."

"But what if the doors won't open below?"

Cameron looked steadily at her. "Then it'll be up to you to get me out," he said.

The glint of alarm that appeared in her eyes gave him pause for doubt, but even as he found himself wondering how she would react if he failed to appear at the car, the sound of footsteps came up the stairway from the lobby. Cameron grasped the rope, swung himself into the shaft, and, feet dangling, felt it tighten and heard the dumb-waiter above him start creaking upward along its wooden rail. Then, praying that the rope would hold, that the brake band of the cab would slow him, and that the ancient contraption would act as counterweight, he began to descend into blackness, groping for toeholds on brackets that supported the rail at regular intervals. Above him, he heard Nina call a greeting. Below him, he felt something come loose from the wall of the shaft, and, hanging still, listened for it to strike bottom. But there was no sound to indicate that the shaft and his journey might have an end. For a second, he wondered if he could make it back to the door. Impossible. He was descending more rapidly than ever now—a function of gravity and a pulley mechanism that he imagined was fastened to the roof above him by the rustiest sort of hook —and, concentrating instead on trying to slow his fall by catching the brackets with the toes of his shoes, he descended faster and faster through the shaft, past a crack of light that must be the opening at the lobby level, and down, down, endlessly down and much too fast, until, shutting his eyes and drawing his knees up to his chest, as if to delay his landing until the last split second, he felt himself settle suddenly and unaccountably to a cushioned stop. At this point, heaving a sigh of relief, he lit a match, saw that he was sitting in a pile of refuse, and listened to the sound of the rope slapping far above him against the sides of the shaft. Then he pushed open the door beside him, and, lighting his way with another match, climbed out of the shaft to find himself in a large room whose walls were lined with racks containing cans of film. When the match petered out, he dropped it on the floor and lit another. This time he could make out a movieola, a workbench, a splicer, and several bins holding racks of hanging film strips. I'm in the cutting room, he thought, and smiled at the idea that even while the director had been down here painstakingly editing him out of the rushes, he had stepped into the picture upstairs as Nina's leading man in a deliciously spontaneous take of their own deepest wish. Now, climbing up on the workbench, he opened a window at ground level, crawled outside, and scrambled on hands and knees across the parking lot to her convertible. She was sitting behind the wheel, and she had brought the face mask, flippers, and the wet suit. Cameron slid in beside her and, with a surge of confidence and strength, took her chin in his hand and turned her mouth to his. The last stunt, he told himself. "I love you," he said.

18

The car radio was playing softly, but at first he was too busy pulling on the wet suit to pay attention to what was being said. Only after he had struggled into the tight rubber jacket did he realize it was a program describing preparations for the next space shot that, weather and the preliminary count-down permitting, would take place tomorrow. If all went well, according to the announcer, the mission would be a giant leap into yet another recess of the universe. Cameron tugged his face mask over his head, and glanced at Nina. "If all goes well," he said, "it'll be the stunt of the century. But if something goes wrong, Gottschalk will be in a bind, won't he? The last thing he must want is for reality to overtake his myth before he can fake a film of it. It would ruin his theory that only art is real."

"Or prove it," she replied.

"The director's full of contradictions, so take your pick," said Cameron with a laugh. "In either case, the only way to stay ahead of his game is to put a happy ending on our story in spite of him. In other words, it's a bad movie, but we don't have to sit through it."

"You mean we can go to Canada."

"Right."

"And d'you think it'll be better there?" she asked. "Any less terrifying?"

He was mulling over a reply when, reminded again of her own story, it occurred to him that the reason she had not been able to fathom the extent of Gottschalk's power was simply that nothing in his domain could possibly seem as terrifying and arbitrary as the split-second act that had deprived her in the world that was forever being described in banner headlines. She's probably felt safer in his film than anywhere else, he thought. Was it any wonder, then, that his discoveries about the director should make her afraid? Yet the thought of her anxiety and tears no longer moved

161

him as before. Did he really care for her? How quickly everything had changed. Yesterday he had fallen in love with her; last night he had succumbed to the temptation of the cameraman's keyhole; and today he was making an accomplice of her in order to figure out the missing links in Gottschalk's scheme and to effect his own escape. She was right, he had changed. In this mood, he wondered if he were capable of loving her. No, it must be the peril he felt around him. Once across the causeway and through the toll booth . . .

"Let's be off," he said gently. "Godspeed to all voyagers, and especially to the astronauts and us."

But even as he spoke, he found himself remembering Gottschalk's description of the Fontinalia scene. *The surfers are wearing those skin-tight black wet suits that, except for color, are similar to the apparel worn by astronauts. Protective suits reiterating the theme of hostile environments, and signaling the imminence of disaster.* The idea descended upon him like a premonition, and as they drove slowly through the streets of the town, he tried to think of some way to shake off the depression that accompanied it.

"Who was coming up the stairs?" he asked. "Just before I went into the dumb-waiter shaft."

"Dalton Roth," she replied. "He was looking for you."

"For me?"

"He said he'd been knocking on your door all day. Evidently, there was something he wanted you to read."

The script, thought Cameron, who glanced out the window and saw that they were passing the gingerbread police station at the top of the avenue. Now, remembering his panicky assumption that it had been either da Fé or Chief Broussard at the door, he smiled and shook his head. So it was only the screen writer coming to show him a script that would tell him what he already knew, and not the cameraman who had turned out to be a seagull, or the policeman who had probably spent the day hunting for the toll collector, who was far too busy indulging in his deepest wish to play the role of informant. Good old Roth. Another example of how quickly things had changed. Was it only last night he had urged Denise to keep the screen writer in the dark, and only this morning he had overheard the director telling Nina that by keeping Roth in focus, he was able to use him to best advantage? Yes, one way or another, Roth was being hoodwinked. Yet he had taken the time and trouble to come to his room with the script. A friend in need, Cameron thought. Except that once he had decided to write himself out of it, there was no longer any need to see the script. . . .

"Look, I don't know if it'll be any better or less terrifying in Canada," he said to Nina. "Or anywhere else, for that matter. In the end, it's best not to know. Otherwise, we'd keep thinking there might be some way to find out what's going to happen in order to change it."

They had left the town behind and climbed over the ridge that separated it from the salt marsh, and were descending the other side to the fork where the causeway joined the old road into town, and where—what an eternity ago it seemed! —he had flagged down the laundry truck. Now, as he retraced his route, he remembered that only yesterday, on the jetty, he had suggested speeding up the projector as a prelude to embracing her. Yes, as recently as yesterday, he had still had faith in the future; today he had lost it; and tonight, as if set in reverse, the projector was speeding him herky-jerky into the past, carrying him in crazy Keystone Kop fashion out of the town, across the causeway, onto the bridge, ass-over-teakettle into the car, in and out of the toll booth, and then, still scrambling ludicrously rearward, through the stunted forest that lined the highway, where the bus still sat like a stranded ark beneath the broiling sun, and the rewound film slapped endlessly in the wheel of the machine. . . .

A sudden deep breath drawn by Nina, who stiffened behind the wheel and stabbed at the brake pedal, brought him back, and, looking through the windshield, he saw that they were approaching the roadblock—a pair of parked patrol cars whose revolving red dome-lights swept the macadam with an urgent glare. Cameron was filled with a curious annoyance, as if the tableau ahead were a waste frame that, instead of having been discarded in the cutting room, had been left in the film by mistake or carelessness. The last obstacle, he thought, and pulled the mask down over his face.

"Let me do the talking," he said. "And remember, we're going out over the causeway so I can practice for a stunt. It's the only way to explain this get-up."

But as they entered the eerie perimeter of illumination surrounding the patrol cars, he began to lose his composure. Flashing red light, harsh with authority and the portent of disaster, exploded off the hood and, penetrating the windshield and the face mask, found its way into his eyes, exposing his own fear as a surgeon's scalpel lays open tissue to disclose a nerve.

Nina had rolled down her window to acknowledge the presence of a policeman whose white ice-cream vendor's hat was reflecting a raspberry glow. The policeman had a young, earnest face that, as he peered into the car and saw Cameron, took on a frown of suspicion.

"We're from the film company," Cameron said quickly, but his mouth had gone dry and the words sounded fuzzy.

"Got some identification, sir?"

Cameron shook his head and tried to manufacture a grin. "None that's waterproof," he replied. "My name's Coleman. Arthur Coleman."

"Where're you heading, Mr. Coleman?"

"Out across the causeway. You see—"

The policeman's frown suddenly deepened.

"—I'm the stunt man," Cameron explained.

The policeman hesitated. "You the one on the whip ride last night?"

"That was for real," said Cameron with a smile. "For the cameras. Tonight it's just practice."

The policeman nodded. "Okay, Mr. Coleman, but I'll have to check. The causeway's supposed to be closed to the public, and our orders are not to let anyone through who doesn't carry identification."

"But Chief Broussard knows about the stunt, and we're only going as far as the bridge."

"I still have to call in, Mr. Coleman. By the way, Miss, may I have your name, too?"

"Mabry," Nina replied. "Nina Mabry."

"Stay here," the policeman said. "I'll be right back."

Cameron watched him walk through the infernal glare of the dome-lights and climb into the nearest patrol car. "Relax," he told Nina. "The chief and I are old friends." And besides, he thought, will the chief not ensure his own deception by suspending disbelief?

But his confidence had begun to unravel once again. What a chance to have taken! Still, if it worked, there would be clear sailing ahead. Canada . . . Don't think about it now, he told himself, and tried instead to conjure up the face of Chief

Broussard, which, he decided, ought to be wearing a grimace of incredulity. Yes, the chief's professional instincts would require him to be suspicious of the odd request being relayed by his patrolman. But upon reflection would he not view it in the context of the other stunts? Come on, Cameron thought grimly, straining to make out the patrolman through the glare. Cut the talk and let's hear the verdict. . . . Never in his life had so much seemed to hang in such fragile balance. Say yes, he thought, as if willing the words from lips that were surely clamped over the ever present cigar. Say yes, dammit. Yes. Yes. *Yes!*

The patrolman had returned and was bending in accommodation to the level of the window. "Chief says okay, Mr.—"

Cameron wondered if the patrolman could hear the sigh of relief that also clouded over his face mask.

"—Coleman, so if you'll just follow me, I'll lead the way."

For a second, Cameron could scarcely believe his ears; then dismay fell upon him like a club. "No need to put yourself out," he croaked. "I know the way."

"Chief's orders, sir. Told me to accompany you and render all assistance."

"Thanks," said Cameron, "but it's really not necessary. All I want to do is test the—"

But the patrolman was already hurrying through the endlessly flashing light to his car.

"—goddam current," Cameron muttered after him, and added a silent string of obscenities in its wake. Then, turning to Nina, he gave a weary shrug. "Well, there's no choice now," he said. "Except to go out there and hope for the best."

"Hope for the best?" she repeated, putting the convertible into gear and starting after the patrol car.

"A chance," he murmured, but he had not the vaguest idea of what he meant until the policeman stopped his vehicle in the road ahead, climbed out, and pulled aside one of the sawhorse barricades that blocked off the causeway. "So the driver had to stop his vehicle, climb out, and pull aside a sawhorse in order to cross the causeway," Gottschalk had said on the very first day, when he had led him step by step, carrot and stick, to the realization of what had really happened. Yes, only art is real. Only art repeats itself. Over and over. Endlessly . . . No wonder the screen writer had suggested that the fugitive kill a cop! But is that the chance I'm hoping for? thought Cameron, who, in a ferment of recollection, was also remembering his imaginary pursuit of the child to whom he had given his autograph.

They had come to the bridge—the bridge that would either once again become a movie set or serve as a bridge to freedom—and he could not help but wonder at the foolishness of the stroboscopic fantasy in which he had crossed it simply by imagining that he could set the projector in reverse. Ahead of them, the policeman parked his car, climbed out, and looked back in their direction, but Cameron was staring at a railing—a brand-new steel railing on the upriver side, which had been painted bright orange to withstand corrosion. So the bridge had been equipped with a railing, which, in spite of the fact that it must have been installed within the past few days, provided one half of the finishing touch that would not only complete but completely change the bridge. Yes, guard rails will change everything, Cameron thought, for in addition to serving as barriers against future accidents, would they not also tend to stand as evidence that none had occurred in the past? But then he saw that the seaward side of the bridge was still open and waiting for the prop men to construct their own railing of balsa or papier-mâché, through which he would go as if through cheese, accompanied only as an afterthought by the soundtrack's spine-tingling scream of tearing metal, by a whopping big splash, and by silent bubbles welling up from the darkness into which he had vanished. . . .

"We're here," said Nina softly.

Cameron got out of the car, walked to the edge of the bridge, and listened to the swift current that was sucking at the concrete abutments and racing out through the dark marsh toward the river mouth, where, long ago, the old counterman had fished out a grotesque appendage of disaster.

The policeman came up on one side of him, and peered down at the roily water. "Jesus," he exclaimed. "You aren't thinking of going into that, are you?"

"Practice makes perfect," Cameron replied.

"But the current's too strong to swim against."

"Not if I wear flippers," said Cameron, who was gauging the distance to the policeman's shoulder and considering the force of the shove that would be necessary to send him over the edge.

On the far side of him, Nina shivered audibly. "No," she whispered. "No!"

The policeman took a half-step in front of Cameron, and nodded in vigorous agreement. "I'm with you, lady. I don't think he should either."

Now, thought Cameron, but when he glanced at Nina, he saw that she was staring at him with the same expression of horror as when he had removed the make-up and revealed his true face to her. For a moment longer, he hesitated, savoring the opportunity that would ensure his freedom even as he felt it slip away.

"There's nothing to worry about," he said finally, and started back to the car to get the flippers.

Only as he sat in the front seat pulling them on, however, did it become completely clear to him that he was not going to cross the bridge. Not unless he killed the patrolman. And he would not be able to kill the patrolman because of that look upon her face, which he would have to carry over the bridge and into whatever future he hoped to find on the other side. So he had come not to a bridge but to an impasse, and the whole notion of not crossing bridges until one came to them was not only figurative but futile. In fact, he might just as well have returned to the bridge under the impulse of the curiosity that is supposed to attend a guilty conscience. Except that one could scarcely return to the scene of a crime if there had been none. Had he returned, then, for some other reason? Out of regret, perhaps, or simply to prove that one could forget the events of a regrettable day? Yes, that must be why, for now a whole parade of sounds came back to him in an order that conspired to carry him over the bridge he would not otherwise be able to cross —the splash he had not heard but only imagined through deduction, the soft, pulpy thud of the rock, the infernal racket of the helicopter, the hoarse, insistent shouting of the toll collector, the scolding of the squirrel, the hum of insects in the stunted forest, the whine of cars hurtling over the highway, and the bored voice of the sergeant who, having grimaced at the sun and wiped a sleeve across his forehead, had told him to take off. . . .

So the first victim of *trompe l'oreille* had been the sergeant! That, at least, was comforting. But was it conceivable that what had happened afterward—all the misfortunes of the past few days—had been initiated by his refusal to interpret the sergeant's order in a vernacular other than his own? At this rate, the whole future of the world could be compromised by the semantic whim of a single moment! No, it seemed much more likely that his encounter with the stunt man simply concluded a series of unfortunate circumstances begun by his impulsive and facetious decision to take the sergeant literally, which, in turn, concluded another series of circumstances. But which of these was first and foremost? The arbitrary withdrawal of his deferment? His subsequent induction? The breakdown of the bus engine? The sergeant's decision to single him out for responsibility? Or could it have been the map that showed the proximity of the sea? There was no way of telling. Who could possibly tell about a game in which everything depended upon the turn of a wheel?

But if he had committed no crime—if he had simply made a perfectly honest, inevitable, and, under the circumstances, natural mistake, why had he even considered killing the policeman, which would surely constitute a crime? And not just any crime, but one that would bear an uncomfortable if not uncanny resemblance to the crime he had not committed. There was no answer to that either, except in the whole series of circumstances that had taken place after he had reached the town. But, make no mistake about one thing, it was uncanny. That was the word, all right. Had he not used it just an hour ago to describe the director's mysterious ways to Nina? And was not the most uncanny thing of all the glimmer of insight which he had derived from the news that the fugitive was going to kill someone he had reason to believe was a cop? Ah, now he was closing in on something! By killing the policeman he would not only commit a crime but also commit himself to the elusive thesis that lay behind the director's film. On the other hand, by not killing the policeman, did he not cut off all chance of escape? Either way, he doomed himself to the same thing, except that now he would have to perform the stunt for which the prop men had yet to make final preparations. Which meant that his descent through the dumb-waiter had merely been another step on the way to an ending of Gottschalk's choosing. Cameron struggled to acknowledge this. Then, as he got out of the car and stood in the roadway, wearing the face mask that concealed his identity and the flippers that made him feel as awkward as a duck out of water, he realized that some part of him had known it all along.

"Take off!" Once again, that ambiguous order rang in his ears as if he were replaying the tape of the first day at full volume. Had he become so immersed in the past that he was beginning to hear things? But the words carried a gruffer intonation than had been given to them by the sergeant's mellifluous voice, and, glancing behind him, Cameron was just in time to see Chief of Police Broussard climbing out of his car, and the patrolman hurrying obediently toward his own. So he had not only not begun to hear things, he had not even heard the chief arrive. And if it had not been for the look on Nina's face, the patrolman might now be thrashing in the current and hollering for dear life instead of driving back to man the roadblock. . . .

Arms akimbo, the chief watched Cameron, who approached at an awkward waddle. Then, yanking the cigar from his mouth, he let his gaze travel from flippers to face mask. Finally, he shook his head as if at a wayward child. "What the hell, Coleman?" he growled. "What the hell are you up to now?"

Cameron shrugged and gave a sheepish grin. "Business as usual," he replied.

"Monkey business," the chief muttered, looking him over again from head to toe.

"I want to test the current."

"In the middle of the goddamn night?"

"A question of the tide."

Chief Broussard heaved a weary sigh. "Look, Coleman, I'm not a nursemaid or a camp counselor. I've got enough on my mind as it is. If you're hell-bent on getting yourself drowned, do me a favor. Go find another river and drown yourself in somebody else's town!" At this point, the police chief turned to Nina. "And just what were you going to do, Miss Mabry? Watch him jump in and wave goodbye?"

"There's no call for that," said Cameron coolly. "It was my idea."

"Some idea. No boat. No rope. Not even a life-preserver!"

"Okay," Cameron replied. "You've made your point."

Chief Broussard clamped the cigar between his teeth, took a deep breath, and blew a cloud of smoke toward the face mask. "The point is that from now on these screwy stunts of yours are going to be cleared through me. I've made that plain to Gottschalk, and now I'm telling you."

"You've talked to Gottschalk?"

"On the telephone. Just before I came out here."

Cameron glanced at Nina, who had turned away and was walking toward the convertible. "Did you mention her?" he asked.

The police chief glanced up at him with quick appraisal. "Wasn't I supposed to?"

"It doesn't matter," said Cameron with a shrug. "It's just that I didn't bother to clear it with him, either."

"So I gathered."

"What did he say?"

"He said you were conscientious but incautious."

"And he suggested that you come out here and talk some common sense to me."

"As a matter of fact, that's just about right."

"Tell me, did he seem annoyed?"

"I couldn't say about that. He's a cool one."

"Yes, a cool one," Cameron murmured.

A tinge of affection crept into the chief's gruff voice. "Look, young fella, I'm sorry if I got you in hot water with your boss. But if I hadn't come out here in the nick of time, you would've been in much worse trouble."

In the nick of time, all right, Cameron was thinking. And you've no idea how much worse trouble. . . . "I guess I ought to thank you," he said.

"Look down there, Coleman. That current must be traveling six or seven knots on this tide. Why, you would've been carried a quarter of a mile before you could even begin to get out of it!"

"You're right," Cameron said. "It was a pretty silly idea."

"Not only that, but there's all kinds of junk down there you could've got yourself tangled up in."

"You don't say," Cameron replied. "What sort of junk?"

"Cars mostly. There used to be a ferry here years ago. Then everybody and his uncle started dumping worn-out jalopies into the river, and finally they built the causeway. God only knows how many old heaps are down there."

So the river bottom is an auto graveyard, Cameron was thinking, where one heap more or less will scarcely matter. . . . "Well," he said with a smile, "there'll be another jalopy down there before I'm through."

Chief Broussard was looking at him quizzically. "You're really going through with it, hanh?"

"It's my job," Cameron replied with a shrug.

The chief peered down at the current and shook his head. "Wild horses couldn't get me in there," he muttered. "For that matter, I don't see why the hell it's necessary. Can't they fake it with models?"

"Sure, but it's liable to look faked, and the director's got a passion for authenticity."

The police chief grinned. "I'll tell the world!" he exclaimed. "He's even asked me to be in the last part of the movie."

"That's a good one," Cameron observed. "You going to have a talking role?"

Chief Broussard gave him a don't-kid-me look and shook his head. "Me and a few of the boys are going to be on the roadblock you run. After you crash it, we open up and you go over the edge of the bridge."

"Open and shut," said Cameron with a laugh. "Kindly remember to use blank ammunition."

"Listen, you'll have enough on your mind without us adding to it," the chief replied. "In fact, this whole business goes against my better judgment."

"Don't worry about my end of things," Cameron said. "I'm a professional fall guy." Who's been perfectly set up, he was thinking.

"Something odd about the way this Gottschalk operates, hanh? I mean, I get the feeling he's trying to copy from the story of the young fella we're after."

"Artistic license," replied Cameron with a shrug. "He draws his inspiration from what he imagines the story could be."

"In my trade, we call it anticipation. You been to college, hanh, Coleman?"

For a second, Cameron could not push out a reply past the breath he had drawn. "Yes," he answered finally. "Why?"

"Just fishing for inspiration," the chief said dryly. "Tell me, if you were this bird, how would you try to get out of town? Assuming, of course, he's still in town."

Cameron considered the question as if it were a trap. "Well, assuming I knew you'd set up the roadblock, I guess I'd try swimming the river or going north along the beach."

"That was my first idea, too, but now I've changed my mind. We've been watching the beach at both ends, and we've turned the town upside down and inside out. Which means that if he's still there, he must have a perfect cover and be moving around right under our noses. Which, in turn, makes me wonder if he won't try to come out right under our noses. Just like he does in the film, hanh?"

Cameron glanced sideways at the chief, who was staring across the vast and darkened salt marsh as if lost in contemplation. "It's an interesting theory," he remarked.

"Yeah," said the chief, who suddenly leaned over the edge of the bridge and spat his cigar into the water. "Well, I'll see you on the job tomorrow."

"Yes," Cameron said.

"And best of luck, hanh?"

"Thanks," said Cameron, looking down at the swift current. So it will be tomorrow, he thought, and the chief, who's on the verge of putting two and two together, will play himself. But was it possible that spitting upon a grave could bring good luck . . . ?

19

~~~

As they drove back to town, he tried desperately to think of some way to break the silence. Then, glancing at her face, he saw a despair that was the aftermath of that other look of hers, which, having stayed his hand from the policeman's shoulder, had placed in forfeit their chance of going off together. No, there were no words to express his disappointment, and none to alter her sadness and resignation. Orpheus and Eurydice with a slightly different twist, he thought, and wondered what kind of ending the director would think up for them now. But how futile to be thinking in terms of endings when Gottschalk believed only in the kind that were endless, such as the astronaut tumbling endlessly through the celestial void, and the sea washing endlessly over rocks at the end of a deserted jetty. Was it posible that his own fate might consist of performing endless stunts—one after the other and each in its way more terrifying than the last—in a limbo delineated by da Fé's camera and described by the director's thesis about reality and art? The idea came to Cameron as they entered the town and started down the broad avenue that overlooked the amusement center, the ocean pier, the dance casino, and the hotels that lined the crescent beach. But the ramshackle conglomeration that had been overwhelmed by the incredibly brilliant sun of the first day now provided a welcoming glow in the dark of night. Was he not somehow relieved to be coming back to this garishly lit coast where terror had been balanced by triumph, where he had survived and overcome the power of the sea, the height of the Ferris wheel, the dizzying centrifugal force of the whip ride, the tormenting heat of the sun upon the roof, and the claustrophobic confines of the dumb-waiter shaft, and where, having perfected his craft by diving, swimming, leaping, falling, and climbing through an obstacle course of infernal proportions, he would now prepare himself to undergo yet another test? Yes, it was not without certain exhilaration that he found himself descending the avenue once again. He was still free, and all the pieces were falling into place. When the puzzle was completed, he would know everything. Then, if he could only get to the end of the gantlet, might he not escape from purgatory purged?

They had entered the parking lot behind the hotel, and pulled into a space beside a hulking black car with a high, hump-backed trunk beneath an oval-shaped rear window—a duplicate of the vehicle he had encountered upon the bridge he would now be able to cross only when it became a movie set again. For a moment, Cameron gazed with misgiving at this sinister reminder. Then, looking up through the windshield, he saw the moon rising above the sea, and imagined the astronauts who would soon be flying out beyond it. Godspeed to all stunt men, he thought again. And a blessing on the vehicles that carry them. . . .

"We're home," he announced. "Take a look and see if the coast is clear."

But as soon as she had gone, he found himself studying the car through the window beside him as if he were peering through a glass case in a museum of natural history at some scaly species of beast that, having been unearthed from the sediment of another age, had been stuffed and displayed for the awed inspection of schoolchildren. What a monster it was! Yet, like all monsters, fascinating. Did its black skin, which gleamed in the light of the moon, seem in better condition, or was it simply that the merciless sun above the causeway had illuminated every defect of its predecessor? No matter. If the other car no longer existed—whether by virtue of having been interred in the graveyard at the bottom of the river, or deleted in the director's cutting room—this one was real enough. Yes, this ancient and virtually extinct model—a grotesque replica from the past—was real because it was the car of the future. A car of the future, thought Cameron, who climbed out of Nina's convertible and glanced around the parking lot to make sure it was deserted. My future . . .

Now, approaching the vehicle in the appraising manner of a prospective customer in a used-car lot, he rapped his knuckles upon its roof and nodded with satisfaction at the lack of resilience they encountered. A well-built tub, he told himself. From the good old days when people built cars with the kind of roof that Janssen and Bakker of the Hague Fire Brigade would be pleased to have over their heads when taking a dip in the murky waters of the Koninginne-gracht. . . . At this point, he opened the door on the driver's side, climbed in behind the wheel, and, even as he pulled the door shut and noted its heavy construction and the solid, comforting click of the latch, was inundated by the musty odor of old upholstery that evoked the brutal sounds of prizefights coming through his father's ancient radio. Skip the nostalgia, he told himself grimly, and proceeded to open and close the windows and vents on either side. So far, so good. Everything appeared to work. The roof seemed heavy and unyielding, the door that would be his escape hatch closed solidly, and the windows rolled up and down without sticking. What else? thought Cameron, lighting a match and lifting up the mats to examine the floorboards, which also seemed solid and bore scarcely a trace of rust.

When he climbed out, a few moments later, Nina had returned and was standing beside the convertible. "Tight as a coffin," he told her with a laugh.

"He's waiting for you upstairs," she replied.

Cameron took note of the apprehension in her voice and rapped his knuckles once again on the roof of the car. "I'll be back for it tomorrow," he said. "But only if he puts a spare in the trunk and gives me good terms with plenty of time to pay." He tried to think of something else to say— some explanation that would set things right—but he could summon up nothing except words to match the macabre bravado that was coursing through him like an electric current. "You go on ahead," he told her. "I'll be coming Douglas Fairbanks style."

The climb to the porch roof was child's play, except for a few prickles he managed to pick up from a rosebush whose trellis he used as a ladder. Cameron plucked the thorns from the palms of his hands, which still bore scars from the barnacles that covered the crossbars beneath the pier; then he crawled around a corner to the ocean side of the hotel, where he raised a window and, grasping the lower part of the sash, swung himself feet first into the director's suite. The inappropriateness of his entry was immediately made apparent by the thump of his feet upon the floor of a room that was dark except for the light of a candle, and bare except for a long, narrow bed where Gottschalk lay in his terrycloth robe, a chair in which Nina sat in shadow, and a small table upon which the candle stood, its flame flickering in a draft from the open window. Cameron felt as if he had intruded upon a scene of funereal serenity, and, reaching quickly behind him, pulled down the sash, which struck the sill with another discordant thump. The impression that he had barged into a burial chamber was heightened at once by the flame of the candle, which flared up and cast its light upon the hawkish face of the director, who was staring at the ceiling with the unblinking enamel eyes of one of those Egyptian mummies whose features have been preserved by injections of wax. It was as if he had stumbled into a forbidden crypt and was looking down upon the bier of a Pharaoh. In this mood, he could not help remembering his first meeing with Gottschalk, when, having rung the service bell that tinkled as if announcing Mass, a face like that of Vermeer's astronomer had emerged from the gloom of the lobby as if from the walls of a museum for the dead. Now, like a clumsy acolyte, he took a tentative step forward.

"You want to see me?" he said.

A smile played at the corners of the director's mouth. "To see you," he murmured, "becomes more and more difficult, my friend. How does one see a man who throws sand in some eyes and pulls the wool over others?"

"I'm here," Cameron replied. "If you don't believe it, take a look."

"So seeing is still believing."

"It's still a handy substitute."

"How consistent you are! D'you remember that when I asked you how I could make you believe the hero would always escape, you replied, 'I'll believe it when I see the film'?"

"That was early in the game," Cameron replied.

"Apparently. For without seeing the rushes of the film, you believe that the hero escaped from the surf and was thrown up alive and kicking on the beach, do you not?"

"Of course."

"Why?"

"Why?" Cameron exclaimed. "Why the hell not?" But even as he blurted out the rejoinder, he thought of himself tumbling endlessly in the vortex of the undertow, only to be reunited with his spirit and rescued by a comber that seemed to be a trick of the camera and a three-dimensional screen. Now, glancing in Nina's direction, he saw that her face was scarcely visible in the shadows beyond the glow of the candle. Remember to believe in her, he thought. And in your knuckles, which have rapped a rooftop that seems solid enough not to cave in under pressure . . . "I've seen the car," he told Gottschalk. "That's enough for me."

"So you believe in something," the director observed.

"I've seen the car, and I've come back to go through with the stunt."

"D'you mean you were thinking of not coming back?"

"The idea crossed my mind."

"What happened to make you change it?"

"You know what happened. I couldn't get across the bridge."

"Perhaps your timing was wrong," said Gottschalk with a smile. "Or the direction you wished to take. Remember Caesar, who taught us the consequences of crossing a certain kind of river."

"Look, I've come back. Not that I had much choice."

"No matter. What's important is that you've come back. Which means you believe in something more than the car, doesn't it?"

Into the esoteric again, Cameron thought. "Whatever you say," he replied wearily.

"But of course!" the director exclaimed. "By returning to do the stunt, you've affirmed your belief in a future in which the hero always escapes."

"Only a fool would believe in the future of a celluloid hero."

"How intransigent you are! But you're right in one sense. Films have no tenses—either past, present, or future. A film is just something that's happening now."

"My chief interest is in what's going to happen next. In other words, the stunt."

"You've read the manual on the techniques perfected by those Dutch firemen?"

"Until I got to the part about how they use aqualungs."

"Ah, yes! I'd forgotten about the aqualungs. Of course, they wouldn't be practical for our purposes."

"Not practical?"

"In terms of the film and its reality."

"How about in terms of my surviving the film and its reality?"

"Yours is a dangerous profession. One assumes you went into it with your eyes open."

"Wide open," said Cameron bitterly. "How else can one be deceived by *trompe l'oeil?*"

"Perhaps by clinging to the belief that seeing is believing."

Cameron stared at the director, whose pale, waxen face once again resembled the mask of a king in his sarcophagus. "You've brought us full circle," he said finally. "Now suppose you tell us what happens if we stop trusting our own eyes and start believing in what you put on film?"

"You'll be happier," replied Gottschalk. "Simply because no one minds being terrified out of his wits or saddened to the point of tears if it's in the movies and not in what he conceives of as real life."

"In other words, we won't mind because the events on the screen are happening to other people."

"Which may also be an illusion."

"Ah!" cried Cameron. "I was hoping you'd say that!"

"But it stands to reason. If the camera is used with sufficient imagination, it can become a character. Then, by extension, so does the spectator, who, remember, not only wants to be deceived but participates in his own deception by suspending disbelief. In this way, a film can dominate the mind in a deeper and more penetrating manner than reality itself, which, after all, is merely an habitual way of looking at things and taking them for real."

"So far so good," Cameron said. "But let's take it a step further. If, by chance, the spectator can also be made to play the role of actor in the unfolding of his own story, the film illusions themselves become habitual and art becomes indistinguishable from reality. That's your whole crazy scheme, isn't it? The ultimate in total cinema!"

For the first time, the director raised his head from the

bed and looked in Cameron's direction. But once again, as when they had first met, his eyes failed in disconcerting fashion to focus properly. Finally, he lay back again—a terra-cotta figure in a shroud—and resumed his steady gaze toward the ceiling. "So you're finally beginning to understand," he murmured. "A question, you see, of accepting one's multiple roles and the infinite levels of reality by perceiving of the self and everything else in terms of double-exposure to some ultimate power. Stunt man, spectator, fugitive, whatever you are—yes, your own case is a prime example!"

"You're insane," Cameron told him.

The director smiled. "Insanity, like double-exposure and soft-focus, is a technical defect that can be turned to artistic advantage."

Cameron walked to the foot of the bed, where Nina sat. "Well, now you know what all that uncanny intuition of his is based upon," he said harshly. "And why we're not supposed to believe what we see. He'd like us to be as blind and crazy as he is!"

The face she turned to him was wan in the candlelight and stricken with doubt. And there was also that look in her eyes again as if he had uttered some irretrievable blasphemy.

"Why not face it?" he went on. "We're here to provide vignettes for his total cinema. I'm supposed to knock myself off in a stunt that will be called an accident, and if he can persuade you to be as depressed as Margaret, you'll end up not just acting before the cameras but committing suicide to boot. The ultimate in authenticity—that's what he's shooting for."

The director gave a soft laugh. "How about the doll we used in the Fontinalia scene this morning? Was that an example of the ultimate in authenticity? Or was it, rather, just another indication of your remarkable persistence in seeing things straight and drawing the wrong conclusion?"

"I was wrong about the doll," Cameron admitted. "And what happened on the causeway, too. But not in imagining that it could have been real."

"Spoken like a spectator! In the cinema, only two of the senses are actively engaged—those of sight and sound—but our spectator's imagination is always operating at full speed. And it's his imagination that holds him prisoner!"

Sight, sound, and imagination, Cameron thought. But there had been something else on the causeway. Yes, there had been something else. . . . For a moment, he struggled to remember what it might have been, but the glimmer that fathered the notion had mysteriously vanished. "What're you going to call the film about the astronaut's wife?" he said.

"*Dead to the World*," the director replied. "As you know, I'm addicted to double meaning."

"D'you see?" Cameron said to Nina. "D'you understand what he's saying and what it means for both Margaret and you?"

The director smiled. "But Margaret's death is inevitable. Disillusioned with the barrenness of the technology that has incarcerated her husband in the sky for perpetuity, and with the hopelessness of a religion that has doomed a child to drowning, she allows the space scientist to seduce her, which, even at the moment of ecstasy, produces another terrifying vision of the past. From then on, her story is one of despair and disintegration until, having inflicted herself with the ultimate debasement, there's no other way out for her. No other escape . . ."

Nina had got to her feet. "But you said the film would demonstrate the sterility of cerebral explanations . . . of all solutions except that of love!"

"I was mistaken, my dear. There's no longer any such thing as love. There are merely substitutes. In the end, Margaret may even become a performer in the kind of cyclical little film Bruno's forever making about his fantasies. Of course, such a scene will have to be done with the right blend of suggestion and explicitness. A question of camera work and montage."

"Which'll make art out of pornography but keep a nice commercial touch," Cameron observed.

The director made a slight gesture with his hand. "D'you have any objections, my dear? For the nude scenes, of course, we can always use a stand-in."

"Not to the idea of playing a nude scene," she replied. "But why has the film changed so? I no longer understand what you're trying to say. As I see her, this woman—"

"—is guilt-ridden and full of despair," Gottschalk went on. "Don't forget that. But nothing's settled yet. I may change my mind again. Let's see how the love scene with the scientist goes. We'll shoot it tomorrow when they launch the space shot."

"Another nice blend of fiction and fact," Cameron remarked. "Almost as subtle as the notion of using Chief of Police Broussard to man the roadblock I'm supposed to run."

"That was Bruno's idea."

"Good old Bruno. So we're both going to end up in his hands. . . ."

"Bruno's indispensable," the director replied softly. "As my vision deteriorates, I find myself depending upon him more and more, which reminds me how fortunate that the sand you threw in his eyes appears not to have done any permanent damage. Your rashness, however, cost us the entire day, which means we're stepping up the schedule and shooting the last stunt tomorrow."

"The last stunt," Cameron murmured. "And then what?"

"Your services will no longer be needed."

"A nice euphemism," said Cameron bitterly. "How convenient for you if it turns out to be the last stunt in more ways than one!"

"You'll have every chance," the director replied. "Every chance you had when you came on the scene."

"Except this time I'm the one who's going into the drink."

"Art repeats itself."

"That's what I'm worried about."

"Then why think of it as the last stunt? Why not think of it in terms of a future you profess to reject—as the last chance to escape?"

Cameron turned to Nina. "Strange, isn't it? How the last way out for both of us would appear to be drowning?"

"Pay him no attention, my dear. He's a desperate fellow. As you must have realized this morning when he tried to blind Bruno."

Cameron gave a harsh laugh. "The only way to blind Bruno would be to take away his camera. As for you—"

"Yes, I'm going blind," the director said. "But I no longer have to see!"

Cameron looked at Nina, and moved his lips in silent exhortation.

The director raised a hand as if in benediction. "A desperate fellow," he murmured. "Unfortunately, the medicine's blurred my vision, so—"

Cameron was pleading with Nina with his eyes.

"—I'll probably not see you again."

Cameron took Nina by the arm and placed his lips against her ear.

"Except, of course, on film . . ."

"Let's get out of here," Cameron whispered.

The director had reached out to the table beside him and was groping for something.

"C'mon while we—"

"My drops," said Gottschalk.

"—still have a—"

"Where are they?"

"—chance!"

For a second, Nina hesitated. Then, nodding in assent, she freed her arm from his grasp, and pointed toward the window. Afterward, she picked up a vial from the table, unscrewed its cap, and, withdrawing a dropper, held it above the face of the director, who stared up at the tiny bell of fluid which, forming at the end of the glass tube, bulged, broke, and fell upon the ball on his unblinking eye.

Cameron stood transfixed, as if he were watching an act of mortification. Then, as Nina wiped away the excess fluid that ran like tears over Gottschalk's cheeks, he retreated to the window, opened it, and climbed back out on the porch roof. A chill wind was blowing in from the sea, and the surf was drumming a cadence upon the beach. Somewhere in the night sky, a gull uttered a funerary squawk. In the dim light of the candle, the director lay upon the bed like some ancient king who, having been confined to his palace with the waning of the moon, waited in sacred seclusion to die before rising with a new moon to begin everything over again.

20

For a long time, he stayed on the porch roof, unable to make up his mind what to do next. Come with me while we still have a chance, he had said, but her reply—that affirmative nod—weighed heavily upon him, for he realized that although he had finally brought her to understand the nature of the web spun around them, nothing was solved. The web remained and they were still caught up in it, suspended between equally hopeless alternatives, which he considered as if he were watching them on a split screen. Below him, the rose trellis led down to the ground and a last chance to make a run for Canada through Broussard's gantlet. Above him, the iron rungs of the fire escape led to his room, where he would have an opportunity to look over the Dutchmen's manual again, and a last chance to get some sleep before taking his chances on the stunt. Impossible gambles, both. In the one, he would revert to being a fugitive; in the other, he would remain a stunt man; and in neither could he possibly subject her to the risks involved. But the idea of leaving her behind was intolerable. There must be some way, he thought. Some way . . .

At this point, Cameron looked up at the Ferris wheel, whose rim was just visible above the adjacent rooftops. When it stops spinning, I'll make up my mind, he told himself, but the wheel continued to spin, and, watching it, he felt his eyelids growing heavy. Sleep . . . that was the most important thing at the moment. He could do nothing without sleep. I've got to get some sleep, he told himself. Now, having made up his mind to sleep, he climbed slowly up the fire escape, stopping at her room to leave a note, and then continued to the top. He was lurching along the corridor toward his own room when a door opened ahead of him, a man stepped through it, and, blinking, Cameron found himself looking into the startled face of the toll collector.

"Where d'you think you're going?" he said.

The toll collector placed a forefinger to his lips. "It's time I got out of here. They'll be finished with the causeway tomorrow or the next day, and I have to go back on duty."

Cameron imagined him making change in the lonely cubicle on the other side of the river—a cubicle that would once again double as a projection booth for his fantasies. "Too bad you won't get to see the film you've starred in."

The toll collector's face sagged with sudden apprehension. "Listen, if the chief should get wind—I mean, they assured me it was just, you know, for private use. . . ."

"Well, it's not exactly the kind of flick they're liable to show at the local drive-in, is it?"

The toll collector gave a tentative smile and, as if hopeful of remaining anonymous, pulled a pair of sunglasses over his eyes. "Then you think there's nothing to worry about," he said uneasily.

"Nothing to worry about," replied Cameron, who once again found himself looking at the reflection of his face in the lenses of the sunglasses. Now, averting his eyes, he realized that the distorted image he had seen on the first day, which had seemed to be nothing more than a freakish caricature of the toll collector's perversity, was also a pro-phetic metaphor for the face he would later press to the keyhole in order to watch the enactment of da Fé's film. For a moment, he had the feeling that he was looking back through an endless hall of mirrors in which—alternately, doubly, and sometimes all at once—he appeared as fugitive, stunt man, spectator, and voyeur. Double-exposure . . . Perhaps the director was not so mad, after all.

The toll collector was watching him intently.

"Nothing to worry about," Cameron repeated. "And no one the wiser."

"It's best that way," the toll collector agreed with a smile. "And vice versa, of course. You know, I bet they ask me to keep an eye open for you out there. Just in case you make it past the roadblock."

"Maybe I will," said Cameron, who remembered that in the first *trompe l'oeil* he had taken the man for a sentry.

The toll collector gave an eloquent shrug to indicate that he considered it a most remote possiblity, and started down he corridor.

"Suppose I do," Cameron persisted.

"No problem," replied the toll collector with a farewell wave. "We only collect from people getting off the highway. You'd be going out the blind side of the booth, where an automatic machine hands you a ticket that doesn't come due until later."

A sentry for the middle of nowhere, Cameron was thinking as he entered his room. And with only a one-hundred-and-eighty-degree view of that. Yes, slipping past the toll collector would be easy. But first of all he was going to have to get across the river. . . .

At first glance, his room seemed exactly as he had left it that morning, when, determined to steal away but unwilling to abandon Nina, he had crawled out the dormer window to wait for nightfall upon the roof. What an agony the day had been! And what a waste that, in spite of all the effort, he should be back where he started. Cameron scarcely knew whether to laugh or cry. In the end, too exhausted to do either, he flopped full-length upon his bed. Then he noticed a book sitting upon the bedside table, which, because it was a hard-cover edition, he knew at once did not belong to him. Propping himself on an elbow, he reached for it and read the title:

RAPTURE OF THE DEEP
And Other Stories
by
Dalton Roth

So the screen writer had not come to show him the script, but to give him a copy of his book. For some moments, Cameron studied the back cover of the collection, which bore a photograph of Roth in younger and cleaner-shaven days, and a paragraph of biography that ended with the sentence, "He is presently in Hollywood writing screen plays." Then, opening the book to the inscription page, he saw that it had been dedicated in a strong and flourishing hand *"To Arthur Coleman, the stunt man, from your friend, Dalton Roth."* Touched and accused, Cameron lay back against the pillows and glanced through the title story, which was about a washed-up film writer who decides to commit suicide by drowning himself in the swimming pool of a producer who has fired him from his job. But just at the point where the writer had jumped into the pool and, weighed down by clothes and despair, begun to drown, Cameron began to drowse, so they sank together, with the light fading and everything dissolving into blur before their eyes.

Thrashing his way to the surface, he burst into sunlight, gasped a lungful of air, and came awake in the incandescent glare of the lamp on his bedside table to find Nina sitting in a chair beside him.

"What time it is?" he asked.

"Four o'clock."

Four o'clock . . . Cameron got to his feet, went to the sink, and splashed his face with cold water. Then he threw open the window, and breathed deeply. The lights of the amusement center had been extinguished, and the Ferris wheel had stopped spinning. In an hour or two, the sun would rise. Dawn. Once again, he found himself anticipating it like a condemned man in a cell. "I've got to think up a way to get us out of here," he said.

"You should have gone long ago," she replied.

"Without you? Did you really think I'd leave without you?"

"I've come here," she said. "So I must have hoped not."

Cameron crossed the room to her side, and, bending down, touched her hair. "Nina, I love you."

She looked up at him. "This morning when you tried to save the child—even though it was a doll—I thought I might be able to love you also. But tonight, on the bridge . . ."

"I was desperate," he told her. "There didn't seem to be any other way out."

She had begun to weep. "Go now while it's still dark. If you wait till morning—"

"If I wait till morning, they'll expect me to go through with the stunt, and you'll have to play Margaret again."

"Again?" she murmured. "No, always."

"Listen to me," he said. "I know why you think you're Margaret. And what you think you're guilty of."

She was weeping soundlessly.

"You were in love with him. Then, after the assassination, you had a nervous breakdown."

She had placed her hands over her eyes.

"And now you feel guilty. But why? For having loved him?"

Nina shook her head.

"Tell me," he said gently. "Tell me so we can get out of here."

She removed her hands from her face and looked up at him. "He was coming to see me. When it happened, he was on his way. As always, he had dismissed his bodyguard."

"On account of you."

"To protect me."

"The same thing."

"Yes."

"So you feel to blame."

Nina gave a tiny shrug. "I'm like Margaret, who's afraid to live."

Margaret's afraid to live and the fugitive's afraid to die, Cameron thought. Yes, they were perffectly cast and still going in circles. So little had changed since they had been together at the end of the jetty. Except time, which was running short. "You and I have no more time to waste," he told her.

"Please," she said. "Go now while it's still dark and you have a chance."

He made no reply, but lifted her to her feet and took her in his arms. A chance for Canada . . . The road unfolded before him in detail. He imagined them leaving the town behind, crossing the river, and then passing through the blind side of the toll booth, where they would automatically be handed a ticket for the highway that led to the border. A ticket to freedom. A flash-forward to a happy ending. How easy it was to dream. And to despair . . . for in the next instant he found himself once again suspended between hope and futility—a stunt man clawing at thin air. Your chance, she was saying. Our chance, he had told her. The last chance, Gottschalk claimed. Did that mean a last chance to escape or simply a last chance to dream about a future in which escape was possible? How submerged they were in the director's world. Celluloid figments. Prisoners of imagination . . .

Her silence needed to be filled, and, kissing her tenderly, he wondered at how she must have struggled against her own sense of hopelessness to have brought herself to hope that he could save her. The sterility of all solutions except that of love, he thought. Gottschalk's first concept. But the director had changed his mind. No matter. He was wrong. And if he was wrong about that, anything was possible, including a reality other than the art that kept repeating itself over and over, endlessly. Another reality . . . which meant a future based upon a script that would give them one more chance. A new script. One that he would write himself. Why not? Cameron thought. Yes, why not, since even according to the director, anything was possible . . . ?

"D'you remember when I told you we could put a happy ending on our story in spite of him?" he said.

"I remember," she replied. "We were going to drive off to Canada."

"We still can."

"But what about the police?"

"They'll be waiting for us with drawn guns—"

She was staring at him with amazement.

"—loaded with blank ammunition."

"I don't understand."

"The stunt," he told her with a laugh. "We're going to go through with it."

Nina was shaking her head in bewilderment.

"We're going to take a leaf from the director's book," he explained. "We're going to improve upon his script and change the story to suit ourselves. In short, we're going through with the first part of the stunt but not the second."

"I still don't understand."

"It's simple!" he cried. "It's so simple I never thought about it until just a moment ago. We're going to crash through the roadblock and keep right on going. Over the bridge and across the river!"

"We are?" she said breathlessly.

"We are," he replied triumphantly. "You and me."

"But how can both of us—?"

"C'mon," he said, taking her by the arm. "I'll show you."

But once he had persuaded her to climb into the trunk compartment of the car, and, having made her as comfortable as possible, closed the door, examined the tailpipe for leaks, and climbed in behind the wheel, his confidence in the plan began to waver. For some moments, he tried to define the sense of foreboding that had come over him. Was it the boldness and simplicity of the scheme, or was it the idea that by attempting to carry it out in a vehicle so similar to the one that had conveyed him into his nightmare to begin with, he was somehow tempting fate? In this mood, his mind subdivided itself in kaleidoscopic fashion, and, like a moviegoer watching images on a multiple screen, he found himself looking at past and future scenes that flashed before him like events of the present. Now, in a simultaneous jumble, he saw a figure lying upon a roadway, which became superimposed upon the murky outline of a car sinking deeper and darker into the river until the sound of metal upon metal signaled its coming to rest in the automobile graveyard. Then, in pitch black at five fathoms, he felt the water rising around his neck as a stream of bubbles fled toward the surface and burst into the harsh light of day which illuminated the panic-filled face of a man racing toward a horizon that kept receding before him. Suddenly, the roadblock loomed up, and, closing his eyes, holding his breath, and clutching the steering wheel in a death grip, he pushed the accelerator pedal to the floor and headed straight for it until . . .

Spots danced before his eyes. He was drenched in sweat and still holding his breath. Now, exhaling all at once, he let go of the wheel, leaned back in the seat, and opened his eyes to find that the first gray light of day was slipping in beneath the night sky. A moment later, he felt a cold breath of air and, turning, saw the door on the passenger's side swing open and someone slide silently into the seat next to him. For a second, he was too startled to react; then the door closed softly, its click bringing him fully awake as if a circuit had been completed, and, drawing a deep, sharp breath, he recoiled from the face of the cameraman, who seemed to have materialized out of thin air. If it had not been for Nina, he would have flung open his own door, whose handle he had grasped by instinct, and bolted from the sight, but the knowledge that she was in the trunk and totally dependent upon him prevented him from giving in to fear. Now, with a sheer act of will, he forced himself to gaze at the ravaged skin and malevolent leer, which, as daylight filled the interior of the car, combined with a pair of inflamed and suppurating eyes to produce a countenance that was mesmerically hideous.

For a time, he held his own; then, unable to continue, he looked away.

Da Fé smiled in triumph. "Nothing to be ashamed of, *caro*," he said. "No one can stare down Bruno. It's a game he never loses."

Cameron thought of Nina in the trunk, and, wondering if she could hear them, girded himself for a second assault. "Last game of the season," he replied grimly, and looked da Fé in the face again.

"Does that mean you're planning to leave?" said the cameraman with a laugh.

"Let's say I'm planning to take an extended vacation."

Da Fé nodded sympathetically. "You've been through an ordeal, *caro*. Your nerves are on edge. What you need is a good long rest and lots of sleep."

"I'm glad you agree," said Cameron. "Where d'you suggest I go?"

Da Fé shrugged. "Why not try some place where you can put your worries aside and forget about things?"

The cameraman's a travel agent for Lethe, Cameron thought. "I don't suppose it's possible to go into the drink without taking one," he said.

"*Caro* . . . ?"

"Just thinking out loud," replied Cameron. "About the stunt."

The cameraman studied him intently. "I, too, have been thinking about the stunt. It's going to be a difficult and unpredictable one, of course, for the simple reason that it can be rehearsed only up to a certain point."

You're telling me, Cameron thought. "It's the kind of stunt that'll have to be improvised," he said. "The kind that once it starts is out of control."

"Exactly, *caro*"

"But it stands to reason, doesn't it? Once the car is driven off the bridge . . ."

The cameraman was squinting at him suspiciously. "Considering the risk, you seem remarkably confident," he observed.

"I've been reading about the adventures of Janssen and Bakker," Cameron replied. "According to them, it's just a question of opening the windows on either side, waiting for the water to create a proper equilibrium with the air, and keeping one's head."

"Then you have no doubts."

"About what?"

"The outcome . . . meaning your ability to come out of the car."

"If I did, would I go through with the stunt?"

"Why does a daredevil defy death?"

"Hard to say," replied Cameron with a shrug. "To prove something to himself, perhaps."

"Precisely, *caro*. To prove to himself that he has no fear of death."

"Or that he can cheat it."

Da Fé was blinking painfully through his bloodshot eyes. "In this last game, *caro,* there'll be no chance to cheat."

No chance to cheat, thought Cameron, who noticed that the cameraman was having trouble seeing. "You mean the game's been fixed?"

"How else can one assure the necessary outcome?"

How else? echoed Cameron to himself. Yes, how else except with a stacked deck that, in this case, consisted of a rigged script? "The outcome," he said. "Meaning my ability to get out of the car?"

"No, *caro,* I mean the outcome of the film—a stream of bubbles welling up from the depths, bursting upon the surface of the water, and then dissolving into the effervescing bubbles in a glass of Coke being served by the waitress to a customer. The waitress is smiling. She believes the fugitive has escaped. The camera pulls away, and the picture comes to an end."

Cameron was shaking his head, for he had forgotten not only about the waitress' role in the film, but also about the film itself. Now, confused between fiction and fact, it dawned on him that by doubling for Jordan in the stunts, he had merely been performing small escapades to liven up a story about which he had only the most fragmentary knowledge and understanding. A moment later, however, he remembered that the film was based largely upon his own story, and that the bubbles which would point up the irony of the waitress' belief that the fugitive had escaped were the same bubbles that had filled him with the terror of drowning to begin with. In this mood, he found himself wondering if the bubbles were anything more than a conveniently transparent cinematic device that served to frame the beginning of his own story and the end of the director's film by creating the illusion that art was indistinguishable from reality and by reiterating Gottschalk's eternal question of what was real. Perhaps the bubbles constituted the most incredible *trompe l'oeil* of all! Now, struggling for focus in a confusion of images in which, once again, he appeared simultaneously as fugitive and stunt man, he thought of Nina in the trunk of the car, and heaved an inward sigh of relief.

"So the waitress is smiling," he said. "Isn't that a rather inconclusive ending?"

"Don't forget the bubbles," da Fé replied. "They tend to provide a certain note of finality, if only by implication."

"In other words, who knows what they mean?"

"Exactly, *caro*. It's the kind of ending that's left to the imagination."

"The kind that's both up in the air and at the bottom of the river."

"Who knows what's at the bottom of the river?" said the cameraman with a smile.

"No one," Cameron replied. "And no one should find out."

"Then it's best to let the bubbles speak for themselves."

"We're agreed on that," said Cameron. "Now what about the rest of the stunt?"

"A question of working out and timing the sequence to fit the requirements of our script. We'll start shooting at this end of the causeway from a truck that will follow your approach to the barricade. A camera on the bridge will pick you up as you crash through the roadblock, record the fusillade of the police, and follow the long, sickening skid that ends with your losing control of the car and going through the guard rail. Then a third camera will take up the final seconds of the sequence, which, of course, includes the splash down, the sinking of the car, and the bubbles whose eloquence we've already discussed."

"The skid's going to be the most difficult part of all," Cameron said. "Suppose I really lose control of the car. I mean, at that rate of speed it would be easy."

"At what rate of speed?"

"Well, I've no idea how fast this crate'll go, but with the pedal to the floor . . ."

"Pedal to the floor!" exclaimed da Fé with a laugh. "You always take things literally, *caro*. Accelerated motion is just another illusion. It's obtained by filming at a slower than normal rate. In this way, the split-second timing of a sequence can appear to be achieved at a much faster pace than is really the case."

"Does that mean I'm supposed to drive slowly?"

Da Fé was studying him through pus-filled eyes. "You seem disappointed."

"Not at all," Cameron protested. "It's just that I assumed—"

"Assumptions are dangerous, *caro*."

"Always," Cameron agreed.

"Moreover, we won't be shooting the scene as a continuous sequence, but in segments. In other words, your approach to the bridge, the crash through the roadblock, the skid, and the plunge into the river will be separate parts of a whole that will only be linked in time and space on the screen."

"Of course," Cameron murmured. "I should have realized."

"Things are never what they seem," said the cameraman with a smile.

"Never," Cameron replied.

"First of all, we'll go through a dry run."

"A dry run," Cameron repeated. "That's a good idea."

Da Fé was rubbing at his eyes with his knuckles. "How agreeable you've become! How cooperative! But let's stop pretending, *caro*. I know very well that you're saying one thing and thinking another."

"You're imagining it," Cameron said.

"No, *caro*, you have a plan. I can't see very well because of what the sand has done to my eyes, but I can tell from the sound of your voice that you still think you have a chance to cheat."

"You're mistaken," Cameron replied. A dry run, he was thinking. The best kind of all. Yes, a dry run accelerated past illusion and timed to fit the requirements of a script that's been improved to assure a happy ending . . . "If you're so worried I'm going to cheat," he said coolly, "why not come along for the ride?"

Da Fé's ravaged face opened into a grin. "Why not?" he exclaimed. "What a brainstorm!"

With a great effort, Cameron forced down his dismay. "Sure," he said. "You can ride in the death seat."

"No, no, *caro*. Your passenger will be an underwater camera that will shoot your descent into the river!"

Cameron heaved a silent sigh of relief that surfaced as a smile, and, gazing into the eyes of the cameraman, felt the elation of Ulysses when, having blinded the Cyclops, he knew he would be able to escape from the cave.

Da Fé was grinning at him as if he were a trusted callaborator. "Tell me, *caro*, what's your name again?"

"My name?"

"Your real name."

Cameron gazed into the inflamed eyes of the cameraman, which looked like a pair of running sores, and gave a shrug. "Cameron," he said.

21

It was going to be another scorcher. Even though the sun was not yet visible above the hotel rooftop, the technicians who were bolting the underwater camera to the back rest of the passenger's seat had begun to sweat profusely. Cameron glanced at the trunk of the car, and was relieved to see that it was still in shadow. By the time the sun hits it, we'll be on our way, he thought. For a few minutes longer, he leaned against a fender of Nina's convertible and watched the preparations; then he strolled across the parking lot and went up the steps of the hotel veranda. He was about to enter the lobby when he heard a shouted command, and, peering around the corner of the porch, was just in time to see Lee Jordan leap off the railing, with arms flung out before him, toward the lens of a camera that was mounted on a tripod on the sand below. The actor landed heavily and got slowly to his feet as da Fé emerged from behind the camera, shaking his head.

"More grimace," he said. "There's got to be more grimace, *caro*. You're fifty feet above the ground. It's your last and only chance. You're desperate!"

Cameron looked at a black backdrop behind the railing, and, realizing that he was watching a pick-up shot that would link the two parts of the stunt he had performed in the amusement center, felt a proprietary twinge of annoyance. But as Jordan prepared to take another dive from the railing, he laughed to himself and turned away. Leap, *caro*, he thought. Leap for your life. . . .

The lobby was empty, but the radio behind the desk in the corner had been tuned to a program about the space flight. "We are one hour and twenty-two minutes into the final countdown," the mission control officer was saying calmly. "Barring last-minute complications, we should have lift-off forty-five minutes from now."

Cameron glanced at his watch—it was nearly eight o'clock

—and went into the dining room, where he found the screen writer reading through a sheaf of manuscript. "How's it going?" he asked.

Roth shook his head without taking his eyes from the pages. "Terrible. I've been up half the night."

Cameron sat down and poured himself a cup of coffee.

"Changes," the screen writer went on. "He's always changing everything. Right until the very last minute."

Cameron smiled. "Don't tell me the fugitive's going to escape."

"Fugitive?" said Roth, who looked up for the first time. aren't you? I mean, except for one last stunt."

"What fugitive?"

"Me," Cameron replied.

Roth leaned back in his chair and laughed. "You know, I've been so busy trying to figure out this crazy scene where Margaret gets laid to the rhythm of the missile countdown, I forgot about the other film entirely. You're almost through,

"Listen, don't you know who I am?"

"Of course I know who you are!"

"Look again."

The screen writer tugged at his melancholy mustaches and regarded Cameron intently. Then he gave a shrug. "I've been up half the night and I'm pretty beat," he said, "but you still look like the stunt man to me."

"Even without make-up?"

"What's a little pancake got to do with it?"

Cameron took a sip of coffee and gave his head a weary shake. "I didn't sleep much either," he said. "I must be tired."

"Well, you ought to get some rest before you go driving off that bridge."

"Too late," replied Cameron, who sensed that Roth was anxious to get back to the script.

"Look, if you don't feel up to it, why not ask for a postponement?"

Cameron finished his coffee. "I'll be okay," he said.

The screen writer was looking at him with concern. "You're crazy to go through with it if you're tired."

"I haven't any choice," Cameron said, and got to his feet.

"Of course you have a choice! What're you talking about?"

"Dramatic narrative," replied Cameron. "An action from

which the hero can't withdraw until things have run their course."

Roth had screwed his face into a grimace of incredulity. "For God's sake!" he exclaimed. "I was talking about a film!"

"Funny," said Cameron with a smile and a farewell wave. "I thought you were talking about whether the fugitive gets away or gets caught."

Out in the lobby, the mission control officer was announcing that the countdown was proceeding on schedule, and that all systems were go for the launch. Cameron watched a pair of prop men lugging a television set up the stairway to the second floor, and decided from their conversation that it must be for the scene between Margaret and the space scientist. Then, he pictured Gottschalk supervising the installation of scenery for an episode that was not going to take place in a film that would never be finished. Talk about *trompe l'oeil!* The tide of illusion had turned, and the director was deceiving himself by furnishing a set with props that would serve no purpose, and by outfitting the bridge with a railing whose deceptively solid appearance would end up fooling no one. A victim of his own theatrical effects, Cameron thought as, once again, he imagined himself and Nina using the bridge to accomplish no other end than the one for which it had been constructed.

Now, glancing through the window beside Gottschalk's desk, he saw da Fé's crew mounting a camera boom on the pick-up truck that would accompany them out across the causeway. Soon it would be time to go. He could scarcely believe it. What an eternity it seemed since he had stood at the counter, making his confession to Gottschalk and receiving the news of his deferment as if it were a form of absolution! And how naïve he had been to think that he could relinquish the ending of his story to a director who not only believed in endings that were endless, but whose films were nothing more than sacraments in which, having suspended their disbelief, the actors did endless penance! No matter, Cameron told himself. Was he not stronger for having performed and survived his ordeals? And was he not wiser for having penetrated and solved the mystery that lay behind them? Yes, wise enough to interpret Gottschalk's

myth to suit himself, and strong enough to defeat the director at his own game. A matter of cunning and confidence—
a question of turning the tables so that the last stunt would
turn out to be an act not of expiation, but of faith in a
future in which the hero always escapes . . .

At this point, the voice of the mission control officer broke
in on his thoughts to say that doctors had pronounced the
astronauts in perfect physical shape for their journey, and
that the space men had expressed themselves confident of
success when they appeared at the launching pad. A good
omen, Cameron told himself, and, glancing out the window
again, saw that everything was ready in the parking lot. Now,
impatient to be gone, he started across the lobby toward
the door, only to hear himself hailed by Denise, who came
hurrying down the staircase. The make-up girl was wearing
her diaphanous white dress and carrying her black bag, and
the sight of her reminded him once again that he was wearing
his real face.

"Weren't you going to say goodbye?" she asked.

Cameron gave an embarrassed smile. "Of course."

"Then you *are* leaving."

"Yes."

"Aren't you forgetting something?"

Cameron shrugged and nodded toward the parking lot,
where the cameraman and his crew stood waiting. "No one's
recognized me so far," he replied.

Denise gave him a glance of professional appraisal. "You
know, it's kind of weird. It must be the bleach in your hair,
but you still look like the fugitive. I mean, the one in the
film."

"Chameleonic change," he told her. "It works both ways.
We become what we pretend and vice versa."

"Well, hadn't I better touch you up a bit? Just to add to
the confusion?"

"Thanks, but I'd rather you didn't."

"So you don't have to wear the disguise any more."

"No," Cameron replied. "From now on I have to get used
to doubling for myself."

"Let's skip the double-talk," said Denise bitterly. "You're
giving me the brush, aren't you?"

"Listen, Denise, just because I don't want to be made
up . . ."

"Sure, I was handy when you had to have another face. But now the heat's off, you don't need me any longer."

Cameron glanced again toward the parking lot. "Look, I haven't got time to explain," he said. "They're waiting for me."

"Run along, stunt man. I hate explanations, anyway."

Cameron looked at her miserably. "Aren't you going to wish me luck?"

"Sure, lots of luck. And thanks for all the thrills."

As he sat in the car and buckled his seat belt, he tried to think of Nina in the trunk and what lay ahead of them, but Denise's dismissal echoed in his brain like an indictment. Now, switching on the radio, he listened to the calm voice of mission control declaring that weather conditions were perfect for the launch. Another good omen. Nonsense. He was giving way to superstition. But everything conspired to put him on edge, including the eye of the underwater camera, which was trained upon his head. An evil presence, he decided. An extension of da Fé himself. Cameron forced himself to look away. The voice of mission control assured him that things were going according to plan. Now, as the cameraman and his crew climbed into the back of the truck, he took a deep breath, turned the ignition key, and started the engine. Then the truck pulled out of the parking lot, and, putting the car into gear, he followed after it.

The streets of the town were stifling hot and nearly deserted, as if the inhabitants were hoping for the amusement center to start up like some giant fan and stir the heavy air. Cameron wiped away a trickle of sweat that was running into his eye and glanced at the Ferris wheel, which stood stock-still against the sky. Next to it the chairs of the whip ride hung limp and motionless from their pole and ring. Everything seemed to be frozen into geometry and suspended in time. Cameron thought of the astronauts strapped in their seats and listening to the minutes of the countdown tick away. Then, following the camera truck, he turned into the avenue that led up the hill from the waterfront, and saw the ocean pier and the dance casino framed in the rectangle of his rear-vision mirror. Ahead of him, da Fé and his crew were maneuvering the boom of the camera to

aim its lens in his direction. Now, as the town receded like
movable background in a process shot, he drove past the
gingerbread police station, whose occupants would be waiting
in ambush on the bridge, wearing the uniforms of ice-cream
vendors and carrying guns that were loaded with blank
ammunition. And, all at once, it was as if he were passing
weightless through a vacuum in which time and space did
not exist. He felt like no man departing from no place on
the way to nowhere. Then he was beyond the ridge, with
the town forever behind him, and descending once again
through a forest of scrub toward the salt marsh.

How vast it seemed in daylight! When he first saw it
through the trees, he was still high enough to make out the
cut of the river that meandered through it, the delicate
tracery of the river's tributaries, and the intricate network
of drainage ditches that had been dug for mosquito control.
As the road continued to descend, however, the river and
the pattern of the ditches were swallowed up by the sheer
horizontal sweep of the marsh, which stretched away like an
immense lawn toward the encircling headlands. Only the
trestle of the causeway raised itself above the incredible
flatness, and now, squinting into the glare of the sun, he
tried to locate the bridge. But the bridge was too far away
to be seen clearly, and he was drawing closer and closer to
the end of the causeway, which diminished his vantage and
foreshortened his perspective. No matter, he reflected. The
bridge was there and real enough, even with its false railing
of balsa and its phony barricade manned by harmless extras.
All that mattered now was to commit himself at the right
time and get across it before anyone could tumble to what
was happening.

The camera truck was slowing down for the roadblock at
the fork where he had flagged down the laundry truck on
the first day, and where he and Nina had sat in an agony of
suspense, the night before, waiting for permission to pass.
The memory was enough to make his heart jump into his
throat. He was even tempted to wheel around and race back
to the safe haven of the town. Too late. He was already
committed. Now, depressing the brake pedal, he came to a
stop behind the truck. At this point, a policeman climbed
out of one of a pair of patrol cars that had been parked to
form a narrow passageway in the center of the road. The

policeman glanced up at the camera crew and, nodding, gave a listless wave of his hand. Da Fé leaned over the side of the truck, pointed toward the car, and said something that caused the policeman to look in Cameron's direction and give another nod and a second lazy wave. Then one of the camera crewmen jumped down, walked back to the car, and, opening the door on the passenger's side, leaned in and turned on the underwater camera, which responded with a whirring noise that Cameron heard together with the sound of his own heart beating and the voice of the mission-control officer, who announced that the countdown had entered its final phase.

The truck had started through the passageway between the two patrol cars. Cameron put his car into first gear and, with eyes fixed straight ahead, followed after it. His hands were trembling on the wheel and his legs felt numb. When he drew abreast of the policeman, his mind made an involuntary leap forward, as if to augment the pistons of the engine, and his foot reacted with a spastic stab on the accelerator pedal. The motor coughed and died. For a second, Cameron froze; then he reached for the ignition key and turned it. The starter ground. From the corner of his stricken eye, he could see the policeman watching him. The starter motor began to screech in protest. The voice of mission control strove mightily for calm. The underwater camera buzzed insistently in his ear. Then the engine caught and, even as he fed it gas, stalled again. The heat was suddenly appalling. Now, lathered with sweat and gasping for air, he turned the ignition key once more. The policeman sauntered toward him. Cameron sat rigidly behind the wheel, hand on the key, in an agony of doubt. If he continued to grind the starter, he was bound to wear down the battery, and if he pumped the gas pedal, he would flood the engine. The camera truck had pulled over to the side of the road, and the causeway stretched ahead of him in open invitation. His fingers tightened on the key. The policeman bent down to his window, and on the periphery of vision, he saw someone climbing out of the patrol car on the opposite side of the road. Now, he thought, and turned the key. The starter ground away interminably. In a frenzy, he pumped the gas pedal. Finally, he held it to the floor. Start, he told the engine, as if to will it back to life. Start! *Start!*

"Camera on?"

"Yes," he said to the policeman who was hovering beside his window.

"Camer*on?*"

"I told you yes," he replied, but the policeman was looking past him blankly, as if the question had come from the other direction, and the accented last syllable was echoing in his brain like the cadence of a wild, implausible melody. Then it died away in the shock of recognition, and, peering around the camera to the window on the passenger's side, he found himself staring into the shining black face and bloodshot eyes of the sergeant.

"Come on out of there, Cameron," the sergeant said softly.

But the command might as well have been given to a corpse, for Cameron's whole spirit had drained from his body and fled through the thumb and forefinger that connected him to the ignition key. For a moment longer, the starter could scarcely be heard above the camera's whirring; then, with a faint whisper of assent, the engine breathed to life, and, revived as if by a reverse flow of energy, he withdrew his hand from the key and placed it on the knob of the gearshift.

"Come on out of there," the sergeant said again.

The words passed through the car a second time, and, like a pulsed beam finding its target, ignited the policeman to an awareness that vied with open-mouthed incredulity as he stared back at the sergeant.

"You mean—"

Cameron tensed like a runner about to jump the gun.

"—this here's the one?"

Then, jamming the car into gear, flooring the accelerator with one foot, and lifting the other off the clutch pedal, he left the question hanging in mid-air, and the two of them gaping at one another across an empty space.

"*T minus ten,*" intoned the hushed voice of mission control as, gathering speed, Cameron shifted into second, shot past the camera truck, and saw . . . *Nine* . . . in his rearview mirror the sergeant and the policeman running toward a patrol car that . . . *Eight* . . . even when he had shifted into third and was rocketing down the track of the causeway, made no move to follow . . . *Seven* . . . which meant that they must be radioing ahead to the bridge . . . *Six* . . . and

that it would be a question of his speed against the reaction
of Broussard and his men, who . . . *Five* . . . would be
shaking out the contents of their revolver cylinders and
fumbling to reload in time . . . *Four* . . . to intercept him at
the sawhorse barricade through which, with a terrific crash
that sent splintered wood flying in all directions, he now
passed onto the bridge and into the realm of total cinema
. . . *Three* . . . where fiction turned into fact, art became
reality, and, running a gantlet of cameras and guns . . . *Two*
. . . . he felt something smash into the side of the car, which
. . . *One* . . . responding as if to a blown tire . . . *Zero* . . .
gave a sickening lurch, spun completely around in the roadway, and . . . *Ignition* . . . went into a long skid that carried
him sideways and soundlessly through the false guard rail
and out into . . . *Lift-off!* . . . a lazy arching flight above
the river during which, watched by the unblinking eye of the
camera, he summoned her name from his throat in a scream
of anguish and terror as he looked down and saw the water
coming up to meet him like the void.

22

His shriek was terminated by the shock of an impact that was accompanied by a stunning explosion, as if the car had struck a wall of concrete. For a moment, he was shaken deaf, dumb, and blind; then, revived by dozens of tiny jets of water that came spurting into the interior of the vehicle, he blinked his eyes, saw a conical-shaped headlight floating away on the current, and, finding his voice again, began to shout her name. Now, in a frenzy, he unbuckled his safety belt, climbed into the rear seat, and, removing the back rest, clawed frantically at the partition that separated him from the trunk. When he was finally able to tear a corner of the partition loose, the water had risen to seat level, and a torrent poured back through the opening. At this point, he glanced behind him, saw that the car was sinking nose first, and, remembering the instructions in the manual, reached back and rolled down the front windows a few inches on either side. The water was swirling around his waist when he resumed his attack upon the partition, and all at once he realized that its pressure would prevent him from making the opening larger. Thrusting his arm into the aperture, he groped for her, found nothing, and, calling her name, got no answer. Then, bending down, he peered into the dark cavern of the trunk until the water rose above his face and he was forced to lift his head for air. Nothing. He had felt nothing, heard nothing, and seen nothing. Could the trunk be empty? Perhaps she had lost her nerve or been discovered by da Fé and his crew. Was it possible that she was even now lying on a bed at the hotel, staring at a television set and pretending to be seduced for Gottschalk's camera? Oh God, please let the trunk be empty, Cameron thought. Let her be anywhere but there. . . .

He tried to sustain himself with this hope, but as he knelt on the seat he felt it being squeezed out of him by dread that, like the water, rose higher and higher around him.

Finally, he climbed back into the front seat and sat behind
the wheel, whose lower rim was now submerged. The car
had broached sideways in the current, and, looking up at
the bridge, he saw that it was lined with spectators standing
on either side of a camera which had been placed at the rent
he had torn in the false railing. Bruno da Fé was staring
down at him from this vantage point with arms akimbo. The
sergeant stood beside him. Next to the sergeant, hands on
hips, stood the chief of police, and beside the chief was the
young earnest-faced patrolman from whose shoulder her look
of horror had stayed his hand the night before. They're
watching it happen, Cameron thought numbly. They're watching it happen and making a movie of it. . . . The idea filled
him with despair. In desperation, he tried to force open the
door beside him until, remembering that the pressure of the
water against it could not possibly be overcome, he gave up
and simply watched them filming him as he floated out upon
the current.

He was amazed at the buoyancy of the car, whose radio
was still working. The voice of mission control shouting "T
plus fifty-six!" came through a steady crackle of interfer-
ence. Fifty-six seconds since he had gone into the river, and
the water had not yet risen to the level of the windows.
When it gets a little higher, I'll give the door another try, he
thought. But even when the river washed over the panes, he
continued to sit motionless behind the wheel, for he had
now passed beyond despair and entered a realm where the
idea of leaving her behind was unthinkable. Instead, he gazed
up at the bridge and heard the garbled voice of mission control, suddenly full of alarm and panic, shout something that
sounded like "Too late!" which was followed by a long rasp
of static and a word that could have been either "aboard"
or "abort." At this point, the radio went dead, and there was
only the sound of air hissing from the car and the underwater camera whirring in his ear. Cameron looked into its
eye with loathing; then, very deliberately, he reached into
his pocket, withdrew a fifty-cent piece, and plugged it into
the lens window. An eye for an eye, he thought grimly. But
what use was there in blinding the Cyclops now?

The car was sinking out of sight. The water had covered
the windows and the windshield, and the interor was filled
with a darkening green glow. Cameron lifted his head to

keep his nose and mouth in the pocket of air that remained, and thought of the roof shining for one last instant in sunlight before it slid beneath the river. Then he heard a crumpling sound as the pressure of the water began to buckle the plating of the chassis, and imagined a stream of bubbles on their way toward the surface, where they would burst in sparkling iridescence before dissolving into the effervescence of a glass of Coke. Sight, sound, and imagination—the spectator's prison. But there had been something else, which came to him all of a sudden now as, descending into darkness, the air pocket became more compressed and his nostrils filled with the singular odor of old and musty upholstery which he remembered from the first day. *Trompe le nez*. How else to explain that pungent smell in two different cars? In which case it was not *trompe le nez* but a question of *déjà senti*, which, in turn, meant that the bubbles he had seen on the first day were the most incredible *trompe l'oeil* of all. No matter. One way or another, he had come full circle and plunged into the river as if to realize his own worst fears and prove the director's thesis in spite of himself. What a fool he had been! To think that he could be so easily tricked . . . But what of the astronauts? Were they not in a similar predicament? And what of Nina, for whom he had implored a different fate? Oh God, he pleaded again. Oh God, please let the trunk be empty. . . . But the light had disappeared, and the director was groping for medicine to relieve the pressure in the hardening lenses of his eyes, and Cameron felt himself swirling cold and weightless through the depths until his ears began to ache with another kind of pressure, and in an agony of pain that drove everything else from mind, he reached the bottom of the river.

The confusing giddiness of narcosis came over him almost at once, which provided an anesthetic for his pain and filled him with a curious sense of well-being. Now, in a state of stupor, he tilted his head back and breathed deeply from the pocket of air above him, like a driver who has succumbed to fatigue and pulled off the highway in the dead of night to catch some sleep. In a little while, I'll be on my way, he thought, and imagined himself passing through the toll booth, where he would automatically be handed a ticket that would assure the future. In this mood, his journey to the bottom of the river seemed not only foreordained but necessary—a temporary detour past which there would be clear sailing and no more obstacles. All he had to do now was stay below until they were satisfied that he had drowned; then, leaving the stunt man behind, he would depart from the car, and, buoyed by Archimedes' principle, rise from the dead to resume his life. For a few minutes more, this feeling of rapture sustained him, but the pocket of air was growing stale and giving out. Hang on, he told himself, and imagined the onlookers leaving the bridge. Not yet, he thought, reaching for the handle of the door. Just a little longer, he prayed when he felt himself beginning to slip away. Now, he decided as, half conscious, he opened the door, slid out from behind the wheel, and relinquished himself to the river.

His return to the surface was not so much an ascent as an ejection, as if he were being expelled from darkness and squeezed by some enormous contraction toward the light. No pain he had ever endured could match the multiple torment that racked him now as, with ears aching, eyes burning, heart throbbing, and lungs constricted to the point of bursting, he exploded from the womb of the river into the warmth of the sun. For a few seconds, he simply floated out on the tide like some ruptured fish that has been dislodged by accident from its accustomed depth. Then, gagging on a combination of salt water he had swallowed and blood that was streaming from his nose and filling his throat, he thrashed his arms feebly, looked back at the bridge, and was amazed to see how far the current had carried him.

The bridge was at least a hundred and fifty yards upstream, and the current was sweeping him along at a rate that would soon carry him out of sight. Cameron watched the mud banks of the river sliding past on either side, and waited until he had rounded the first bend; then he struck out for the nearest shore and tried to pull himself out of the water. Twice his fingers found purchase in the slime, but at this stage of the tide the banks rose almost vertically to the level of the marsh grass, ten feet above him, and both times he slipped back into the river when he attempted to make the climb. He tried a third time and a fourth, but he was tiring himself to no avail, and soon it was all he could do to stay afloat. Then he thought of himself caught forever in the toils of the river's meanders, and decided to expend his remaining strength on one last effort. Once again he managed to haul himself partway out of the water only to lose his grip on the slick mud wall that rose above him. When he fell back this time, he went all the way under, and when he came up, it was only to go under again. He was finished, done for, and ready to accept the verdict. So ready, in fact, that when he felt bottom a moment later, and lifted his head to find that the river had washed him into the mouth of one of the drainage ditches that crisscrossed the marsh, his disbelief was tinged with annoyance, as if his deliverance were some kind of dirty trick.

The ditch contained only a couple of feet of water, but when he tried to move he discovered that his legs were mired in a deep bed of ooze at the bottom. Now, panicked by the fear of sinking into muck, he thrashed about until he managed to extricate himself. Then, half swimming and half crawling through a mixture of water and slime, he started into the marsh. After a few yards, he collapsed in the mud, utterly spent. His nose was bleeding again, and even as he watched the blood drops staining the murky water, he saw dozens of tiny minnows attracted like piranha fish to the smell of it. At this point, it occurred to him that he must have punctured his ear drums during his descent to the bottom of the river. He was deaf. The idea horrified him. And, even more terrifying, something had stirred beneath him. He started to recoil, but the muck held him fast, and, all of a sudden, he realized that the ditch was crawling with an incredible abundance of life. Snails, slugs, eels, minnows, water bugs, bloodworms—all these plus species of living things he had never seen or even imagined were thriving in the primordial ooze that surrounded him. It was as if the marsh were an intermediate station in the eternity of evolution. Something moved again beneath him, and this time Cameron gave a mighty wrench that broke the sunction of the muck, and watched a pair of large, linked horseshoe crabs crawl slowly out from under him. For a second, he stared in horror at these bony-plated prehistoric spiders which had gone unchanged for millions of years; then he saw that the mud along the banks of the ditch was swarming with them, and imagined himself impaled upon their dagger-like caudal spines. Suddenly, the ditch became as terrifying as the sinister rivers that flow through jungle films, and the horseshoe crabs seemed as ominous as the inevitable crocodiles that glide from their banks and, showing eyes of implacable intent and trailing almost imperceptible wakes, converge silently upon the helpless swimmer. Cameron thought of himself locked in mortal combat with a succession of giant crabs, which he dispatched in Weissmuller style by wrestling them into a ventral position and stabbing them again and again until the slime flowed crimson with blood. Then, with the strength born of fear, he hauled himself out of the ditch.

A merciless African sun beat down upon him. The mud on his body began to dry and cake almost at once. He got to his hands and knees and started to crawl, but dropped to his stomach when he thought of how visible he must be in the vast carpet of spartina grass that surrounded him. Now, raising his head to orient himself, he looked along the line of the ditch which paralleled the causeway, and saw the marsh stretching out before him. From his angle, it seemed incredibly beautiful. In the distance, the spartina grass gave way first to fields of swamp marigolds and heather, then to acres of tall reeds and cattails that harbored flocks of blackbirds, and finally to headlands dotted with thickets of sumac, clumps of cedar trees, and stands of pitch pine and scrub oak. The sight filled Cameron with hope, for the ditch, which ran straight as an arrow toward this last horizon, would provide him with the cover necessary to reach it undetected. Then, glancing behind him and gauging his position in relation to the causeway, he realized that he was still on the wrong side of the river.

With a sigh of despair, he flattened himself in the grass and began to weep. A horde of insects buzzed around his head, and the sun beating down upon him began to bake him like a piece of pottery in a kiln. Finally, when he could bear the heat no longer, he rolled off the shelf of grass and into the bottom of the ditch. The cool slime revived him. Behind him, the river he must somehow get across continued flowing swiftly toward the sea. Cameron struggled to his knees and shook his fist at it. Afterward, he felt calmer. The river was the thing. One way or another, he had to get across it. But he would have to wait until the tide was at ebb. Yes, he would wait an hour or so, until the current subsided. In the meantime, he would explore the ditch in the hope of finding a plank or a piece of driftwood to float upon.

He started off slowly, sloshing his way through knee-deep muck. When he had gone about fifty yards, he came to an intersection where the ditch was joined at right angles by a shallower trench. For a moment, he paused at this cross-road; then, taking the easier route, he changed direction. For the next half-hour, he wallowed in a checkerboard pattern, turning right or left as the spirit moved him, but always with the idea of working his way farther and farther from the bridge and the causeway. Finally, he came to a tiny creek, which he decided to follow in the hope that it would lead him back to the river. The creek joined a larger creek that flowed in a deep, winding gully through layers of muck that gave off a pungent aroma of decay which mingled with the fragrance of salt hay. For a short while, he followed its serpentine course; then, rounding a bend, he came upon a heron standing one-legged and stock-still like a sentinel in the mud. The heron rose out of the marsh with a ponderous flapping of its wings, and, fearing that he had given away his position, Cameron turned off into another of the drainage ditches. Once again, his journey took on right-angle proportions, as if he were a piece being moved over a grid-squared game board. But the marsh had become a maze and the sum total of all his twistings and turnings seemed to be leading nowhere. Looking behind him, he saw a trail of black holes where his feet and legs had sunk into the muck. The tide was at ebb. If he were going to cross the river, now was the time. But where was the river? Cameron crouched in the ditch and tried to make up his mind which direction to take. Impossible. He was hopelessly lost. If he were to get his bearings, he would have to lift his head above the level of the marsh, and risk the chance of being spotted. He came up slowly and peered through the grass for the causeway. At first, the headlands seemed equidistant all around him. Then, turning in a complete circle, he located the causeway behind him, and saw a long line of men fanning out from it as they advanced across the marsh.

Obeying his first impulse, he fled headlong down the ditch until the forward momentum of his body yielded to the tenacious grip of the muck upon his feet and he went sprawling face down in the slime. Now, half blinded by mud, he staggered to his feet and continued to the end of the ditch, where he tumbled into a deep creek bed. Which way to go? The few inches of water in the creek was covered with the oily scum of decaying vegation, and flowed neither one way nor the other. Cameron bent down, studied it closely, and decided that he could detect a faint trace of current. Then, following in its direction, he sloshed and slogged his way along the bottom of the creek bed until he came to a bend and saw that the gully narrowed. Here, confused, he lifted his head for another look and found that he was heading toward the line of men, who, fanning out from the causeway, had been joined by another line that was sweeping across the marsh from the direction of the town. Cameron watched the tiny figures advancing slowly through the spartina grass, half a mile away, and realized that they were in the process of forming a great half-circle with anchor points at the bank of the river on either end. Then he turned and retraced his route, following his own footprints back through the slime. Their trail was unmistakable—a dead giveway that only the incoming tide would erase. Cameron imagined the first triumphant shout the sight of them would evoke. But it would take time for his pursurers to follow all his twistings and turnings, and the tide had turned to help him. Somewhere ahead lay the river. Everything depended on how quickly he could reach it.

When he came to the end of his own trail, a few minutes later, he plowed on resolutely through the mud until the creek bed widened, and, looking ahead, he saw an opening. Keeping his head low, he proceeded cautiously as the water rose over his knees and up to his waist; then, plunging forward, he swam the last few yards against a gentle current, and came to the mouth of the creek. Here, treading water, he tried to gauge the distance to the marsh on the other side of the river. A hundred yards at most. And the river at this stage of the tide was placid. A hundred yards . . . Cameron took a deep breath and studied the smooth expanse of water that lay before him. Once on the other side, he would keep to the ditches and make his way to the headlands in the distance. Dry ground. How he yearned for it! But there was still the river—this river that had defeated him at every turn. For a second longer, he hesitated; then, just as he was about to commit himself, a shadow swept over the water, and, squinting into the glare of the sun, he saw the helicopter.

The helicopter was skimming just above the river, as it had on the first day, when he had seen it from the bridge. Cameron took a gulp of air, pinched his nose between thumb and forefinger, and sank beneath the surface. When he came up for air, the machine was hovering in the sky, a quarter of a mile away. Then, tilting on end, it flew in a lazy arc that carried it behind him, as if delineating the half-circle of men who were advancing across the marsh. At the end of the arc, the helicopter repeated its flight upriver, and once again Cameron held his breath and ducked beneath the surface. There was no question of crossing the river now, and even as he realized this, he turned and, swimming underwater, made his way back into the creek. When he came up again, the helicopter was starting another lazy arc out over the marsh. Cameron imagined the pattern of its flight growing smaller as the net of his pursuers tightened. It was hopeless. There was not a chance for him. But as he considered giving up, the helicopter finished its second arc and started upriver again. Cameron crawled out of the water and hid beneath a clump of grass that hung over the bank of the creek. Then, rolling in the slime, he smeared himself from head to toe with mud, and charged off through the creek bed until he came to one of the drainage ditches. Now, belly down, he wormed his way into it and waited for the helicopter to fly by again.

Several minutes passed. Then, remembering that he was deaf, he lifted his head and found that he could scarcely see because of the slime that covered his face. Hopeless. He thought of giving up once more, but continued squirming his way along the ditch, which was filling with water as the tide came in. Something rose out of the marsh ahead of him, and, rubbing his eyes, he made out a small hummock covered with a growth of cattails. His last chance. If he could use one of the stalks as a breathing tube, he could bury himself in the muck and let his pursuers pass him by. It was a desperate gamble and he had little faith in it, but he continued to inch his way along the ditch until, warned by another shadow, he flattened himself face down. This time he could feel a faint wash from the helicopter's rotor blades and hear a dull echo of the engine's roar. When it diminished, he raised his head an inch or two above the slime. Just a few feet more and he would reach the cattails. An agonizing distance. How diminished his perspectives had become. Everything had shrunk around him. He no longer even thought about the river. The cattails loomed ahead like a sanctuary. The sun seared his back, and even the muck had grown hot beneath him. Using his elbows, Cameron crept forward and closed the remaining gap. Ten feet. Eight. Five . . . He was nearly there. The shadow of the helicopter swept over him again. He waited a few seconds; then, reaching out, he grasped a handful of stalks. And, suddenly, the thought of burrowing into the ooze was intolerable to him. Half blind, nearly deaf—had he not suffered enough? And for what? The unfairness of it overwhelmed him. He wanted to rise out of the muck and, like some blackened specter, shout defiance to the sky. Instead, clutching the stalks for support, he crawled from the ditch and hid himself among the cattails. Perhaps he would be lucky, like baby Moses among the reeds. No, there was not a chance. But he had finally reached some semblance of dry ground. Let them come now. At least he would be able to stand on his feet and greet them with contempt.

When he parted the reeds, he saw that the half-circle formed by the search party had diminished greatly. Soon the figures of his pursuers would be only a few feet apart. And, finally, they would close in on him shoulder to shoulder. Now, running his eyes along their ranks, Cameron made out the chief of police, the sergeant, and the cameraman, whose crew was carrying its equipment and struggling to keep up. So they were going to film this, too. The idea enraged him. He thought of making a last desperate run for the river, but that would be just what they hoped he would do. No, he had suffered enough, and the thought of swimming a river whose depths had claimed her was insupportable to him. He would wait where he was. Yes, he would wait in the cattails and hope that the first man to come within arm's reach would be da Fé.

The helicopter was no longer flying the half-circle pattern above the marsh. Instead, it seemed to be following the course of the creek bed that had led him to the river. Cameron watched the machine draw closer, and knew that his footprints had been discovered. The helicopter hovered for a moment at the end of the ditch that led to his hiding place; then tilted sideways and swung slowly toward him. The sun glinted off its plexiglass canopy, and the spartina grass danced in all directions beneath it. Cameron turned his head away and crouched in the cattails until it was almost upon him and he could feel the cold breath of the rotor blades. Then he looked up as if at an avenging angel, and found himself staring into the face of the director. Now the machine came over him, the cattail stalks flattened away around him, and, filled with a wild hope of escape that co-mingled with a fierce desire to pull Gottschalk out of the sky, he coiled himself, gave a great leap, and, reaching out with his hands, grasped one of the runner skids. There was an eerie moment of equilibrium as if man and machine were somehow evenly matched. Then, legs dangling and arms outstretched, Cameron was plucked from the marsh, raised up, and, like Icarus in reverse, lifted higher and higher into the sky in a spiraling flight that led straight toward the midday sun into the hope and despair of whose blinding light he dissappeared from sight.

THE END

About the Author

PAUL BRODEUR was born in 1931, in Boston. He was graduated from Harvard College, served in the Counter Intelligence Corps in Germany, and since 1958 has been a writer on the staff of *The New Yorker*, to which he has contributed short stories and many nonfiction pieces. Other stories by him have appeared in the *Saturday Evening Post, Show Magazine, Seventeen,* and the *Michigan Quarterly Review.* His first novel, *The Sick Fox,* was published in 1963 and received critical acclaim here and in England. His most recent work, *Downstream,* is a collection of his short stories.

PAUL THEROUX

"... will successively startle you ... shock you ... impress you ... but never, never bore you!"*

Available at your bookstore or use this coupon.

——PICTURE PALACE   28042   2.50
Come behind the camera's eye into the extraordinary world of Maude Coffin Pratt, whose life is a picture palace of passions, intrigues, seductions, and obsessions. "Absolutely brilliant!" — New York Times.

——THE FAMILY ARSENAL   25751   2.25
A nightmare of I.R.A. terrorism set in London. "The most evocative suspense novel in years!" — N.Y. Times Book Review.

——THE CONSUL'S FILE   27297   1.95
A "funny, knowing, ironic" (Saturday Review) record of the Consul's stint in Malaysia.

——GIRLS AT PLAY   25754   1.95
Four white women in an East African outpost devise little games to while away the time — games that change from play to hate to violence ... "Harrowing ... Stunning." — Cleveland Plain Dealer.

——THE BLACK HOUSE   25753   1.95
Set in the misty English countryside — a contemporary ghost story filled with tensely mounting horror! "A horror story definitely not for children ... first-rate!" — Boston Globe.

——SAINT JACK   27708   1.95
The bawdy adventures of Jack Flowers — the most resourceful and most endearing pimp in modern-day Singapore! "There's never a dull moment!" — San Francisco Chronicle.*

——THE GREAT RAILWAY BAZAAR   25191   1.95
From swinging London to seething Asia — aboard the world's legendary trains. "The most consistently entertaining book ... in a long time." — N.Y. Times.

BB   **BALLANTINE MAIL SALES**
        Dept. LG, 201 E. 50th St., New York, N.Y. 10022

Please send me the BALLANTINE or DEL REY BOOKS I have checked above. I am enclosing $.......... (add 35¢ per copy to cover postage and handling). Send check or money order — no cash or C.O.D.'s please. Prices and numbers are subject to change without notice.

Name_____

Address_____

City_____ State_____ Zip Code_____
       Allow at least 4 weeks for delivery.   G-7

The most fascinating people and events of World War II

Available at your bookstore or use this coupon.

____**ADOLF HITLER, John Toland**   27533 3.95
Pulitzer Prize-winning author John Toland's bestselling biography of Hitler based on over 150 interviews with the numerous survivors of his circle of friends, servants and associates.

____**A MAN CALLED INTREPID, William Stevenson**   28124 2.50
The authentic account of the most decisive intelligence operations of World War II - and the superspy who controlled them.

____**CYNTHIA, H. Montgomery Hyde**   28197 1.95
The incredible, but fully-documented true story of a brave, shrewd sensual woman's contribution to the allied victory — in World War II's most unusual battlefield.

____**PIERCING THE REICH, Joseph E. Persico**   28280 2.50
After 35 years of silence, top-secret files have been opened to reveal the stupendous drama of the most perilous and heroic chapter of intelligence history.

 BALLANTINE MAIL SALES
Dept. NE, 201 E. 50th St., New York, N.Y. 10022

Please send me the BALLANTINE or DEL REY BOOKS I have checked above. I am enclosing $. . . . . (add 35¢ per copy to cover postage and handling). Send check or money order — no cash or C.O.D.'s please. Prices and numbers are subject to change without notice.

Name_____

Address_____

City_____State_____Zip Code_____
Allow at least 4 weeks for delivery.   NE-13